HUNGRY
INDEPENDENTS

TED HILL

A PERMUTED PRESS book

ISBN (trade paperback): 978-1-61868-318-2
ISBN (eBook): 978-1-61868-319-9

PERMUTED
PRESS

For Big H
You make me smile everyday.

1.

HUNTER

Hunter teetered on the edge of teeth-gnashing insanity from the pain. Most of the time his shoulder felt numb and he was able to cope. Other times, like this one, he wanted to rip his arm from the socket and beat the pain to death. He wished he was at home in his nice big bed next to Molly, instead of messing around in a rainstorm.

The pain flared up as he climbed the rusty ladder to the grain elevator's roof in Cozad, Nebraska. A late-summer thunderstorm lashed upon him violently in the dark hours after midnight, while sheets of water cascaded down the white concrete wall, making the climb more treacherous than anticipated. At least the rain provided good cover. The kid up top would be oblivious to Hunter's approach in this mess.

Hunter reached for the next rung and his foot slipped, his body dropped, and his right arm took the weight. Pain seared through his shoulder. He clamped his other arm around the ladder, trembling with fear from the thought of ping-ponging all the way down the safety cage. Rain pelted the hood of his waterproof jacket, loud and harsh in unison with his terrified panting. The ground waited to catch him fifty feet below. Another fifty feet of climbing and he'd reach the top where the sniper roosted.

Five months ago when Hunter had died, all his cares and worries had been washed away. He was saved when his older brother, Jimmy, made the ultimate sacrifice. That gift would be wasted if he fell and crash landed on his head.

Earlier that day, he had slowed his motorbike as he approached the small town of Cozad, visiting as an emissary from Independents to find out if Cozad's food crops were also suffering from the infestation of grasshoppers. That's when the shots rang out, throwing up puffs of dirt around him from the bullet impacts. Hunter understood the message perfectly—Go Away!

The warning shots had ticked him off. Jimmy didn't give up his life so some yahoo could take Hunter out by accident or otherwise. Whatever reason the kid had for scoping him with daddy's deer rifle, he was about to learn the terrible consequence of jacking with people in the Big Bad.

With his grit back in check, Hunter climbed the rest of the way with no more thought about his shoulder. He peeked over the top, where a hundred yards of puddles collected the rain on the flat surface. Thick drops clattered on the metal roof of a narrow structure that housed the spouts where the elevated grain filled the different bins underneath. No one was in sight.

Hunter stepped up and moved away from the edge before he was blown off like a kite in the gusty wind. He huddled against the narrow building and worked his bad shoulder, lifting his arm and rolling small circles. It still hurt, but that was expected. He could manage.

A taller outbuilding at the other end of the grain elevator was barely visible through the curtain of rain. Maybe the sniper was inside cleaning his gun, or maybe the kid went home at night, and maybe Hunter would just have to wait until morning. He had lived through worse weather out in the open.

Hunter caught a rotten whiff and pinched his nose. Whatever remained in the grain elevator had definitely turned. He crept alongside and peered with his right eye into the dirty windows of the lower building and saw only darkness. He lost sight in his left eye the day he lost his brother. He'd gotten used to the change in depth perception, but still struggled with Jimmy's absence. That was going to take a while.

He closed within fifty feet of the other end, where a dark form huddled on the edge. A loud, thunder-like crack reverberated around the rooftop of the elevator. After a brief fire-flash, Hunter realized he'd been shot as the bullet ripped through his stomach and knocked him backwards into the building. He doubled over in agony that quickly subsided, and lifted his shirt in startled amazement. The bullet hole closed without one drop of blood escaping.

When Hunter had been beaten to death—a broken, bleeding and checking out for good kind of whooping—the ultimate sacrifice his brother made involved Hunter being healed by a little girl named Catherine. Right then, Hunter thought the healing had some residual effect. Cool for him. Bad for the guy holding the gun.

He advanced and another shot fired, catching Hunter in the shoulder. He spun off-balance and landed in a giant puddle. Hunter screamed for one excruciating moment before the pain ceased, reverting to its normal dull ache, with no blood and no bullet hole. The only thing he felt was a boiling desire to kill.

Hunter pushed up to his feet and sprinted for the kid, but something wasn't right. He skidded to a stop on the wet roof and wiped water from his eye. The boy's clothes were drenched and his exposed skin rippled like ever-changing waves on a pond. He stared at Hunter with clouded eyes the color of milk.

"You!" the boy-thing hissed. "How did you get here? You won't stop my master."

Hunter wiped his eye again. Sure enough, he'd been shot by some kind of gun-toting demon-kid. If little girls could heal people back from the dead and some kid could unleash a plague that killed every adult around the world, then demons—why not? Hunter searched the sky for a guardian angel and was rewarded with a fat drop of water in the eye.

"You just shot me. Twice!" He poked his belly, then his shoulder, and frowned at the holes in his jacket. "Look what you did to my brand new jacket!"

"That is nothing compared to what my master will do. He will rend your flesh and eat because he hungers. He always hungers."

"It sounds like your boy needs a pizza. I don't deliver. Now, drop the gun."

The creature rushed for Hunter, wielding the rifle like a club. Hunter ducked as the swing cut through the rain above his head. He tore the rifle from the little demon's hands, hurling it over the edge to the ground below. He lifted the creature up and plowed it against the building, imprinting a nice demon shape in the sheet metal.

The demon sank its teeth into Hunter's shoulder and tore away a bloody chunk of skin. Hunter screamed, more from horror than the quickly subsiding pain. Again his body healed, but now he had an even bigger hole in his jacket.

He gripped the thing by the throat and bashed it in the face repeatedly before releasing it with a final punch. The demon scrambled away from Hunter's fury.

"You've ruined my brand new jacket my girlfriend made me. Now I'm going to hear all kinds of crap about how I never appreciate anything she does for me."

Hunter grabbed the back of the demon's shirt and dragged it across the roof with every intention of throwing it after its rifle. The pounding rain washed away some of the madness, and Hunter hesitated. The creature jumped with inhuman speed, flipped behind Hunter, and shoved him from the roof. Hunter caught the edge and his shoulder popped.

Dangling by his fingertips, he watched the demon pace in quick, tight circles. It smiled and its forked tongue lashed out, flicking blood at him.

"You don't have your wings. The fall won't kill you, but it will hurt."

The demon lifted its bare foot, clawed toenails sharp and threatening. Hunter strained to pull himself up, but his bad shoulder wouldn't allow it.

Thunder roared as a bolt of lightning streaked across the dark clouds and blasted into the demon kid's chest.

The air smelled of ozone and burnt toast. Hunter strained harder, his boots finding traction and his bad shoulder holding. The other arm hauled the rest of him over the edge. He flopped onto the rooftop and rested a cheek on the cool, wet surface. The rain lessened, with giant drops splashing in puddles. A grasshopper twitched three feet away and then flittered into the open air. Hunter closed his good eye and considered taking a nap.

"What are you doing, silly?"

He opened his eye. "Catherine?"

"Huh? Not even."

Hunter flipped onto his back and sat up. A teenage girl in a white T-shirt and blue jeans dropped the demon kid's limp body onto the roof. Behind them, a large smoking hole had been blown into the grain elevator. He gagged from the overwhelming stench of rot.

"Stinks, don't it? Try living down there. I'll never get that smell out of my hair."

"Who are you?" Hunter asked.

"I'm Barbie," the brunette girl said, flashing a bright smile. "Thank you for finding me."

Hunter fell back in a puddle and watched the clearing storm shake the last raindrops from the clouds. "You've got to be kidding me."

2.

HUNTER

"What the fuck is this thing?" Hunter prodded the inert body of the gunman with his foot. "And why doesn't he have a big hole in his chest from the lightning?"

Barbie looked up from her examination of the creature. "Watch the potty mouth, mister. You're in the presence of a lady."

Hunter crossed his arms and his bad shoulder offered a twinge in protest.

Barbie rested on her knees and continued checking the thing's pulse and temperature. She brushed its wet bangs away from its closed eyelids.

"This thing is a little boy who got into some trouble, but we can fix that. He's possessed by a demon and apparently it's impervious to lightning strikes."

"Who are you?"

"I told you that already."

"Yeah, Barbie, I know. But where did you come from?"

"You may be cute with the eye patch and smoldering good looks, but you come off a little thick." She pointed back to the hole in the grain elevator where the stench still emanated, and wisps of smoke climbed into the night sky. "What else?"

"Excuse me?"

"What else do you want to know, or can I go ahead and exorcise this demon before he wakes up and we have to go through it all over again?"

"Are you related to a little girl named Catherine?"

"I used to wheel around with a Catherine," Barbie said, followed by a girly giggle.

Hunter rubbed his forehead, anticipating a future migraine. "I think we're talking about the same person."

"I'm sure we are, Michael." She smiled, pulling her long dark hair back. She produced a hair band from her pocket and wrapped the length into a ponytail. The front of her wet T-shirt stretched.

Distracted, Hunter watched. When he returned his gaze to her face, she winked at him.

"Wicked thoughts?" she asked.

Hunter burned with embarrassment. He shook his hands out, rotated his bad shoulder, and tried to rid himself of impure ideas. "How did you know my name?"

Barbie flashed a fascinating, lip curling, gleaming teeth in the darkness smile at him. She tapped a finger against the side of her head.

Hunter sighed. "Yeah, we're definitely talking about the same person."

The possessed boy moved his legs and shifted his body. His skin rippled again as his eyelids began to flutter. He opened his mouth wide and his pointy teeth glistened with bands of saliva stretching between his lips.

Barbie snapped her fingers twice at Hunter. "Hurry, hold him down!"

Hunter dropped to his knees, straddled the boy's stomach, and clamped his hands over the demon's arms. Milky eyes popped open and a rush of wind hammered the top of the grain elevator. The demon screeched when it saw Barbie.

She rubbed her hands together like she was about to perform a neat trick. "Yes, yes, it will all be over soon. Lie back, relax and Aunt Barbie will make all the badness go away." She patted Hunter on the shoulder. "You got him, right?"

Hunter winced. "Yeah, just don't tap me on *that* shoulder. It hurts like hell."

"I thought you knew Catherine?"

The demon boy bucked and Hunter added more pressure to keep him down. Sharp teeth snapped at him and the forked tongue flicked at his good eye.

"Less talk. More action."

"Yes, master." Barbie rested her hands on the demon boy's head. The contact sizzled and popped like an electrical current.

White sparkling light encompassed her arms and hands. Her ponytail fanned out, standing on end, and her eyes glowed.

The wind pounded them again, swirling up puddles and spraying water in their faces. Where the water touched Barbie, sparks flew and water transformed into steam.

A shock raced through Hunter, leaving his body tingling and constricting his muscles. He shifted his arms slightly, afraid of electrocution from Barbie and all the water. The demon bucked harder.

"Hold him down!" Barbie's voice clapped like thunder.

Hunter fought through the panic and shoved the thrashing demon back down.

Barbie flickered like an old fluorescent bulb, back before the worldwide electrical system winked out. Then she powered up and shined like a newborn star.

Hunter focused on the boy's face, not wanting to go blind, but also not willing to close his eye and allow the creature an opportunity to try something. Barbie murmured a chant in a language Hunter didn't understand. Skin on the demon's forehead smoked. The crackling hum illuminating Barbie continued to make Hunter nervous.

The demon boy's features rippled and then something separated. A translucent mask of the demon lifted like a smoky apparition, rising above the anguished face of a young boy. A pulse ran through the image as Barbie's light snapped up a notch and the apparition expanded. The demon's teeth gnashed together, eyes wide in what appeared to be fear, and the struggle ended with a final gust of wind stripping away the demon and leaving only the sleeping boy.

Barbie removed her hand from the child's head, revealing his smooth, unmarred skin. She touched Hunter, who still held the boy's arms tight. He flinched, afraid of being electrocuted, but her hands were freezing and she shivered all over.

"You can let go now. He'll be fine."

Slowly, Hunter relaxed the pressure and held Barbie's hand as he lifted himself off the boy. He stood and helped her off the ground. She wobbled and fell against him, pressing her icy cheek against his neck.

"I'm so cold, Michael."

"It's Hunter. My parents called me Michael, but they're gone."

She gazed up at him with sad, confused eyes. Her lips parted, but she remained silent. Hunter fought an impulse to kiss her, and then looked over the dark horizon instead.

She sighed. "Whatever. I'm so cold."

Hunter copied her sigh, opened his brand new jacket that his girlfriend had made, and allowed Barbie inside. She was cold and wet and felt very, very nice.

3.

MOLLY

Whenever Molly's dad went out of town on business, her mom would let Molly sleep in their bed, saying the bed was too big without him. That was a long time ago, but lying in bed in the middle of the night worrying about Hunter, Molly now knew exactly how her mom had felt.

Finding sleep impossible, she rolled out from under the sheets. She pulled on her jeans and a T-shirt and left her lonely bedroom to shake the nagging feeling that something was wrong. She lit a candle in the living room and looked over her bookshelf containing twenty-seven books ranging from self-help to anger management. Molly had read them all twice and wanted more. It was nice to be passionate about something that benefited Independents.

Unfortunately she wasn't in the reading mood. Nervous energy had her up and going, so she tied on her tennis shoes and headed out the door of her apartment, down to the cobbled pavement of Main Street, Independents. Grasshoppers jumped about as she disturbed their slumber. Moonlight reflected in the potholes that had yet to be repaired. A rainstorm had passed through, filling them up like little ponds.

Curfew began at eight unless something special at Brittany's kept kids out later. As one of the older kids and a member of the town council, Molly didn't worry about getting busted. Especially since her brother Mark was the sheriff and enforcer of the curfew.

Plus, she knew Mark's new job wiped him out—watching his son all day while his wife, Vanessa, taught the young ones at school. Still, Molly decided to go the opposite way of their house, just in case.

The scent of wet grass brought a refreshing bounce to her steps. She found herself following old paths that led her to the rubble of a house where she used to live. She had created the rubble in a blaze of rage, longing and sorrow. Hunter's old house was a reminder of all the terrible things Molly had been responsible for ten months ago and the strides she'd made since Catherine had healed her troubled mind.

She left one house for another. This house had different memories. It stood on the edge of town overlooking the fields where all the vegetable and fruit crops grew for the kids of Independents. Molly used to come to this house a lot too, but she'd never gone inside. This had been Jimmy's house, Hunter's older brother. Jimmy died so Hunter could live. Hunter carried the weight of that event on troubled shoulders, refusing to share the load with anyone, not even Molly. Someday she would break through and convince her boyfriend that what happened wasn't his fault, but until then she'd keep researching ways to help until something clicked.

The front door opened and she considered running like a child caught doing something naughty. Samuel was just as startled.

"Holy crap!" Samuel jumped when the screen door slammed behind him. "Why are you creeping around out here? You scared the hell out of me."

Molly laughed at the older boy in the tie-dye shirt. "I'm sorry, Sammy. I couldn't sleep."

Samuel stooped over and collected his work boots by the door. Molly noticed the other pair left behind. Samuel sat on the porch steps, slipped his feet inside the boots, and laced up. He stomped on a grasshopper and kicked it off his concrete step.

"You couldn't sleep, so you came out here to visit old Sammy." His mouth stretched into a giant smile, and Molly could almost read his mind. "Hunter isn't back yet, is he?"

"No, he's supposed to get back tomorrow."

"Uh huh, good luck with that. Jimmy never learned either."

"Never learned what?"

Samuel leaned back like he was hoarding all the good information. He sucked on a tooth; a real unattractive habit. "So, I get it now. Hunter's gone and you're feeling lonely, but before you get all hot and bothered, I must warn you that Hunter is one of my best friends and I will not allow you to cheat on him with me more than once... maybe twice. After that you'll just have to tell him that it's over and that you've found a real man."

Molly smiled. "Do you realize how dumb you are?"

Samuel stuck out his bottom lip and looked on with droopy eyes. "No. But I hear about it all the time. One day I'll find someone who takes me seriously."

Molly sat next to him on the steps. "What are you doing up this early?"

"I'm going to kill some grasshoppers if I can find the right pesticide. Those bugs keep destroying our crops faster than the Brittanys are able to can them. Besides, I'm up this time every morning. A lot of us hard working types are early risers. John and Alex are collecting eggs and slopping hogs by now, Frank, Sarah and Jessie are tending to the goats, sheep and cattle, and Dylan is probably out setting trotlines. I bet the Britts are already in the kitchen cooking breakfast."

"Why not wait until daylight?"

"Because I like to finish the tough jobs before the sun pops up. It still gets hotter than hell out in the fields by noontime. That's when I go take a nap in the shade."

"I knew you didn't work all day. Hunter's convinced that Jimmy never took a break. I think it's what drives him."

Samuel sucked on his tooth again. "Well, Hunter's right. Jimmy was a workhorse. He never took naps. I've got three extra field hands doing the work that Jimmy used to do."

Molly leaned over and bumped him shoulder to shoulder. "You're kidding?"

"Not about Jimmy." Samuel tied a blue bandanna around his head. "See, Hunter and I have a lot in common. We both had tremendously hard working brothers that accomplished a lot during their short lives. Greg led us here and Jimmy kept us fed."

Molly gazed at Samuel, seeing the hurt and pain in his eyes that he kept tightly shut off from everyone. His brother and his best friend were gone. Both of them lived in this house with him. Jimmy moved in the day Greg died. Now Samuel lived alone, refusing any new housemates.

He broke eye contact and looked over the crops to the horizon. "Try living up to that."

The sound of shifting grass broke their conversation and Molly and Samuel stood up on the porch. A massive black dog lumbered out of the field next to the house. The creature shook its bulk and snorted, like allergies had gotten the better of it. Then four more giant dogs joined the first. Bright red eyes gleamed in the darkness, locking on Molly and Samuel. A deep growl rumbled from their chests and the leader padded forward, lowered its muzzle, and bared its teeth.

"Get in the house," Samuel whispered.

Molly trembled. She told her stupid foot to step back, but the sight of those terrible beasts with their giant maws kept her feet planted on the porch steps. The leader moved closer and the other four widened their positions in case someone chose to run away from the house.

"Molly, get into the freaking house," Samuel said it louder this time.

The lead dog barked and snapped at the air, showing them what it had in mind. Samuel reached over and retrieved a shovel leaning against the railing. He brought the long handle up and held the spade high. The metal glinted in the moonlight like a mystical sword created for putting down such trouble.

The lead dog paused now that an actual threat had presented itself. The others continued closing the loop on long skinny legs with their skin stretched tight over protruding ribs. Their tails hung straight and low without swaying.

Samuel stepped down in front of Molly. The leader leaned back on its haunches and barked another loud warning. The others stopped and watched for Samuel's next move.

"Molly, get in the house. I have your back. Slam the door shut when I come in behind you. Wait 'til I'm inside."

Molly liked the plan. She knew she should do exactly what Samuel instructed. Her mind was screaming at her, but her body refused.

"Molly!"

"I can't, Samuel. I can't."

"You have to!"

The lead dog took another step. The other red eyes watched for what would happen next. Their rumbling chorus resumed.

Samuel made a quick move off the porch steps onto the walkway and screamed a challenge. The dog slinked back a couple of feet. The others watched and waited. Samuel swung the spade back and forth, slicing through the air. The lead dog stayed out of range, baring its teeth and growling, saliva spilling from its mouth. Samuel screamed again and the dog rose to the challenge with a series of furious barks. The rest began to circle Samuel like they were separating him from the herd, but he caught on. He tripped backing up, and whacked his head on the bottom step.

The shovel clattered on the walkway as the lead dog charged.

4.

MOLLY

Finally, Molly snapped into action. Fear coursed through her limbs, but she pushed through the barrier when the lead dog closed over Samuel like a juicy pork chop. Molly jumped off the porch and kicked the beast in the head with a sickening thud. She snatched up the shovel and jabbed the spade into the rows of teeth as the dog's head swiveled back. The dog yelped in pain, retreating behind the others in the pack.

Samuel lay motionless on the ground with his eyes closed.

"Samuel! Samuel, are you all right? You have to get up!"

No response. The two dogs in the middle separated and crept forward, wary now that Molly had shown her backbone. The injured dog slinked off to lick its wound and await the outcome.

Molly gripped the shovel's worn handle with slippery palms. Afraid to dry them on her pants, she hoped she could hang on until Samuel came around. She nudged him with a toe. He moaned once, but nothing more.

The dog on her right sprang forward and she stepped over Samuel to meet its charge. The beast stopped and crouched again. On her left, the other canine came in low at her legs. Molly stabbed the shovel blade down and caught it in the neck. The cutting edge bit with force and another whining shriek echoed in the darkness. The animal rolled over and Molly struck its side, penetrating its body.

She lifted and twirled back as the dog on her right attempted to sneak up. In the motion of her spin, the shovel hit the post that supported the porch overhang, sending vibrations through her hands and arms. Exposed without the shovel between them, Molly stumbled when the dog bowled into her side and knocked her against the railing. She slipped her hands up the handle and drove downward into the animal's back as its menacing teeth sought her legs. Molly hammered the canine repeatedly with the blunt handle, screaming as fear fueled her strikes. The attempts to bite her ceased and Molly kicked the dog's side, spun the shovel around, and buried the spade in its back. The animal whimpered, fell and bled.

With Molly out of position to protect Samuel, the last two dogs pounced on him. One bit into his leg while the other bared its teeth close to Samuel's throat and watched Molly with red, intelligent eyes.

Molly didn't pause to think. Using the shovel as a lance, she charged the animal biting Samuel, spearing its side and taking the beast all the way to the ground. The other one slammed into her and this time Molly was knocked off her feet into a flowerbed.

She lost her grip on the shovel from the hard landing. The dog followed, its heavy body pinning her, foul hot breath on the back of her neck. Trapped, she clawed at the dirt and flowers in panic. She waited for the sharp pain that would carry her death close behind.

A tremendous roar sounded and the weight lifted off her with a giant clash and a surprised yip. Molly pushed up and regained her feet, searching for the shovel's protection. She found it in the flowers and spun to help her defender.

Her brother Mark, in nothing more than his striped boxer shorts, wielding an aluminum bat, clubbed the black beast until nothing moved. Mark breathed like a thing possessed and searched for more dogs to strike. Four furry bodies lay sprawled in the moonlight.

"There were five," Molly said, trying to breathe and contain the adrenaline spike that carried her, "...five of them."

Mark nodded and stalked through the front yard, searching for the fifth. The lead dog that first tasted the blade of Molly's shovel.

More boys, similarly clothed as her brother, arrived with bats of aluminum and wood, like they were about to have late night batting practice.

"There's at least one more dog out here," Mark relayed to the others. "Get in teams of three and find it. Molly, do you know which way it went?"

Molly dropped to the soft, wet ground, crushed under the weight of fear and exhaustion. She kept her grip tight on the shovel. "They came out of the field. The missing one is wounded."

"Half of you take the field," Mark said. "The rest, search around every house. Luis, check on Samuel."

Boys left in all directions. The ones who took to the field crashed into the high grass that bordered the crops with little worry for the monsters lurking there. Molly found that very brave and very reckless, but was thankful all the same for their courage.

One of the dogs in the yard squirmed and whined, and Molly cried out. Mark walked over and smashed his bat into the animal's head with a disgusting, mushy 'thunk.' The beast laid still, its red eyes dimmed. Molly's stomach flip-flopped. She retched on the flowers, wiped her mouth, and used the shovel to push away from the smell.

"I need light and a pair of scissors," Luis said.

"Are you okay?" Mark asked Molly.

"I'm fine. Get what he needs."

Mark jumped onto the porch and ran into the house. The screen door slammed shut behind him.

Samuel breathed in shallow puffs, his face pale in the moonlight, his jeans torn and dark with blood. Luis shook Samuel's shoulder but the injured boy did not respond.

Luis bent over for a closer inspection. He touched the wounded area and blood gushed, soaking the jeans more and pooling on the broken concrete walkway.

"He took it in the femoral artery. There's no time." Luis patted his naked chest and the waistband of his underwear. He looked up at Molly. "I need your shirt."

Molly removed her shirt and handed it over. She covered her breasts with one arm, holding the shovel handle in the crook of the other as Luis set to work applying pressure to Samuel's wound. Blood, more than Molly had ever seen, flowed everywhere.

A deep growl sounded. The lead dog broke away from the shadows at the side of the house, all salivating jaws and terrible teeth gnashing.

Molly swung the blade of her shovel up from the grass and screamed in defiance at the hungry, desperate beast. The red eyes faltered. Molly leapt forward and cleaved the shovel blade down into the back of the beast and it crumpled to its belly. She raised the shovel again, readjusted her hold, and stabbed it through.

Blood gurgled from the dog's mouth.

Mark tore through the screen door, bat held high, and charged to his sister's rescue. He came to a halt when there was nothing left for him to do.

Molly smiled. "I got him."

Mark wrapped her in his arms and hugged her fiercely. "You sure did, sis. You got him good."

They hugged for about six seconds and then separated when realization struck that Molly and Mark were both topless.

Mark blushed and Molly smiled at his embarrassment. "Awkward," she said.

Mark scratched the back of his head and averted his eyes. "Um, yeah."

"Oh for crying out loud. We used to take baths together!"

"We were four! Things have changed."

Luis had lit a candle and cut a seam right up the leg of Samuel's jeans, exposing the terrible gash where blood flowed freely, but something else felt horribly wrong. Tears flowed from Luis's eyes as freely as the blood, and then Molly knew.

Luis looked up and said, "He never really had a chance."

Molly knelt, joining Luis's sorrow. A breeze wrapped around them, extinguishing the candlelight.

"What are you sillies doing?" A small hand rested on Molly's bare shoulder. Catherine stuck her head between theirs and looked gravely at Samuel. "Haven't you learned by now there's always a chance when I'm with you?"

5.

SCOUT

All the noise woke him up. Scout quickly dressed and tied on his Converse All-Stars.

"Where are you going?" Raven asked, rolling over in the sheets. Her eyes remained closed in their dark apartment.

"Someone's outside yelling."

"What are they yelling?"

"I have no idea. It's gotten further away. I better go check it out."

Raven didn't respond. Her breathing turned heavy as she settled back to sleep.

Scout stepped outside and down to the street. Moonlight spread through the sky like a giant white nimbus, making it easy to see the recent rain on the damp bricks of Main Street. Scout jogged toward the distant sounds that led him toward the edge of town. A flurry of grasshoppers scattered at his approach. He wondered why no one thought to wake him up to help.

A yellow light penetrated the darkness like the single headlight on his motorbike. The light was tinged with a soft pinkness that Scout had never seen in one of Catherine's previous healings. He sped up, knowing that something serious must have happened if the little girl was working a miracle.

Scout raced the last hundred yards towards Samuel's house and skidded to a stop as Catherine's light shot from her eyes into the heavens. She slumped to the ground, and so did Molly, who appeared to have lent Catherine her strength for the healing.

The first thing he noticed was Molly's boobs.

"Close your mouth, Scout. That's my sister."

Scout's eyes whipped up to Mark standing next to the three unconscious kids with his arms crossed. "Billy, run into the house and find some blankets."

Billy nodded, shaded his eyes from Molly with his left hand, and stumbled up the porch. The screen door slammed shut after he went through. "Sorry," he called from the dark interior.

Luis bent over and wiped blood off Samuel's leg. Whatever wound had caused the mess was healed. He shook his head. "Sometimes I wonder why I'm still studying medicine."

"You're still studying in case Catherine isn't here when we need a miracle," Mark said.

Scout surveyed the yard. Five big shadowy heaps lay scattered about the perimeter. Farther out, boys were hanging around in their underwear, carrying baseball bats and watching the fields. They talked in low, excited tones.

"So what'd I miss?" Scout asked.

Mark hooked a thumb in the waistband of his striped boxers. He shouldered the thirty-four inch Easton aluminum baseball bat that Scout had given him for his seventeenth birthday. Blood spattered the end of the barrel. He smiled at Scout.

"And why is everybody naked?"

Mark's smile grew bigger. He looked back and caught Luis staring at his sister. "Luis! Samuel's fine now. Come over here with us until Billy gets back."

Luis's skinny body leapt up like he was strapped to a rocket. "Sorry!" He hurried over, eyed Mark's bloody bat, and stood closer to Scout.

Mark shook his head. "Why couldn't I have had a twin brother?"

Scout inspected one of the dead heaps of fur lying in the flowerbed. "This is a big animal. Are they dogs or wolves?"

Mark came up beside him. "Whatever they were, they killed all of the chickens and hogs. Alex and John woke me up after they found all their animals dead, and I got everybody else to start searching. I don't know what Molly and Sam were doing out here this early, but I barely arrived in time. Molly said that one bit Samuel on the leg. It was a mess."

"He died," Luis said from the other side of Scout. "He bled to death right in front of me. And then Catherine was here."

"Praise the Lord," Scout said. He bowed his head and prayed, thanking God for watching over them and bringing Catherine into their lives.

Mark prodded the dog with his bat. The dead animal smelled like rotten eggs. "We need to bury these carcasses before the kids start waking up. They're scared of enough things without seeing the Big Bad Wolf."

"This is the Big Bad," Scout said, referring to the world in which they lived. He and Mark shared a glance. "I'll start digging a hole to bury them. Are these all of them?"

"Yes."

Scout whistled, rubbing his hand over his tight afro. "And you got every one?"

Mark shook his head and pointed. "I got that one there."

"Samuel must have put up a heck of a fight."

"No, Molly said he tripped and got knocked out. She killed four of them with the shovel. I got here right before that one ate her. She finished off the last one while I was inside the house looking for stuff."

Scout whistled again. "I didn't know Molly was such a badass."

"She's not when it comes to dogs. A Doberman bit her arm when we were five. It was pretty bloody. She had twenty stitches afterward. She's been terrified of dogs ever since."

"Not anymore from the looks of things," Scout said.

Mark shrugged.

Billy returned and the screen door slammed again. "Sorry." He looked over the bundle to where Molly lay sprawled with her breasts exposed to the moonlight. He squeezed his eyes shut.

"Just stay there, Billy," Mark said. "I don't want you stumbling off the porch." Mark hopped over the unconscious group and retrieved the blankets. He covered his sister first. "All clear everybody."

"Can I make a comment?" Scout said.

Mark scowled, as if daring Scout to try.

Scout waved him off. "Forget it. I'll go dig that hole."

"Great idea," Mark said, and finished covering Catherine and Samuel from the early morning chill. "Billy, go tell those guys to take turns getting dressed before they catch cold. Tell them to go in teams. I don't want anyone wandering out here alone."

Scout picked up the shovel and noticed that the spade was stained by greater quantities of blood than Mark's bat. He walked to the side of the house to find a good burial plot that wouldn't tear up Samuel's front yard, but still close enough so he didn't have to drag around a bunch of heavy dog carcasses. Scout scanned the darkness for a good digging spot. He considered torching the dogs with gasoline because burying them might draw other scavengers, but gasoline needed conserving. Deep holes were easy to create with time and effort.

One of the boys from the rescue party walked through the yard toward Scout, twirling his bat round and round. Scout frowned when he recognized Dylan.

"Hey, Preach. You're up kind of early. Too bad you missed the fight, as usual."

Scout stabbed the shovel into the ground. "What's that supposed to mean?"

Dylan leaned on his bat like a walking stick. He wore a pair of red gym shorts. His ropey limbs were knotted with muscles from hanging around the weight room that Hunter had set up in one of the buildings on Main Street. Dylan smiled. "It's nothing. Why are you digging a hole?"

"I volunteered for burial duty. Want to help?"

"Nah, I got to keep my eyes open in case anymore doggies come around. Too bad they're so skinny. We could have made some wicked stew."

"Is that what Brittany served the other day for lunch? I thought it was chicken."

"You'd know all about chicken, wouldn't you, Preach?"

Scout stepped forward. "What's your problem, Dylan? You've been on my back for three months."

Dylan straightened and readjusted his grip on the bat. "I don't have just one problem with you. My biggest, though, is that you went out and got Jimmy killed then you came rolling back here like you're some kind of holier-than-thou fucker. I think you're full of shit."

Scout's pulse raced and his jaw clenched. "I went out there and risked my neck for Jimmy so he could rescue Catherine. He's the one that chose to die. I had nothing to do with that. I tried to stop him."

"That's not the way I heard it. I heard you jacked up the whole operation by going after your girl, what's-her-name."

"What's going on over there?" Mark called out from the corner of the house. Billy stood beside him.

Dylan spoke so only Scout could hear. "Oh, look. It's big brother to the rescue. See you later, Preach, when we can talk in private." Dylan turned and waved. "Oh, hey Mark, we were just talking about where Scout should dig his hole. I'll keep looking for dogs."

Scout watched Dylan spinning his bat as he walked away.

"Are you all right?" Mark asked, coming over. "What's got you all worked up?"

Scout looked past Mark to where Billy still stood at the corner of the house. The deep pocket of night's shadows hid the little boy's face. Billy turned and ran after Dylan, who patted him on the back like they were old pals.

"Scout, what's wrong?"

He shook his head. "It's nothing. Where should I dig this hole?"

6.

SCOUT

By the time the second splinter tore into his hand, Scout hated digging. He gave serious consideration again to burning the dogs with gasoline. Forget saving gas—not at the expense of his palms. Luckily, this splinter stuck out far enough for him to pull it out with his teeth.

Every so often, raucous laughter carried in the early morning darkness, setting Scout further on edge. Dylan and the couple boys hanging around him were busy doing nothing except talking. Scout couldn't shake the feeling that the general topic of their conversation involved him. How were rumors spreading that he'd got Jimmy killed? Jimmy got Jimmy killed. Scout had just been along for the ride.

The conversation with Dylan depressed him more than he wanted to admit. Only the constant attention to the hole he was digging allowed him to focus on something else, but once he found a good rhythm with the shovel, he only thought about one thing: Did he get Jimmy killed?

Scout stood at the bottom of a two foot hole that was eight feet wide, and a lot of shoveling still needing to be done. He wanted somebody to come over and help him, but after Dylan's accusation he didn't know who to ask or who to trust.

He struck the blade into the ground and hit something hard. His palms skidded down the worn handle and splinter number three slid into his thumb.

"Damn it!"

Laughter followed from Dylan's little huddle. "Hear that, boys? I think Preach is working on his next sermon. It sounds a little dismal. I might have to skip that one."

Dylan's pals hooted and slapped him on the back, like he couldn't get any funnier.

Scout sucked on the splinter in silent embarrassment, mad at himself for letting the curse word slip. He wanted to set an example of a godly life since he preached about it every Sunday, but the change from the way he used to live took time and obviously more attention.

"You should put these on." Samuel held out a pair of leatherwork gloves for Scout. He wore a pair himself and another shovel rested in the crook of his arm. "You should always wear gloves when you dig, especially if you're going to use Jimmy's shovel. It's tossed a lot of dirt."

Scout took the gloves and continued gnawing the splinter out of his thumb. Samuel dropped into the hole and got to work, shoveling with a precision and speed that Scout found amazing and could never possibly match. Smooth steady strokes came one after another, and full scoops of dirt tumbled into piles around the rim. Scout tore out the splinter and spat into the hole. He pulled on the work gloves and took a side, negotiating out of Samuel's way.

Scout began again, working to match Samuel's productivity. It wasn't happening, so he tried to make a good showing.

Samuel tapped Scout on the shoulder. "How 'bout you sit the rest out? You got a good start. I'll take us home from here."

"Are you sure, man? I mean you were a little..." Scout wanted to be sensitive, but there really wasn't any way around the subject, "...dead about thirty minutes ago. Shouldn't you get some more rest?"

"Dude, I got to work or I'm going to go crazy thinking about what happened. Plus, I feel awesome. I've never felt this good."

"All right. I'll hang around for moral support." Scout stepped onto a pile and the dirt tumbled back into the hole.

Samuel scooped it right out again. "Just don't knock over any more piles."

"Sorry."

"Don't worry about it. But seriously, back up two feet." Samuel smiled and dug in.

It took about a minute for Dylan to notice the change. "Nice going, Preach. You found a way to get out of work again."

Samuel stopped shoveling and looked at Scout. Scout leaned on Jimmy's useless shovel and inspected his shoes.

"See guys, I told you Preach was soft."

"Hey, Dylan," Samuel said. "Is it true what they say about lifting weights?"

"What's that?"

"Does it just make your dick smaller or does it also affect your brains? See, cause if it was the other way around, I might be into it."

Dylan took a couple steps toward them, slapping the barrel of his bat into his hand. "That's not cool, man."

"What are you going to do about it?" Samuel drove his shovel in the ground and climbed out of the hole.

"Dylan," Mark called from the front of the house. "I think we're okay here. You guys can go on home and get some sleep before breakfast."

Dylan and Samuel glared at each other, separated by twenty feet of grass. Samuel puckered and blew him a kiss. Dylan squinted hard, trying to deduce what Samuel just did in the darkness. Then he turned and stalked off, followed closely by his posse. Samuel dropped into the hole, retrieved his shovel, and got back to work.

Scout sighed. "You didn't have to do that, man."

"Excuse my language, Scout, but that's bullshit. You don't let a jackass like Dylan give you a bunch of crap. If that starts then you might as well get ready for a heap of trouble. Guys like Dylan don't quit until you put your fist into them."

Scout stayed silent as a strange sense of weariness seeped into him. It might have been a lot better if he had stayed in bed instead of running into this mess. At least he wouldn't know what they were whispering behind his back. He leaned harder on the shovel and closed his eyes.

"Dylan's full of crap. Nobody believes you had any part in Jimmy's death."

Scout's knees shook, but he caught himself before falling to the ground. Did everybody know the alternate version of how Jimmy died? And how many *did* believe it?

"I knew Jimmy better than anyone," Samuel said. "If he had his mind made up about something, then nobody could get him to change it."

"I didn't get him killed," Scout said, just to hear the words.

Just to convince himself that he did everything he could to keep Jimmy alive.

"I wouldn't let you wear his gloves if I thought you did."

Scout looked at the leatherwork gloves covering his hands. They were well used with permanent dirt stains in every crease and stitch. He flexed his fingers. The gloves were big for him but would have fit Jimmy perfectly.

Scout thought about the last words Jimmy had spoken to him. "You're in charge, Scout." You don't leave the person who killed you in charge.

Tears filled his eyes, clouding his vision. He wiped them away with the backs of Jimmy's gloves, leaving dark splotches on the tanned hide.

Samuel cranked out the rest of the hole, taking it down another four feet in a quarter of the time it had taken Scout to complete his part. When he finished, he laid his shovel over the top and leapt up, pushing himself out. He removed his gloves and beat the dirt off them on his cut-up jeans.

"Luis ruined my favorite pair of button fly Levi's. I hope you or Hunter can find me another pair in my size."

Scout just nodded.

"Let's get these dogs in the ground. The sun will be up soon and the last thing we want is smelly dead dogs lying around when the kiddos come out to play."

Scout followed Samuel to one of the beasts Molly had killed. Samuel put his gloves back on and they each grabbed legs. The big dog's head fell back and its snout dragged the ground between them.

Samuel one-armed the creature and covered his nose with the other. "This smells worse than Hunter's underwear after he's been out riding for a week."

Scout smiled because it was true.

"See, I knew I'd get you to smile if I bagged on Hunter."

"I'm picturing you sniffing Hunter's underwear."

Samuel grinned. "You shouldn't knock it."

They heaved the carcass into the pit and left to find the next one. Around the front of the house, they discovered Molly was now awake, sitting up on the porch with a shirt on, thankfully. Of course the thankful part depended on whether or not her brother was still around—which he was.

"Hey there, Molly," Samuel stopped cold and Scout bumped into him, but he barely noticed. "Is that my Nirvana concert T-shirt?"

Molly pulled down the front where a naked baby boy swam after a dollar bill. "Mark gave it to me."

"But it's never been worn. That shirt is a classic."

"What's a classic?" Molly asked.

Samuel looked around for support but his friends were all blank faced. His head dropped in defeat. "First my parents, then Greg, and now this..."

"Don't be so dramatic. I can wash it."

"Don't wash it!" Samuel's voice cranked up an octave.

Everyone looked at him like he was bonkers. Scout sort of understood. He was slightly bonkers about his own special stuff, but that was baseball gloves, not some stupid shirt.

"Just bring it back the way it is after you take it off." Samuel took a deep breath and released it slowly. "I guess I should be thanking you for saving my life."

"It wouldn't have needed saving if I had gone inside the house when you told me too. I'm sorry. I have this thing about dogs."

"Well, those dogs had a thing about you that didn't end well for them. But what I'm really upset about is missing all the good parts."

"What good parts?" Molly asked.

Samuel waggled his eyebrows at her and Molly's face turned as bright as a tomato.

"Knock it off, Sam," Mark said. "I shouldn't have even told you."

"Yeah, right, because now I'm all disappointed and stuff."

"Not to mention deprived," Scout said.

"Good one," Samuel said, offering Scout a fist bump.

"Are you guys done digging the hole?" Mark asked.

"Yeah, we're rounding up the doggies now," Samuel said.

"They're hellhounds."

Everyone looked at Catherine, who had propped herself up and was stretching her little hands above her head. Her mussed blonde hair required a good brushing. Bags under her eyes showed her need for more recovery time from her latest healing.

"Hellhounds will turn to ash when the sun comes up."

"Wish somebody would have told us that before we dug the hole," Samuel said. "I guess I could plant a tree or find some treasure to bury."

"Why don't we fill it with water for a swimming pool?" Scout said.

Samuel nudged him in the shoulder. "You're two for two, bro."

Mark stared them down into silence. "Catherine, when you say hellhounds, you mean..."

"Exactly the way it sounds. Those hounds were sent here from Hell to hunt. Judging by who they attacked, I'd suggest Molly keep her night wanderings to a minimum."

Catherine shifted her attention away from the group. "Well, hello there! When did you get here?"

Scout searched the direction Catherine spoke toward and found no one else in the hazy dawn.

"Yes, yes, I won't say a word. I think you're right. Secrecy would be best right now."

"Who are you talking to?" Scout asked.

Catherine combed fingers through her hair, pulling out the tangles without answering the question. Her eyes grew big and she pointed behind the small assembly. "Lookie, lookie!"

Everyone followed her excitement and turned. The first rays of sunlight found the hellhounds. Their bodies smoked, a dark purple swirl drifting in the sun's rays. The skin under their fur bubbled and boiled and the reek from their bodies smelled like Brittany's the morning after chili night. Daylight cut a bright path through the end of nighttime. The dogs popped with a concussive blast, and a blinding flash made everyone cover their eyes. When it was safe to look again, they found four piles of purple ash sitting on the ground, topped by wisps of smoke.

"What about the dog we threw in the hole?" Scout asked.

"Hellhound," Catherine corrected him. "Will the sun hit it?"

"I kind of doubt it," Samuel said. "I guess we could just bury that one."

Catherine shook her head. "No good. Once the sun goes down it will just claw its way out and go hunting again. You better drag it out into the sunshine."

Scout turned to finish the gruesome task. "I should have stayed in bed."

7.

HUNTER

Hunter's weary eye burned when the first rays of sunshine shot over the east. Thankfully he sat facing south on top of the grain elevator with his back against the metal building, staring at Interstate 80 running parallel to the muddy Platte River.

Barbie stirred under his arm where she slept after exorcising the demon from the little boy. Hunter stayed up all night watching over them both, half afraid that the demon would return. That thought alone was enough to keep him up, but he couldn't stop thinking about his new special ability.

Was he truly invincible? And how did one test the extent of invincibility without carrying it too far? The demon thought the hundred foot drop from the grain elevator wouldn't kill Hunter. And how the hell did the demon know that?

The little boy lay on the concrete with his face to the sky. The same position he was in when the demon was ripped out and dissolved in a screaming fit as it was sent back to wherever. Hell? Hunter never used to believe in Heaven and Hell, but too many unexplainable things had happened in the past year for him to ignore the possibilities.

Hunter worked free of Barbie and laid her against the sheet metal wall, making sure she wouldn't fall over. He draped his jacket, now full of holes, over her and she continued sleeping huddled inside. Hunter stretched his back. He walked around stiffly, trying to jumpstart the feeling in his legs. His shoulder ached, but that was no surprise.

Sunshine crept over the tower's edge, illuminating the little boy. His eyes popped open and he hollered, "I'm me!" He burst up and lifted his arms towards the blue sky. "I'm me again, I'm me! Yippee!"

Hunter smiled. You didn't see a lot of ecstatic joy these days in the Big Bad. If Hunter didn't feel like hell, he'd consider sharing the boy's excitement by jumping around and giving his own shouts of jubilation.

The boy raced around the grain elevator, sprinting back and forth while steering clear of the edge. He passed Hunter a couple of times before giving him any notice and slid to a stop. He flashed Hunter an innocent smile that looked very different from the soulless milky eyes and the pointy teeth that tore into his shoulder earlier.

"Who are you?"

"I'm Hunter. We helped you out of your... trouble."

The boy grabbed his hand with his two tiny ones and pumped it like he was airing up a flat. "Thank you so very, very much!" The child pulled hard and wrapped his arms around Hunter, giving a tight hug that reminded him of another little kid.

"Who's giving out the hugs?"

Barbie stood and held out her arms. The boy broke from Hunter and rushed over to greet her.

"Hunter said you guys saved me. Thank you so much!" He squeezed and she squeezed him back. Hunter was happy he hadn't been caught in the middle of that embrace.

"You're very welcome. I'm Barbie. What's your name?"

"Wesley, but you can call me Wes. Only my sister calls me Wesley anymore. Oh gosh! I hope Carissa is okay."

"Do you guys live in Cozad?" Hunter asked.

"Yes. We came here after the plague."

"Well let's climb down and go find her. I bet she's worried about you."

"Climb down? Where...? Oh gosh!" Wes scrambled away from the edge like a pack of giant spiders had crested the top looking for food and he was it. He pressed his back against the metal building. "Oh gosh, oh gosh! Too high! Too high!"

Hunter and Barbie shared a look. "I think Wes is afraid of heights," he said to her.

"Guess you're going to have to carry him down."

Wes closed his eyes and kicked his feet, shoving back against the building so hard that the sheet metal warped and popped. Given enough time, he might have torn a second hole in it.

"I don't suppose we could knock him out for the trip down? It's going to be hard enough without him squirming in fright."

"Leave everything to me," Barbie said. She caressed Hunter's cheek with her index finger. "Big boy."

"I have a girlfriend." Hunter blurted the statement out for two reasons: he wanted her to know so there were no misunderstandings, and he needed the reminder.

Barbie paused, turning her head back to regard Hunter. "I'm sure you do." She looked him over, toes to top and back again. "Jealous." She laughed and continued walking. Hunter swore her hips swung wider on the trip over to where Wes was still trying to escape the scary distance to the ground.

Barbie knelt and laid her hands on the sides of his head. "Wes, we're going to need you calm so we can get down from here."

"Down! I'm not going anywhere!"

Barbie bowed her head and her hands crackled with electrical sparks. Wes looked shocked. Hunter expected the boy's head to explode, releasing a hardboiled brain, but Wes smiled up at her as his feet stopped squirming and his eyes drooped. She helped him stand and leaned him against the building.

"Time to go," she said.

"How long will that last?"

"Long enough, but let's not dally."

"C'mon, Wes. Let's go find your sister," Hunter said.

"Okay," Wes said, sounding half-asleep.

Hunter led them to the taller building that capped the end. He jiggled the doorknob and bumped it with his good shoulder to break the lock, but nothing doing. They were going down the hard way. He looked over a different ladder than the one on the opposite side, figuring out how the hell he would climb down with a limp body draped over him. Wes stood close by, oblivious to the dangerous height.

Barbie opened the locked door with a simple turn and whistled Hunter over. "Hey, I think there's some stairs in here if you want."

Hunter patted Wes on the back. "What do you know? Something is going right."

Wes gazed at him in an open-mouthed stupor.

"Never mind. Just stay close to me."

Hunter led the way inside where a control panel for operating the grain elevator occupied one wall and the smell of rotten grain overpowered everything. He lifted his shirt to mask the stench. No help. Murky light crept in through filthy windows, but the light was enough to navigate the flight of stairs leading down. Hunter went first, followed by Wes, then Barbie.

The trip ended with ease as Hunter found the unlocked door that led outside.

"Fucking great," he said. "I didn't even try this door. I thought the ladders were the only way up."

Barbie narrowed her eyes at him.

"What?"

She covered Wes's ears. "I wish you would not use language like that, especially in front of the child."

Hunter frowned, but conceded with a nod.

Barbie's hands crackled on the side of Wes's head. The little boy's eyes opened wide and he smiled when he noticed the ground. "Hey, how'd we get down?"

Hunter wiggled his fingers at him. "Magic." He used his best mysterious voice.

"Don't tease him." Barbie punched him in the shoulder.

Hunter dropped to his knees and screamed. "Motherfucker, don't hit me there!"

Barbie took Wes's hand and dragged him away. "C'mon, Wes, let's give Mr. Potty Mouth time to recoup."

Hunter's face hovered an inch from the ground as he sucked in air, blinking back tears. Pain spiked in his shoulder. Half of him wanted to die and the other half wanted to ride home and leave freaking Cozad and crazy Barbie in the dust. But he couldn't. Samuel needed information or they'd risk losing their food crops to a bunch of grasshoppers and starving through the winter.

He stood on shaky legs, rubbing his hurt shoulder with the opposite hand, and staggered after Barbie and Wes. They were stopped in front of a sign that Wes pointed out.

"This is the 100th Meridian sign. I'm not sure, but I think it's important."

"Oh it's very important, Wes," Barbie said.

"Why the..." Hunter coughed. "Uh, why is it important?"

Barbie gave him a blank look. "Well, duh. It's the 100th Meridian."

Barbie and Wes began walking again.

Hunter waited a moment until they were safely away. "Stupid bitch."

"That's very hurtful," she yelled back. "C'mon, we got stuff to do."

Hunter jogged up behind them as they entered onto Main Street, Cozad, which looked like Independents, right down to the growing number of potholes. A scrawny brown dog barked at them from the shade of a storefront. Hunter noticed the faces peering at them from the windows. Then he saw recognition on one of the faces, and a girl tore out of the building.

"Wesley, oh Wesley," the girl cried. She ran to Wes and scooped him up, swinging him around, laughing and crying along with fourteen other emotions dancing across her face.

Barbie wrapped her arm around Hunter's waist and laid her head on his good shoulder. "It always feels so nice to do good deeds for people. This is the reward: happiness, full and abundant. Am I really what you said?"

"What?" Hunter asked, distracted. "Oh. No, I'm sorry about that. I have a lot of pent up aggression. At least that's what my girlfriend keeps telling me."

"She sounds smart. Are you sure things are working out between you two?"

"Very."

"Well, we'll see once we get you home. Won't we?"

"Guys, guys, this is my sister, Carissa. Carissa this is Hunter and Barbie. They brought me back."

"Thank you so much for saving my Wesley. I wish there was some way I could repay you for your kindness."

"Something to eat would be great. I'm starving. Then I need to speak to your farmers."

"You want something to eat?" Carissa repeated in a hollow voice.

That's when Hunter noticed her emaciated form, veins corded along the skin of her bony arms, her sunken cheeks below big round eyes. Then the rest of the kids in the building shambled out front onto the walkway. A couple kids stumbled off the curb and were assisted back to their feet. One chased after the dog in an attempt to do something. Hunter wasn't willing to speculate.

"Just take me to your leader," Hunter said.

8.

HUNTER

They crowded around Hunter like a pack of zombies and he knew his brains would not be enough to satiate their hunger. The clothes draped over their bodies would have fit kids twice their size. Their skin, drawn and grey, reminded him of all the dead he'd stumbled across after the plague first hit. The starving kids stared at Hunter with their mouths opening and closing like they were eating oxygen. No way did he have enough food in his backpack to feed this crowd.

Carissa fussed over Wes's bangs, brushing them to the side as she focused on his features. Wes looked healthy and Hunter guessed it came from his time spent possessed by the demon.

"Carissa," Hunter said. "Which one is your town leader?"

Carissa stopped stroking Wes's hair. She looked at the ground. "She died."

Hunter's stomach dropped. He hated this. "How did she die?"

Carissa glanced at the hollow faces of her fellow townspeople. None met her eyes. They stared at Hunter like he offered them hope on a giant silver platter with extra pickles. He maybe had two tortillas left, some jerky and an apple. Not what you would call a bountiful buffet. This crowd would tear each other apart for a single bite.

Carissa turned dark eyes on Hunter. "She got eaten."

A chill swept over Hunter. His hands trembled and he tightened them into fists. His stomach flipped like a kid on a trampoline who doesn't make it all the way around. Needing immediate clarification, his words came slowly.

"What—do—you—mean—eaten?"

An older boy broke from the pack and rested his hand on Carissa's shoulder. The boy nodded at Hunter. "My name's Henry."

"Hunter."

"Where do you come from?"

"Town like this one called Independents. It's southwest of Lincoln, just north of the Nebraska-Kansas state line. I was sent here because we're having troubles with grasshoppers eating our crops, but first I had to deal with your sniper."

Henry scratched his head and flakes fell like a heavy snow. "That wasn't our doing. You met the creature controlling Wes."

"This is Barbie. She chased it away for good, right?"

Barbie nodded with heavy sadness in her eyes, creasing her brow. Hunter guessed her magic was capable of many things, but figured it couldn't produce a stack of pizzas.

"If you did, then thank you," Henry told Barbie. "We knew something was wrong with him, but we weren't prepared for it. He kept us penned in here for the past two weeks."

"What did she mean when she said your town leader was eaten?" Hunter asked.

Henry's sad eyes searched the crowd. "That's why we haven't left town."

The kids in the middle of the pack stared intently at Hunter and Barbie. Their eyes burned with a gigantic need. It was the kids on the edges that made Hunter worry. They appeared uninterested in the discussion. Their eyes were locked up and down the street, flickering to the shadows and the rooftops. Something else besides a demon sniper terrified the kids of Cozad.

"Are we safe out here in the streets, Henry?"

The skinny teenager shook his head. "We're not really safe anywhere."

"Is it safer back in that building?"

Henry shrugged. "It's better than nothing."

Hunter nodded and began moving toward the building. He passed Carissa and she reached out, wrapping her stick-like fingers around his arm.

"Thank you," she said.

Hunter smiled at her. "You're welcome."

A sudden howl tore through the quiet street. Hunter shivered in the morning heat. The crowd around him sprang to life. Wide eyed and fearful, they moved with a shambling gait to the better-than-nothing safety of the building. A couple kids fell and were trampled by others in the panicked surge. Furious at what happened, Hunter ran to the nearest fallen little girl and helped her stand. Her nose bloodied, she broke away toward the building as another howl erupted, louder, closer and a whole lot more chilling.

Henry ushered people through the door, giving instructions. "Twelve and under to the back. Everyone else, you know what you have to do."

Hunter heard the fear in Henry's voice, but the boy's eyes were steady, focused. The last of the kids filed inside with Carissa and Wes bringing up the rear. Hunter and Barbie waited while all of Cozad packed inside the building. The older ones lined up, pressing against the large windows and looking out. This was not suitable protection from whatever howled.

"Henry, what the hell is going on?"

Henry looked inside, his eyes stopping on Wes in the back with the twelve and under crowd. Carissa left him there and went to the window in silent tears.

"About two weeks ago in the middle of the night, six kids went missing, including my little sister. The next morning after breakfast, Wes started shooting anyone who tried to leave the diner." Henry looked down the street. "Later that day, this tall kid comes walking down the street with our missing six, and when our town leader went out to see what was going on, the kid killed her and then they ate her on the spot."

"You're fucking kidding me?" Hunter checked Barbie, expecting a rebuke, but she stared at the ground.

Henry continued like he hadn't been interrupted. "I don't know how or why but that tall kid turned six of our youngest kids into man-eating monsters."

Hunter's head spun around the idea. He leaned against the building before he crashed into the sidewalk. Another howl tore through the town, and this time Hunter realized why it was so disturbing. The person making that sound couldn't be more than nine. He wiped the sweat off his brow and dried his hand on his shirt.

"It's been two days since they last fed."

Frustrated, Hunter's anger sparked. "Why don't you fight back?"

"We tried. They slaughtered half of us like we were a bunch of little kids instead of the other way around. The creature leading them was the worst." Henry scanned the kids as if he didn't want the wrong people hearing. He turned back to Hunter. "He ripped off people's limbs."

Hunter looked around the street for signs of the carnage that wasn't there. "Where have the bodies gone?"

"I don't know. Every night we hear a bunch of growling in the streets, like a pack of dogs or something, but we've been too scared to look. Every morning the bodies are gone. Last night the rain finally washed all the bloodstains away."

Hunter regarded Barbie. She still stared at the ground, watching ants go by in their fruitless search for a picnic. "Barbie?" She didn't respond. He shook her shoulder, breaking her trance. Slowly, she lifted her head and met his gaze. "What are we dealing with here?"

She opened her mouth, but nothing came out. Her eyes fluttered like butterfly wings. She tried again, her voice croaking the first word. "His... name is Famine. He feeds on starvation, creating more in his image, and they will spread his sickness across the land. As food sources are destroyed, the people will consume each other until nothing and none remain."

A screech sounded from nearby and Hunter turned in the direction. A little girl the size of Catherine stood in the middle of the street at the end of the block. She raised her head, throat exposed, and howled like a lost soul. The girl lowered her head and glared at them. Slowly, the other five filtered around the corner and stopped in line with the girl.

A strong wind stirred up the dust lying around town and blew through the street like a big brown specter, momentarily blinding Hunter. A spray of dirt struck his face, and when it stopped he chanced a peek. There was now a seventh person standing behind the other six. He was tall and gangly, with a mop of oily black hair on his head.

"Inside," Henry said. "Go to the back with the young ones. You'll be safe with them."

"What do you mean?"

Henry held the door open and pointed. "You'll see inside."

Hunter followed Barbie into the Cozad building and was greeted by a wave of putrid smells as if a bag of dirty socks exploded in there and barfed before taking a dump. A couple of tables and chairs were spaced throughout. The older kids lined up against the window. Some of them wept, bodies trembling, and all of their knees shook with fear. Whatever was about to take place, Hunter knew it never should. The little kids in the back of the building whimpered in a mass huddle. The look on their faces showed a terror that Hunter never believed possible.

He turned back and found Henry taking a spot at the window that must have been reserved for him. "What happens next?"

"One of us is chosen."

"Chosen for what?" Hunter asked as other faces stared back from the opposite side of the windows, and Hunter knew. This building housed a meat market filled with a selection of cold cuts, and the lunchtime crowd had just arrived.

The tall gangly kid with the oily hair passed by the first window and Hunter's mind grappled with recognition, but he couldn't be one hundred percent sure. By the second window, the percentages rose. The kid had grown two feet taller since Hunter had beat the hell out of him and then Patrick banished him into the wilderness.

"Tommy the Perv!"

Tommy came to a halt, turning his head at the sound of his name. His smile revealed horrible pointy teeth. Black, dilated pupils absorbed every inch of Hunter. Then Tommy pointed.

Henry gasped. "You've been chosen."

Hunter trembled with one part rage and two parts terror. "Yeah, I'm lucky like that."

9.

HUNTER

The crowd on this side of the window gave a collective sigh. Hunter watched the cannibal children leave the window outside and move to the street. Only Tommy the Perv remained. He looked hungry, licking his lips and smacking his chops. Like the demon that controlled Wesley, Tommy's teeth were sharpened into tiny, unnatural points.

Tommy knocked on the glass, signaling for Hunter to come outside like they had a play date scheduled and Hunter was bringing the snacks. Creepy Tommy didn't scare Hunter, but those six little kids out there made him want to run and huddle in the back. What could possibly turn them into hideous killing machines? How do you hurt kids, even ones that want to eat you for dinner?

Hunter considered his newfound invincibility. How was that working, and how many bites could he surrender before the portions ran out?

The scared kids of Cozad, unable to stand at the window looking at Tommy and the six, turned away without making eye contact with Hunter, like he no longer existed.

"Henry?" Hunter said. "Do you guys have transportation?"

"We have a bus if we could get to it, but the battery needs charging."

"Great."

"So what's the plan?" Barbie asked. Her narrowed eyes fixed

on Tommy, showing she intended to go with Hunter. He hoped this might work out after all.

"What are you bringing to the party?"

Electricity crackled around the tips of her fingers. "Watch and see."

"Maybe I should do that from in here."

"I wasn't chosen."

Hunter wished he'd looked around the grain elevator for the rifle before they left. "Do you have any guns in here?" he asked Henry.

"No. We kept them locked up, but they all disappeared when that guy showed up."

Hunter rolled his sore shoulder and popped his neck. "Fine, let's do it then."

He moved toward the door and grabbed a broom leaning against the wall. The thick handle felt heavy and comforting. Before he opened the door, he stomped down and snapped the head off, leaving a jagged edge. He smiled at his pathetic weapon even as he grabbed the door handle with a shaky hand.

"Don't worry, Michael," Barbie said. "God is with us."

"I hope so." Hunter pulled the entrance open and walked into the sunlight.

Tommy had moved away and towered over the children gathered around him, like a deranged babysitter. They all looked confident and hungry. It was the hungry part that had Hunter calculating the run to his hidden motorbike.

Beads of sweat ran down his back and each step felt like he dragged a pair of concrete shoes. Hunter stopped twenty feet away and Barbie pulled up beside him. He wished the sky was filled with clouds, maybe a giant thunderhead, so Barbie could work some serious magic and end this quick with one bolt of lightning, but all he saw was pure blue. It would have been a beautiful day if not for the six drooling kids and the perv.

Tommy cocked his head. "I know you."

"We met once, back in Denver. You were putting your hands on my brother's girl."

Tommy's chuckle rang hollow in the space between the store fronts on Main Street, Cozad. "I've done that to lots of girls." He sounded like he was talking through a pipe. "What made your brother's girl so special?"

"She was the last one in Denver before Patrick kicked you out." Hunter hefted the broomstick to his shoulder. "I beat your ass right before that."

Tommy wiped the corner of his mouth with a solitary finger. "She was your sister?"

"That was a cover story."

Tommy tilted his head and narrowed his eyes, moving them sideways to stare at Barbie. "You will not stop us, little sister."

"I'm not your sister."

"I wasn't referring to our relationship, only to your higher calling. It will satisfy me greatly to savor your flesh, in more ways than you can imagine."

"All right, dude. Number one, gross, and number two, she's not your type."

"Everyone is my type." Tommy looked at the two little boys and a girl on his left. They returned his gaze with eager anticipation. Tommy closed his eyes and nodded. They sprang from their spots and rushed Hunter and Barbie, howling, with tiny hands stretched out like claws.

Hunter stepped back and gripped the broom handle tightly, trying to figure out who to stick first and whether he should even do it.

Barbie stepped forward, hands sizzling at her sides with white balls of hot fire. The light show did not deter the kids from the tempting meal. Barbie shot low and thin electrical bolts struck their knees. The current climbed their bodies, turning their eyes into white orbs. Realization struck their faces that dinner plans had changed. They dropped to the ground in spasms.

Hunter gagged and tried hard to keep from screaming and throwing up at the same time. Those poor kids didn't deserve to be roasted either.

Barbie looked back at all the noise Hunter was making, sensing the reason for his discomfort. "They're just unconscious," she told him. "But they will wake up. You better finish this quick."

Hunter wiped his forehead and pointed. The other three kids had been unleashed and were almost upon Barbie. She sidestepped the closest and the girl flew into Hunter, bowling him over, snapping her teeth at his throat. The stick clattered out of his hands and across the pavement as he fought to keep the girl from biting him. He grabbed both sides of her head. Her fingernails raked his arms, searching for his face, while her knees pummeled him down below.

Hunter rolled and carried the girl over onto her back. Quickly he pushed up, but the moment he released her head she bit into his wrist. Hunter screamed and tried to yank free. The girl reached up and slapped his face, raking her fingernails across his cheek. Hunter pushed his free hand against her face. She took the bait and bit his other hand.

Then Barbie knelt beside him and touched the crazy cannibal's small head. An electric pulse rippled through her, causing the unfortunate reaction of chomping on Hunter's hand before she fell unconscious.

Hunter backed away and tripped over one of the other five kids sprawled on the street. He scrambled away in panic as pain burned his hands. He regained his feet and inspected his wounds as they started to heal. Glancing up, he remembered Tommy, but the perv had not moved from his spot. Barbie retrieved Hunter's lost stick.

Tommy smiled.

"Quit screwing around and zap this asshole!"

Barbie tossed the stick at Hunter. He caught it, wincing because he half expected his hands to hurt. They didn't.

"He's different. It only works on the innocent."

"So what are you saying?"

"This is your fight, Michael. It's why you're here."

Hunter looked from her to Tommy. Tommy's smile widened. Hunter looked back at Barbie. "You're not making any sense. I'm nobody. Just some dumb kid who got his brother killed. This is some kind of freaky, supernatural shit. I mean, look at this dude! He grew two feet in four months and didn't have sense enough to find clothes that fit."

"Michael, you didn't get your brother killed."

His anger swept him away for an instant. "Stop calling me that! My name is Hunter!"

Barbie placed her hands on her hips. "You didn't get your brother killed. He died so you could be reborn as God intended."

"Bullshit!"

Barbie marched over the unconscious kids in her path and got right up in Hunter's face. "You are too good to use language like that!" She rocked onto her tiptoes, wrapped her hands around the back of his neck, and kissed him hard on the lips. "Now go kick his ass!"

Barbie stepped around him without another glance, leaving nothing but the cracked pavement between Hunter and Tommy, the very hungry looking perv. Hunter hefted the stick in his hands, trying to find the passion to fight, but all his anger had fled after rolling around on the ground with the possessed girl biting his hands. A steady dose of horror and revulsion filled him, but not a willingness to throw down. That was not good. Without anger fueling him, Hunter could pretty much kiss his chances goodbye.

He took a deep breath, wishing Tommy would say something to piss him off. Tommy stood there flexing his fingers and licking his lips. Hunter looked elsewhere for strength. The six little kids frightened him. His sight swept over the unconscious group and settled on the girl who bit him.

Her breaths came in rapid pants, like she suffered from an overactive jolt of energy that even in sleep wasn't enough to slow her down. She wore a thin summer dress covered with a yellow flower print. Her small feet were dirty and bare. Traces of Hunter's blood smattered her lips. Her hands were perfectly small, curled up next to her face as if any moment she would fold them together and pray.

Tommy chuckled, deep and hollow. Hunter felt a spike of what he needed.

"You like her, don't you?" Tommy said. "If you join me in the feast, I will let you have her, if you know what I mean."

Madness swelled in Hunter. He gripped the stick and ran, jagged point leading the charge. He screamed as he sprinted down the street, with Tommy waiting to receive him. Hunter pushed ahead and met empty air where he hoped a skewering impact would take place, but Tommy spun out of the way and chopped Hunter in the back of the neck. Hunter hit the ground and skidded over the pavement on his chest.

Tommy leaped on top of Hunter and clawed his back, cackling like a loon. Each rip of flesh through Hunter's shirt sent searing pain as Tommy flayed him open.

Tommy gripped Hunter's hair. "This used to be shorter," the perv said, reflecting on the last time they met. "Your sister had the big boobs, didn't she?"

Hunter bucked. "She's not my sister!"

Tommy held on strong and rode him out. His other hand stretched in front of Hunter's face. Long, dark fingernails, with who knew what underneath, dropped towards Hunter's throat. Tommy's hot, rancid breath fanned the back of Hunter's neck.

"I'm going to drain your blood right here for your little saint to see. Then I'm going to eat her too."

The dark fingernails flicked. Hunter jerked his head forward and then rammed backward. He felt the solid crunch of something soft.

Tommy screamed, standing up. Hunter scrambled for the stick, rolled up, and found Tommy holding his busted, bleeding nose. He rushed forward, but instead of trying the impaling trick again, he hit the brakes and swung. The broom staff smashed against Tommy's head. Quickly, Hunter spun the staff around and crashed it on the other side of Tommy, right in the hip. Then it was a one-sided sword fight, swinging at random targets, with Tommy trying to guess where the staff was headed next and always protecting the wrong spot.

Tommy would not go down and Hunter found himself slowing from exhaustion. Then Tommy got it right. He caught the staff and yanked it from Hunter's hands.

Tommy staggered on his feet, holding Hunter's weapon. Hunter wavered, out of breath and energy. The staff blurred in Tommy's thrust and the broomstick pierced Hunter's stomach. Tommy yanked the staff out and Hunter knew his intestines followed as his stomach burned. He hoped his invincibility was about to kick in because the pain exploded into his brain and he cried in anguish, falling to the ground and waiting, waiting...

Tommy scuffled over. "You almost had me there, but not quite..."

A brick flew by and smashed Tommy in the face, followed by more rocks and debris. A dozen angry voices yelled threats. He hoped Scout had come to save him with a group from Independents. Jimmy would be mad. Hunter lifted his head, but his eyesight blurred the small forms rushing at Tommy. His head bounced off the pavement as he remembered something important before fading out.

Jimmy was dead.

10.

MOLLY

Mark followed her through Independents. It was really kind of sweet, but Molly hoped he didn't expect to make it a habit. It would be inconvenient when she had to use the outhouse or wanted to take a bath or, God forbid, have "cuddle time" with her boyfriend.

At least her twin brother didn't object to her relationship anymore since Hunter had proven himself worthy. Molly smiled. She was the one who had to prove to everyone in Independents that she was good enough after her betrayal involving Catherine's kidnapping last November. But Catherine had made Molly good again. And that was enough.

Molly stopped at the corner of a street. Mark walked right into her and barely had time to catch her before she fell.

"Mark, really, I'm fine. Catherine said that the hellhounds only come out at night."

"Yeah, well, what if something else is out here to get you? I'm not taking any chances."

"I don't even know why Catherine thinks they were after me. I'm nothing special. Not like the chickens and pigs they killed before finding us. They could have been going after Sam."

"Why would they go after Sam?"

She sat on the curb and retied her shoe. "He's the one that feeds this town now. Without him, I don't think the other kids working in the field would know what to plant where and when it's time to harvest." She stood and brushed off the back of her jeans. "Besides, the dogs bit him first."

Mark raised an eyebrow and rested his hands on his hips.

Molly shook her head. "At least go home and put some clothes on. Those boxer shorts aren't leaving a lot to the imagination. Vanessa is going to have your butt. Plus, you're starting to draw a crowd."

Mark followed Molly's line of sight to the group of little girls dismally failing to hide behind a bush at the house across the street. They pointed and giggled until they noticed that Mark had spotted them and then they scattered every which way.

Mark adjusted his boxers and blushed. "Let's head over to my place so I can change, then we'll go to breakfast. It might be a long time before we eat ham and eggs again."

"I have something else to do."

"What?"

Molly pointed. "I'm going over to talk with Catherine. She took off way too fast before I could ask her why she thought the hellhounds were after me. I want to get to the bottom of this."

"She *was* being a little spooky talking to the air and stuff."

"Yeah, there's that too." Molly glanced over Mark's shoulder. "They're back."

Mark spun around. The girls had regrouped behind a tree a couple houses down. "There's nothing to see here! Move along!"

They disbanded in a confused pattern again. Squeals of glee rattled off the surrounding houses. One named Emma held her ground and gave a wolf whistle.

Mark turned back, even redder in the face.

"I've always liked Emma," Molly said. "She's going to be trouble when she's older."

Mark frowned. "Going to be?" He hitched his shorts up higher, which didn't help his situation. He sighed heavily. "All right, you go see Catherine. I'll run home, change, and check in with Vanessa. Then I'll come over and escort you all to breakfast."

"Aren't you watching David today?"

"I'll ask Reese to babysit. Just plan on having me around until we get this settled."

"But, Mark..."

"End of discussion. If you want, I'll just lock you up again." A smile spread across his face, but Molly knew he wasn't joking.

She stuck her tongue out at him. "You're not funny."

"David thinks I'm a riot when I stick veggies in my nose."

"I'll see you in a bit. Go put some clean underwear on, please."

"What are you talking about?" Mark said, twisting around for a better look at the back of his shorts.

Molly covered her eyes. "Mark, you're poking out!"

The little girls started hooting and clapping from the corner house on the street.

Emma hollered, "That a boy!"

Mark ran for home.

*   *   *

Molly walked up to Ginger's house that had become her home away from home. The yellow paint glowed in the morning sunlight like a warm pot of honey. Flowerbeds filled the yard in patterns and swirls, perfectly maintained and full of life and color. Bees busied themselves dipping into petals here and there, having found their personal Shangri-La for harvesting nectar to return to the hive. The smells were intoxicating.

Whispering came from the porch and Molly noticed the swing creaking back and forth on its metal chains. She stopped beneath the green shade of Ginger's pear tree to eavesdrop, wondering who would be talking so quietly.

Catherine looked up over the hedge, but she must not have detected Molly for she continued her conversation when she ducked back down on the swing. "I don't know why she didn't see you. I thought we had a 50/50 chance, but you never know with this sort of thing."

There came a short pause before Catherine answered some unspoken question.

"Yes, she is very beautiful. I think that has something to do with the pregnancy."

She paused.

"I'm glad that makes you happy. Everyone has been supportive. He will have a wonderful reception when he's finally born."

"Oh, I'm sure it's a boy. I know these kinds of things." Another pause followed. "He's out of town on a mission. Samuel has him out doing something about the grasshoppers. You don't need to worry. Michael is very responsible now."

"I meant Hunter. I flip-flop with all the nicknames, except for Raven, of course. I don't want her to hit me." Catherine laughed her innocent little girl laugh.

Molly smiled, even though the conversation disturbed her greatly. Catherine obviously suffered from some sort of dementia. Molly wondered if the child's guilt over not saving Jimmy had become greater than Hunter's guilt over being the one who was saved in his place. She wanted to sneak back home and check her books before confronting the little girl's delusions. Granted, Catherine was not an ordinary child, but something could still be seriously wrong with her. Everyone was susceptible to mental anguish, especially in these times.

Catherine's conversation continued. "Oh you saw her aura. It's been getting brighter over the past month."

"No, she doesn't remember who she is yet, but I suspect the time is getting close. The hellhounds must have seen her glowing and that's why they attacked."

"She's what?" Catherine shot up off the swing and peered over the hedge.

Molly stood out like a garish garden gnome beside the narrow trunk of the tree.

"Don't you know it's impolite to spy?"

"I wasn't spying. I didn't want to interrupt."

Catherine frowned and looked back over her shoulder. "Yes, I'm being analyzed this very instant."

Another pause and Catherine nodded. "I know. It is frustrating."

Molly ducked out from beneath her hiding spot and walked up onto the porch. Catherine patted the seat next to her. Molly looked around the empty porch. Then she shrugged and took a seat.

Catherine hopped down, pushed the seat of the swing back, and then spun around and hopped up, releasing the swing into motion. "Keep us going, please. My feet don't reach."

Molly wrapped her hand around the metal chain and kicked off the porch. They swung higher and Catherine folded her legs up on the bench, looking pleased to have someone doing all the work.

"So?" Molly hesitated.

Catherine's head snapped around to give Molly her full attention. "Questions?"

"Uh, yes, I have a few."

"My favorite color is pink. I like the number seven and eleven best because they both rhyme with Heaven. My favorite food is bread. I'm partial to grape juice, although not the kind that Samuel makes because too much of that can lead to temptation. I don't remember my mother and don't know how long she breast fed me. I don't remember my biological father either, but my real Father watches over me from His Kingdom in Heaven and, no, He would never do anything inappropriate."

"Why's that?" Molly asked for lack of anything smarter to say.

"He's incapable." Catherine leaned back. She signaled with her hand for Molly to keep the motion going.

Molly kicked off the porch. "Who were you talking to a minute ago?"

"Do you see anyone?"

Molly looked around the porch again. "No, I don't."

"Then I was talking to no one." With a giant twinkle in her blue eyes, Catherine appeared to be having a good time. "My turn. Why were you at Samuel's in the middle of the night?"

Molly pulled her shirt, Samuel's shirt, down. "I couldn't sleep."

"Hunter's only been gone a couple of days."

Heat rushed into Molly's cheeks. She leveled her gaze on the smiling, happy girl. "I couldn't sleep. I didn't say I went looking for comfort in Samuel's bed."

"So defensive."

"My turn. Why would hellhounds be after me?"

Catherine stared at her for a long moment. The swing stopped swinging.

"You want the truth?"

Molly nodded. "Of course I do."

Catherine bit her bottom lip and motioned Molly to start swinging them again.

Once they were going high enough, Catherine said, "I can't tell you everything. One, I don't know it all, and two, you wouldn't believe me anyways. Some things are going to happen to you, and it will all make better sense when it does. Right now, if I tried to tell you everything, it might affect the outcome. Understand?"

Molly shook her head slowly. That, with the swinging and Catherine's explanation, left her feeling dizzy. Not to mention lack of sleep and the fight with the hellhounds and the help she lent reviving Samuel.

Catherine groaned. "This would be a lot easier if you remembered who you are."

Molly hedged back from the unexpected statement. She sort of remembered who she was before Catherine *fixed* her. "Do you mean when I was evil Molly?"

"No, before that. In your past life."

Molly straightened her knees and halted the swing. "My past

what?"

The front door opened. Ginger waddled out in her golden maternity blouse stretched tightly across the round life resting inside her belly. She glowed in the morning light.

"Molly, are you okay? Catherine told me what happened."

Molly looked from Catherine to Ginger and back to Catherine. "My past what?"

Catherine smiled at her like Molly was simple and patted her hand with what must have been patience. "It's called reincarnation."

11.

MOLLY

Obviously, one needed a ton of patience when dealing with Catherine. Molly rubbed her forehead. Catherine could and had done some amazing things, like basically raising the dead or at least not letting Hunter, and now Samuel, slip too far away before bringing them back. And the world had grown a whole lot weirder since Catherine's arrival. Between a boy named Chase being responsible for the plague that killed all the adults, and now hellhounds evaporating in sunlight, reincarnation was just another pill to swallow. Except this giant pill had Molly's name written across it and she never took her medicine well.

"Reincarnation, right," she said, pouring sarcasm into the words. "So what was I before, a flower?"

Catherine frowned. "If you're not going to take this seriously then what's the point?"

Ginger stepped over, belly leading the way. Molly stood up and offered her side of the swing. All the swinging motion was making it difficult to talk to Catherine and maintain any type of concentration.

"I can stand," Ginger said.

"Luis put you on bed rest didn't he?" Molly held the swing steady.

"I had to get out of my room for a bit." Ginger took the offered seat. "I get anxious lying around all day. You know how I like to stay busy."

Catherine placed her head next to Ginger's belly and nodded like she was listening to the daily news on a radio. "Oh, really? Well then, I think you should come out when you're ready."

Ginger shared a look with Molly and shook her head. "Our morning ritual."

Catherine lifted her head and smiled at the belly. "Okay, I'll let her know."

Ginger rubbed Catherine's back. "What's the status report?"

"He's still worried about being cold. He says he's just about ready but he's having a hard time finding his way out."

"Tell him not to worry about the cold. It's been a sunny August so far and Luis has everything we need to keep him warm. As far as getting out, tell him to head down."

Catherine relayed the information then nodded again.

Ginger shifted and held her hands around the lower portion of her belly. "Oh, my goodness."

Molly stood up from where she leaned against the house. "What is it?"

Ginger's face twisted. "He's really moving." She blew out a long breath of air and sucked back in an equal amount. She narrowed her eyes at Catherine. "What did you do?"

"I'm just the messenger." Catherine glanced down at the belly like she just heard a shout and pressed her ear against it. "Okay, I'll let her know."

Ginger huffed and puffed like a bellows at the fireplace. "What?"

"He's having a hard time turning around."

Ginger's face pinched in discomfort. "What?"

"He says he's tangled up in something."

Mark ran up to the house like a pack of hellhounds were having breakfast on the porch. His heavy breathing matched Ginger's perfectly. He wore a pair of denim cutoff shorts and an orange T-shirt with "BRONCOS" written across the chest in navy letters.

"What's wrong?"

Molly knelt next to Ginger and held her hands. "She's having the baby. We need something to take her to Luis's."

Luckily, Mark had been through all of this before. He didn't even hesitate. "Give me three minutes." And he was gone, sprinting across the yard and down the street, pumping his arms as his legs churned like a galloping horse.

Ginger gripped Molly's hands in a tight squeeze, wincing from pain Molly could only imagine. Ginger's face reddened and finally she relaxed her grip. Molly waited for the feeling in her hands to return.

Catherine scooted off the swing and held it steady. She stepped close and placed her small hand on Molly's shoulder. "We're going to need you sooner than I thought, Margaret."

Molly straightened up. The name jingled inside her mind, like the tinkling of familiar sleigh bells from Christmases long ago. Her back became uncomfortably cold and she wiggled in an attempt to shake off a frosty shiver. Memories flooded her mind, but she couldn't make sense of the sequence.

Catherine settled her palm over Molly's forehead. A warm sensation seeped into her, flowing with the pulse of her heartbeat, carrying itself into the core of Molly's soul. She closed her eyes.

A shining light stood at the end of a long tunnel. Molly's hands lifted and stretched toward the light. Her feet walked with a purpose and conviction that she never knew she possessed. The closer she came to the light the more brilliant it burned, and that warmth she felt from the small hand on her forehead was nothing compared to the searing fire that blazed from this illumination. She found it odd that her eyes weren't smoldering in their sockets and that her flesh did not fry off her bones.

Molly found herself, at last, standing in front of a golden cross, the source of the light. She fell to her knees and clasped her hands together, zapped by an electric realization, rewiring and then recharging her mind and spirit.

"I am Margaret."

*   *   *

Someone shook her awake, but she held her eyes shut, wanting to remain in the dream.

"Do you think you should be doing that?" A familiar male voice asked. "I thought you said she hit her head."

Little hands grabbed her shoulders and shook again. "It was just a bump, silly. Nothing to worry about at all."

"Yeah, but..."

"I don't have time for this. We need her in the other room."

"What can Molly do in the other room that Luis and you can't?"

"She has a special talent for these sorts of things."

"What, childbirth? What in the world does my sister know

about delivering babies?"

She waited for the answer, but one didn't follow. She remembered being inside the stifling foul belly of a dragon once. She remembered that her devotion and prayers to the Lord were rewarded with freedom. Not to mention the golden cross she wore had irritated the beast's belly. She smiled in her feigned sleep.

"Now you're just faking. Get up, Margaret. You got work to do."

"Why did you call her that?" the male voice asked, rising concern evident in the way his timbre trembled. "What's going on with my sister?"

Margaret opened her eyes and recognized the handsome young man with the troubled brown eyes. He stood over a girl with shiny strands of golden hair. She knew them both right away, and then she knew herself completely, like the closing of a circle, tying itself off at the ends and containing everything within.

The girl pressed him back with her tiny hand. "It's just a little head trauma. Nothing to worry about." The girl, Catherine, spun around and grabbed Margaret's shoulder and shook her roughly. Catherine stopped, catching Margaret staring up at her, and placed her hands on her hips. "I knew you were faking."

Margaret covered her yawn and stretched. "Hello, Catherine. You're smaller than I remember."

"How's the head?"

Margaret sat up from where she'd been resting on the big yellow sofa in the waiting area of Luis's clinic. She felt fantastic, like she had slept for years and her body was reborn in the spirit. She patted her chest and became worried when she couldn't locate her cross.

Catherine reached into the pocket of her jeans and pulled out the golden chain with the cross dangling at the end. She twirled it on her finger. "I had Scout pick this up for you. I knew you'd want one as soon as you came around."

Margaret reached out and took it from her in mid-swing. "You shouldn't treat it like that."

"Molly, what's going on? Are you okay?"

Margaret gazed at her twin brother, Mark. She felt a pang of regret, knowing this was all going to sound very confusing to him. Mark believed only what he could see, and what she had to explain was so much more than visual.

"I'm fine." She rubbed the back of her head and found nothing. Catherine was just coming up with an excuse as to why Margaret was unconscious. Mark's eyes were filled with concern, so Margaret shrugged. "Just a little bump."

"Why was she calling you Margaret? I thought you hated your full name."

Molly did hate the name, but Margaret didn't have the same issues. Molly hated the old fashioned stuffiness of Margaret. Old fashion suited Margaret just fine. All this thinking in two different mindsets felt weird. Molly had a separate life of seventeen years, but now that Margaret had returned, Molly would have to acclimate.

"Oh, it's not so bad when Catherine uses it."

The door that separated the actual clinic side to Luis's swung open. Vanessa held the knob, looking very much in control, but worry filled her eyes. She wore a blue sterile gown, a matching cap, and a mask covering her mouth. She'd been through a pregnancy before and knew the large amount of risk associated with bringing a life into the world for both the child and the mother. Vanessa would have bled to death when she delivered David if it hadn't been for Catherine's timely arrival. Margaret knew timing had nothing to do with it. Everything was related and timed to the second according to His plan.

Vanessa pulled the mask down. "Catherine, you better get in here and tell us what's going on. Luis is concerned because Ginger's having contractions but her cervix is not dilating."

Margaret reached for Catherine's hand. "What is it?"

"He's tangled in the umbilical cord."

Margaret sighed, stood up, and brushed off her jeans. She looked down at the print of a naked baby swimming after a dollar bill on her shirt. She smiled when she remembered Samuel's reaction to seeing her wearing it. Now she thought the shirt was very appropriate, even though she didn't understand the part about the dollar bill.

"Wrapped umbilical," she said, walking toward the door. "Is that all?"

"Um, Molly," Vanessa said, blocking her way. "I don't mean to be rude, but I think Catherine is the one we need right now."

Catherine stepped up beside Margaret. "No, this is all Molly. She has a knack for this sort of stuff. Trust me."

There was little trust in Vanessa's hardened, worried expression.

Catherine reached out and patted Vanessa's hand. "Trust me," she said again with a smile. "I'll be in there too if that will help your confidence." Catherine took Vanessa inside and Margaret followed, leaving Mark standing by the yellow sofa.

12.

MARGARET

Ginger lay on the narrow hospital bed in discomfort. Lines from the struggle of childbirth were drawn on her face. Her hair hung in sweaty strands, pasted against her cheeks. But that was not the thing that stopped Margaret dead in her tracks.

The transparent form of Jimmy hovering next to Ginger's side nearly keeled her over.

Catherine nudged Margaret in the ribs. "What's wrong?"

Margaret gave Catherine a slow look.

"Oh, you mean him. Yeah, he crossed back over with Samuel. Nice timing, right?"

Margaret held up her cross and kissed it, then tucked it down the front of her shirt, letting its comfort rest against her skin. She stepped closer to the group around Ginger and avoided looking at Jimmy as long as she could. Finally the compulsion overwhelmed her. She glanced straight into his eyes just in time to see Vanessa walk through his chest and make a comment about how chilly the air felt. Jimmy's ethereal form swirled with Vanessa's passage then reinstated itself. He smiled at Margaret.

His face held that same concern and worry that often accompanied it in life. Would it always mark him or was there peace with death? Margaret thought she should remember, but had she ever truly died?

Jimmy's hand fell through Ginger's wrist as his attention drifted back to the only girl he'd ever loved. Margaret, or rather

Molly, had wished for Jimmy's affections. She smiled when she realized it was a year ago. Time worked in slow, meandering cycles, especially if you lived multiple life spans in the service of God. Jimmy had made the right choice.

Ginger groaned and twisted in bed. She reached out and gripped Margaret's hand. Margaret squeezed it reassuringly and prayed. The Lord granted her a steady dose of His power and light to ease Ginger's pain.

Ginger's eyes opened wide. "Molly?"

"How do you feel?" Margaret asked.

"Better, but how? Are you doing this?"

Vanessa and Luis stood on either side of Jimmy. The two living people glanced at one another and then, along with Jimmy, turned curious eyes on Margaret.

Catherine beamed one of her brightest smiles. "They always seem so shocked."

Margaret shrugged at the group who believed she was still just Molly. "There's been a small change. Let me help Ginger deliver her baby then I will tell you what I can."

Incomprehensible expressions remained and, in Vanessa's case, it might have worsened. Margaret avoided further delay and gave Ginger her undivided attention.

Ginger's belly quivered with life. Her breath came in rapid pants as she fought through another wave of labor pains. Margaret supplied more light to help her cope with the contractions. Vanessa gasped. A soft pink light pulsed in Margaret's hand as she held Ginger's.

Catherine circled the bed. "Excuse me," she said to Jimmy's spirit, and stepped through him next to Vanessa. She patted Vanessa's hand. "Why don't you have a seat? It's about to get a lot brighter and I'm going to be helping out. I don't want you to fall and hit your head."

Vanessa nodded and found the chair next to the wall. Margaret guessed it wasn't everyday you found out your sister-in-law had a brand new bag of tricks.

Luis rustled in his blue gown. "Do I take a seat too?"

Catherine shook her head at him. "Don't be a silly. We need you to catch the baby."

"Catch?" Luis wavered in his stance.

Catherine rushed over and supported him. Jimmy's ghost swirled in her passing.

"It might be best if you keep the jokes to a minimum,"

Margaret said.

Catherine stuck her tongue out at her. "Party pooper." She hugged Luis. "I was only teasing. It will be a normal delivery. We need you to do your normal part. Okay?"

Luis sighed. "Okay, no problem."

"Thank you," Catherine said and winked at Margaret. She moved to her original position past Jimmy, where Ginger's sweaty head rested on the pillow. She settled her hands lovingly on her housemate's pale forehead.

Margaret laid her hands on Ginger's stomach and closed her eyes. She spoke calm soothing words inside her mind to the child struggling to be born. She felt his agitated thoughts return quickly. He was ready to enter the world but the umbilical cord, which had sustained him these many months, held him tight and he couldn't proceed. Margaret knew from experience how deadly this predicament could become to the child. In earlier centuries, she had saved many children from this type of fate. Medical advances had solved the problem over the last century, but those advances were gone again with the coming of the plague. Margaret prayed for guidance and help. His answer rushed over her like a jolt of confidence and holy energy.

Margaret concentrated, speaking calmly to the child, guiding him through the tangles of umbilical. The cord had wrapped around his neck. Margaret used the child to lift the cord and unwrap himself, moving the baby closer to the placenta to give him the slack he needed to work free. The child grew excited as the tangles loosened and fell away.

Margaret kept her eyes closed and her hands in contact with Ginger's belly as she maintained a mental connection with the child. "Luis?"

"Yeah?"

"Get ready to receive the delivery."

Margaret told the baby that it was time and he kicked with pleasure and excitement, causing a smile to creep across Margaret's face. She missed the simple joy of being inside a baby's mind. They didn't require much—just warmth, food, sleep, and a clean bottom.

Ginger squirmed under her hands as the contractions ramped up their frequency. "Oh my goodness!"

"You're doing great, Ginger," Catherine said. "It won't be long now. How are you doing back there, Vanessa?"

"Her hands... her hands are glowing..." Vanessa said. "Her

hands are glowing pink."

Margaret fought off another smile at her sister-in-law's confusion. She knew a long conversation with Mark and Vanessa was coming in the near future, and did not look forward to all the explanations she would circle around. Hopefully Catherine would be there for support.

"Yes, yes, Vanessa," Catherine said. "Don't worry. Molly's got everything under control. Don't you?"

"Like riding a bike," Margaret said, focusing on the task at hand. She instructed the baby to turn so he could go out headfirst. The baby squirmed in the embryonic sack as he did a tuck and roll.

Ginger's legs kicked out.

"Ouch!" Luis said.

"Sorry," Ginger said between pants.

"You know how to ride a bike. Lucky."

"Not now, Catherine," Margaret said.

Now in the right position, the baby set himself up for the final push. His glee roared in Margaret's mind like a merry-go-round loaded with four-year-olds. She relayed instructions for him to keep moving forward; he was doing great. The baby was thrilled by her praise.

"Good job, Ginger. Keep breathing," Vanessa said.

Margaret peeked and saw her sister-in-law standing across from her, holding Ginger's hand. Vanessa gave her a nervous smile before transferring her full attention to Ginger.

"Control your breathing like we practiced," Vanessa said. "Work through each contraction as they come." Ginger worked in rhythm, like she was moving coal along a railroad. "That's it. Just like that. Very good."

Before closing her eyes, Margaret noticed Jimmy pacing frantically behind the living crowd. There was nothing for him to do that wouldn't freak out everybody else in the room, so Margaret just let it go and closed her eyes.

"Everything's fine, silly," Catherine said. "You'll evaporate if you keep that up."

"Who are you talking to?" Vanessa asked.

"Nobody," she told Vanessa. Then she added, "I was just teasing about evaporating. You don't have to worry about that. Unbelievable!"

"The head is crowning," Luis said. "Get ready to push on the next contraction, Ginger."

Margaret spoke to the baby silently. "Are you ready?"

The baby gave a cry of enthusiasm in her mind that created a mini-migraine. He kicked out as the final contraction began.

Ginger grunted with all her might. Her belly tensed along with every other nerve and muscle in her young body. Vanessa cried encouragement.

"Welcome to the world, little one," Margaret said.

Luis pulled away with the small red bundle of life. The umbilical cord connecting mother and child, that caused so much trouble earlier, no longer posed a threat.

Luis quickly unplugged the child's nose and mouth and gave the baby a pat to kick start his life on the outside. The baby wailed, but Margaret interpreted his cry of joy.

"It's a boy!" Luis said.

"Told you," Catherine announced proudly.

Jimmy's spirit smiled brightly over Luis's shoulder as he looked down upon the child he brought into this world before his death. Margaret wanted to weep for his life that had been cut short, but was overjoyed that he was able to experience this moment.

Luis walked over with the child and laid him in his mother's arms.

Ginger beamed as her baby boy opened his eyes and gazed straight into her soul. "Hello, James. I'm your mother."

13.

SCOUT

Scout gunned the throttle on his motorbike, pushing the speed, hoping the wind would blow away his anguish. So far he swallowed three grasshoppers and was pelted in the face by another six, but the anguish hadn't budged. Even with the noontime sun and the white puffy clouds hovering here and there, nothing cheered him out of his dismal mood because someone claimed that his actions had gotten his friend killed.

He bounded over bumps, soaring above the ground. He landed and rolled the throttle harder, looking for more jumps. Finally the ride consumed him the way he wanted. Concentration became critical, blocking out everything else. One mistake and he'd flip through the prairie like a flung action figure; only plastic didn't snap and bruise like bone and flesh.

His yellow Suzuki tore through the dirt trail. Patches of wildflowers dotted the prairie where tall Nebraska corn once grew in abundance. Every few miles, a windbreak would mark an abandoned farmhouse gutted of valuables this close to Independents. Scout knew them all for twenty-miles around, having personally walked through every door.

Solitary farmhouses were easy pickings. Small towns and cities had been avoided for two reasons: diseases and gangs. Rotting bodies had left behind the diseases. Gangs had formed for protection and would attack anybody stupid enough to stray close. Almost seven years since the plague, neither disease nor gangs posed a threat anymore. Both met up with the same fate: time. Bodies decomposed, leaving nothing infectious behind. Gangs learned how to survive for themselves or disbanded.

Scout carved a path to a farmhouse through the high native grass. He killed the engine by the porch before slipping his water bottle out of his bag and taking a big guzzle. This house used to have baby furniture and a sewing machine that had been acquired last year for his nephew and Ginger. Scout leaned his bike against the railing and went inside to browse.

Light followed him through the door, casting his shadow into the interior. The last time he visited this place was in the cold of winter, but now the August heat stifled his lungs. Sweat beaded along his skin. He pushed the curtains apart to allow sunshine through the dusty glass panes. Then he opened the windows, giving the heat passage outside. A couple of panes refused to slide without a fight. Scout won most of the battles and soon a breeze found its way inside.

Dusty furniture was pushed aside at funny angles from a barren spot. Scout remembered the rug that occupied the empty space. The rug he had rolled up, took home, and placed in his room. The rug, which had burned after its first night when Molly torched his house after Hunter broke her heart.

If Scout was hoping to find something to cheer him up, following that line of memories was not the way. He left the living room and climbed upstairs to the baby's room. A wallpaper border surrounded him on all sides with a yellow bear in a red sweater, a little pink pig, and a tiger bouncing on his tail. Forgotten toys lay scattered across the floor. Scout poked through the pile and retrieved a Jack in the Box, a stuffed Elmo doll, and one of those toys that made various barnyard animal noises. He loaded the toys in his backpack for Ginger, knowing she'd appreciate the gifts when the baby came. He cursed himself for thinking it would somehow make up for Jimmy's death.

"I didn't get Jimmy killed," he said to the empty room then finished stuffing his bag. He zipped it closed. "I didn't," he said, softer.

In his dark mood, Scout stalked over to the closet and opened the accordion-style door. Clothes hung on the bar, and stuffed animals were propped into one corner opposite a box. Scout drug out the box and slit through the tape with his pocketknife. His heart quickened and his smile grew wide when he saw the contents.

He reached in and pulled out the Boy Scout uniform. An American flag was sewn on the shoulder and the green troop number, 17, was sewn under the Nebraskan Council patch. Scout gently touched the eagle patch sewn on the front pocket, like it might shock him, and then he started jumping around the room.

"I found one! I found one! Yes, yes, yes! That's right! It's all mine!"

Scout slipped his arms into the khaki sleeves and straightened the collar around his neck. The oversized shirt engulfed him but that was just fine. Plenty of room to grow.

He reached deeper into the box and found the blue scarf and neck slide. He dug farther and felt patches attached to something else. Then he pulled out the olive sash covered with thirty-three merit badges stitched in orderly rows. Some he recognized immediately, especially the eagle-required ones circled with silver thread: First Aid, Citizenship in the Community Nation and World, http://scouting.org/boyscouts/advancementandawards/meritbad ges/mb-COMM.aspxPersonal Fitness, Emergency Preparedness, Environmental Science, Personal Management, Swimming, Camping, and Family Life.

He touched each one with loving reverence and thought about the lucky kid who earned all these at summer camps, ceremonies and celebrations that Scout had dreamed about since finding his Boy Scout handbook.

A library lay at the bottom of the box, containing a well-used Boy Scout handbook like the one Scout kept in his backpack at all times, and twenty or so merit badge books, ranging from American Business to Woodwork. Scout had struck gold.

He rolled the blue scarf and draped it around the back of his neck, holding it in place with the eagle emblem metal slide. He looped the olive-green merit badge sash across his chest. He tucked the shirttail into his cargo pants, looked around the room— no mirror.

He dashed into the hallway and opened the next door he crossed. The bathroom. He pushed open the window to bring more light inside. He stood at attention and stared at his reflection as sweat ran down his face. Nothing could banish his bright smile.

When the reality of his discovery struck, Scout took to a knee right there on the linoleum and prayed.

"Thank you, God, so much for this Boy Scout uniform. I know I probably don't deserve it, but thank you for giving this to me, and I promise to show my faith in all my actions and words. Thank you, God. Thank you so much. Thank you for the many, many blessings. Thank you, God. Amen."

Scout stayed on his knees, repeating his prayer until the tears came and he sobbed without knowing why. Scout wept until he shed every emotion he possessed, and then he left the bathroom without looking at himself again.

He went back into the baby's room to inventory his find. There was one thing missing that he wanted. He pulled the olive green pants and belt out of the box and the worn olive socks. He set a stack of Boys' Life magazines next to his growing pile on the floor.

The last thing in the bottom was a wooden box. Opening the lid, he found all the patches of rank that came before eagle. Everything but the one thing Scout really wanted: the medal that a Boy Scout earned when he achieved the rank of eagle. He rifled through the contents of the wooden box until satisfied that it wasn't there. It wasn't in the larger box either.

Scout stood and scratched his head. The baby hadn't earned this stuff. His father had saved his scouting experience to share with his son one day.

He walked down the hall and opened a different door leading to another familiar room. This once held the sewing supplies that Scout had given to Ginger. A quick but thorough search brought no medal.

He turned to the last door upstairs and remembered the haunted look on Mark's face. He told Scout not to go in. Scout had listened then, but now was different. Now he needed to find something. Scout needed it more than whatever horror waited for him behind that door.

Scout opened the door. The trapped heat sucked the air out of his lungs again. Sunlight outlined the perimeter of curtained windows. Scout spread the curtains and opened the windows. He breathed in the cool air outside and turned.

Three dried husks lie on the bed. Father and mother rested in peace with their little boy between them.

Scout pounded the wall in blind rage as a fresh supply of tears filled his eyes. "Damn you, Chase!"

He circled the room, looking in the dresser and the armoire—furniture that appeared to be antiques from a different era. He wasn't finding it. So he opened the closet and ripped through the contents, overtaken by madness to find the medal. Scout faced the nightstand next to the man, thinking if he had worked hard to earn something so special he'd keep it right beside him till death.

He forced himself to ignore the nightmare lying a few feet away, then he filtered through the dust buildup on the nightstand. On the surface, there was an empty glass, the man's watch, wallet, and keys, an alarm clock, a mystery novel, a bible, but no medal. The single drawer contained papers, greeting cards from forgotten Christmases and birthdays, an old comic book, a box of condoms, pictures, a pocketknife, ear plugs, a plastic deer call, a stopwatch, loose change, but no eagle medal.

Scout breathed deeply and turned his head. He looked at the man, decayed beyond recognition. Faded clothing contained whatever was left after rot destroyed the man's body. No medal.

The plague did not kill children. The plague only killed those who were eighteen or older. Scout was afraid to think about what killed this child. Afraid to think about what this child experienced before it succumbed to death. He looked at the boy and his heart shattered into a million pieces.

Inside the boy's tiny grip lay the eagle medal that Scout coveted, with its red, white and blue ribbon.

Scout rubbed his dry mouth slowly.

He reached out.

He stopped.

The husk of the dead kid lay curled between his dead parents.

Scout hadn't earned this man's badge. He wasn't worthy to take the one thing this little boy had held onto in death.

Scout grabbed a gym bag from the closet and hurried to the child's room. He removed the uniform and packed all of the Boy Scout stuff inside the bag. Wearing his own backpack once again, he carried the gym bag downstairs to his bike and secured it to the end of his seat and rode away, leaving the eagle medal behind where it belonged. Maybe someday he would earn his own.

14.

SCOUT

Scout rode underneath the afternoon sun that covered him like an extra blanket. Halfway home, he shook off the tension and sadness, his excitement growing from the recent discovery. Scout reached back, assuring himself that the gym bag was still fastened down and still very real—the contents of his dreams packed safely inside.

He reduced speed when he arrived in town and turned onto the cobbles of Main Street where a crowd had gathered outside Luis's clinic. He parked the Suzuki and unstrapped the gym bag. The crowd would keep until Scout secured his treasure inside his apartment. Besides, Raven would know if something important was going on.

Scout climbed the steps two at a time and opened the door. He walked inside, ready to show off his awesome Boy Scout shirt to his girlfriend.

Raven turned from the window, eyes rimmed red. "Where have you been?"

Surprised by her harsh tone, Scout set the gym bag on the table. "I went for a ride. What's wrong?"

"What's wrong? Samuel came over here to check on you. He said some guy was giving you a hard time. I hadn't seen you since you took off in the middle of the night. I didn't know what to tell him."

Scout hurried over and sat beside her. She flinched when he

touched her arm. He settled his hand in his lap, thinking that this wasn't like Raven at all. "I'm sorry. I should have told you where I was going."

"Yes, you should have." She turned back toward the window and ignored him.

Scout waited, wondering how to make things right and wishing he could break out his new stuff and show it off. The crowd mingled in front of Luis's and Dylan looked up at Scout's window. Scout thought about closing the blinds, but decided he just didn't care right now. Then he noticed the pile of toys, baby clothes and flowers propped against the front of the clinic.

"Ginger had the baby?"

Raven sighed, her whole body rising with the effort. "About an hour ago. It's a boy. She called him James." Raven used a white handkerchief to blow her nose. "Samuel told me."

"I missed another birth. I should go down there and offer a blessing to Ginger and little James." Scout smiled. "James! That's fantastic!"

"I've wanted to go down there all morning, but not without you."

"Why didn't you just go on down there by yourself?"

Raven spun her head around, startling Scout with the glint in her eyes. "Because I've been an outcast ever since we got back from Denver. No one talks to me, other than your sister, Molly and Ginger. Everyone else in this town acts like I'm not even here."

"That's crazy," Scout said. Her hard look indicated he'd chosen the wrong word. "I mean, I'm sure everyone is still getting to know you."

"I've been living here for almost a year now. We're way past introductions, but I still feel like a stranger in this place."

Raven was blowing the situation out of proportion. Scout knew she was having a hard time making friends, ever since she'd first arrived as the enemy. But she had proven her loyalty by taking them to Denver and helping rescue Catherine.

Scout had an irritating thought. He looked out the window and watched Dylan laugh with his group of buddies—the hunting and fishing crowd. Billy huddled with them, smiling along with the boys. Dylan patted him on the shoulder.

Scout stood up. "Let's go. We should go see how Ginger and the baby are doing."

Raven's face brightened and she blew her nose again. "I'm a mess."

"Yes." Scout smiled at her frown. "But you're my mess."

She hopped up and punched him in the stomach. Luckily, Scout anticipated her favorite target and tightened his gut in time.

"Impressive," she said.

"I hope you didn't break your hand."

That brought a smile. "Hardly. I need to fix my face before we go." She left for their bedroom, where she kept the face fixing tools.

"Okay, but we don't have all day." Scout chuckled until a familiar white object with blue stripes whizzed past his head. "Hey, that's my pillow!"

"Leave it on the couch. You'll need it later. What's in that bag you brought in?"

Scout's excitement rushed back. "Oh! You're not going to believe what I found! It's incredible!" He ran over and unzipped the gym bag.

Raven returned, wiping her face with a damp washcloth. "It's not another baseball glove, is it?"

"No, even better!"

Scout pulled out the shirt, holding it up to his chest and grinning like he'd just found a tanker full of fresh gasoline. "Can you believe it? What do you think? Awesome, right?"

"Is that an army shirt?"

"What? No, it's not an army shirt." He turned it around and inspected it, making sure he pulled the right one out. The eagle patch stared him in the face. He smiled back and returned the shirt to his chest. "It's an official Class 'A' Boy Scout shirt with an eagle patch."

Raven looked unimpressed.

Scout held it out for her to inspect. He shook the uniform to emphasize that this was a big deal. Scout's shoulders dropped when Raven didn't take the bait. "I've been looking for a Boy Scout uniform for five years now. I finally found one."

"That's nice. I'm very happy for you," Raven said, brushing her dark hair in front of the mirror by the door. "I'm ready to go."

Scout refolded the Boy Scout shirt and placed it back inside the bag.

"Let's go." He followed her out.

*   *   *

Talk on the street was loud and excited as Scout and Raven

moved to join in the celebration. What a fantastic time to be in Independents. Not only were they surviving in a nice clean town with plenty of food, but their community was also thriving. This was the second child born in Independents, their birthdays coming a little over a year apart, and who knew which couple was going to have the next one. Scout would have laid money on it being Hunter and Molly—if money had any value. Maybe he would wager one of his fifty baseball gloves, but certainly not his Boy Scout shirt.

He would have believed that he and Raven could be the next proud parents in Independents, but his latest conversation left him frustrated. Raven didn't understand him at all. Preoccupied, Scout rubbed his brow, totally missing Dylan walking out to greet them.

"Whoa there, Preach. You have some big balls showing up here."

"Leave me alone, Dylan. I'm here to see Ginger and the baby."

"You mean the poor kid that's going to grow up without his father just like the rest of us? Only it didn't have to go down like that. But thanks to you, he's just one more little bastard in the bunch."

"What's he talking about, Scout?"

"Yeah, Preach. You might as well tell her what's up since she's also to blame."

Scout's anger swelled close to the breakpoint. He wanted to swing at Dylan so badly that his fists had already clenched involuntarily, ready and willing. Beating up Dylan would feel so good and so right that it scared him. Scout closed his eyes, lowered his head, and said a silent prayer for mercy.

He opened his eyes and sought Billy among Dylan's crowd. The boy smirked at him. Scout knew exactly where he had picked up that expression.

"Billy, you know that's not the way things went down. You were there. You know Jimmy did what he did to save Hunter. You stood right next to Raven with tears in your eyes and watched Jimmy drive away. I had nothing to do with it. His death was his decision."

"Hey, Preach. Leave the kid out of this. We all know what you did."

"Billy, please. I forgive you. Tell the truth."

"I said leave him be, Preach," Dylan said, and shoved Scout in the chest.

Scout stumbled to the ground, skinning his hands across the cobbles. The impact shocked him—madness consumed him. No prayers would be offered now. He sprang from the ground and flew into Dylan, who stood like he never expected Scout to fight back.

Scout led with a quick jab, popping him under the left eye. Stunned, Dylan bent over. Scout should have stopped. He grabbed Dylan's shoulders and brought his knee up into the staggering boy's face. Dylan toppled backwards and his eyes rolled white. No need for a ten count. The kid was out.

Three of Dylan's friends rushed Scout and tackled him. The blows came from every direction, but Scout clawed and rabbit punched and bit whatever he could to strike back.

"Stop it! Get off of him!" Raven screamed, coming over to help. Then she cried out, collapsing to the ground with blood seeping from a cut across her forehead.

Scout went ballistic, beating whatever and whoever so he could get to Raven.

Shouts interrupted the fight. Mark and Samuel arrived, throwing Dylan's friends off. They backed Scout's attackers away, releasing him so he could go to his girlfriend's aid.

Raven's hand was pressed to her head to stem the bleeding. She sat in the street, her eyes wide with shock and confusion.

"Are you okay?" Scout asked.

She nodded and handed him a rock.

He gripped it so tight the edges bit into his palm. He jumped up and turned on Dylan and his gang. "Who threw this at her?"

Dylan was still stretched out on the ground. The rest of his group refused to meet Scout's eyes—all but one.

Billy smirked at Scout and nodded slightly.

Scout dropped the rock and tore after the kid. "You son of a bitch. I'll kill you!"

Before he reached Billy, Mark wrapped him up and carried him off, cursing and screaming across the street. Billy continued smirking at him as Scout was forced upstairs to his apartment.

15.

JIMMY

Watching Ginger breastfeed his son amazed Jimmy just as much now as it did when he was alive. Of course that had been Vanessa, and Mark had been sitting right there, and Jimmy hadn't been invisible. Not that being invisible mattered now. The baby was his son after all and Ginger was his girlfriend. Well, his girlfriend when he'd been alive.

Catherine came up next to him and whispered, "Close your mouth, silly."

Breaking his gaze, Jimmy clapped his mouth shut and regarded the little girl. Things looked different in death—from Catherine's pulsing yellow aura to Molly shining a bright rosy pink. Jimmy looked at his own body and saw the floor through it.

Activity had cooled in the maternity ward. Ginger was busy bonding with James. Luis moved around the room straightening up like he had another delivery scheduled for the afternoon. Outside, the soft rumble of the generator supplied energy to run the heat lamps and beeping heart monitor. Jimmy remembered when he had laid on that same hospital bed and Luis poked a tube through his chest to drain fluid and re-inflate his lungs. Good times.

Vanessa departed to take care of her own little one, but not before she made Molly promise to talk to her soon. Catherine said they'd get together after dinner, and it didn't appear to please Vanessa that the little girl had invited herself along, but she shrugged and left.

All that remained were Catherine and Molly and their glowing auras. Molly fidgeted with the hem of her shirt like she had a lot on her mind. "Can I speak with you in private, Catherine?"

Catherine patted Ginger's arm. "Are you going to be okay for a bit?"

"I'm fine. Right, Luis?"

"You're in perfect health," Luis said. "They don't mention recoveries like this in my medical books. But they also don't mention divine intervention either."

"Divine," Catherine said, and winked at Luis. "You say the sweetest things." She kissed baby James on the head and he cooed before returning to his food source. "We'll be around if you need us."

Catherine followed Molly to the door then she cleared her throat. Jimmy glanced up from his inspection of the breastfeeding. Catherine motioned her head for him to follow before she walked out and shut the door. Jimmy frowned—that was so un-cool.

He glided over to the wall and held his breath. Well, he didn't actually hold anything but the action felt better. He closed his eyes and continued the glide, tugging his way through what no living person could possibly pass.

"You can stop now, silly."

Jimmy opened his eyes. He'd almost hovered through Molly, who looked as unnerved as he felt by the situation.

"She can see me now?" Jimmy asked Catherine.

"Yes," Molly said.

Jimmy glided back a step and waved. "Hey, Molly."

"Hunter misses you terribly."

Jimmy removed his hat and played with the crease in the bill. Then he realized he'd been wearing a hat and stopped all together. He replaced the hat and stared at the floor. "I've missed him. Where is he?"

"Don't worry. He'll be back sometime."

Jimmy smiled and caught Molly returning his smile. "You shouldn't tease the dead. We like to haunt, you know?"

"How's the whole dead thing working out?" Catherine said. "Did you like the clouds? I find it too bright myself. How are Father, J.C. and the Spirit?"

"Catherine!" Molly said, like the floor was about to open up and swallow everyone standing there. "You shouldn't refer to the Holy Trinity that way."

Catherine pinched Molly's waist and Molly spun from her reach. "I'm devout, Margaret. I said my prayers this morning. What about you?"

"I was busy defending myself against hellhounds."

Catherine offered Molly a wicked grin. "I'm still a virgin."

Molly covered her mouth and gasped. Her eyes widened in what looked like fear and then slowly melted into shame. "I hadn't even thought about that."

For a dead guy, Jimmy felt awfully uncomfortable. First the breastfeeding and now talk about his little brother's apparent sex life.

Molly dropped onto the yellow sofa in the waiting room and her face fell into her hands.

"Ooh, muffins!" Catherine ran to the table and shoved a muffin in her mouth, pocketed another, and poured apple juice in a plastic cup. "Do you want one, Jimmy?" Crumbs shot out of her mouth.

Jimmy shook his head, but couldn't believe how incredibly hungry he felt.

Catherine finished her muffin and brushed her hands off on the front of her white T-shirt. "Sorry, didn't mean to bring up food. The hunger thing is the worst part about being a ghost. Forget I mentioned it."

"How do you know?"

"Oh, I've been dead lots of times, silly. So has Margaret, right?" Catherine looked at Molly around Jimmy like he was as solid as an oak tree.

"How could I have lost my virginity?" Molly said through her hands. "An eternity of abstinence and then the apocalypse comes and I'm giving it away without a second thought."

Catherine straightened and grinned at Jimmy. "She was going to have to deal with this sooner or later." Then the girl and her yellow aura walked over and sat next to Molly and her pink one. Jimmy stared at the muffins a moment longer.

"You didn't give it away for nothing, Margaret. I mean, really, you've been the saint of pregnancy forever. Maybe He thought it was time for you to discover more about your profession with a little on-the-job training."

Molly raised her head, her face lined with haggard creases. "Please don't blaspheme to me, Catherine."

"Look, what's done is done. You might as well get over it and have a little fun. What's it like anyways?"

"Catherine, please!" Jimmy shouted. His son started crying in the other room.

Catherine hopped up with her hands on her hips and gave a stern expression. "Now see what you've done?"

"He heard me?"

"You've got a lot to learn, Mister."

Jimmy glided next to the wall and held his hand close to the white paint. He wanted to stick his head through for a peek, but the overriding fear of getting stuck in the wall won out. "So tell me."

"You go first. What happened when you died? Where'd you go? Who'd you see?"

Jimmy closed his eyes, surprised by the darkness when he did. "I remember floating away from my body with Ginger still holding me in the front seat of that truck. Then I floated through the roof towards the sunshine. Next thing I knew I woke up by a big tree with a shovel lying next to me. Every day I woke up next to that tree and every day, for whatever reason, I dug a grave, and in the evening I would lie down in the grave and go to sleep only to wake up and do it all over again."

Molly rose off the couch and stood next to Catherine. "It's happening, isn't it?"

Catherine shushed her. "Let him finish. Keep going, Jimmy."

"Well, today I woke up early, still in the grave, and I found Samuel by the tree looking down at me. I was excited to see him, but then there was the light that I thought was the rising sun. I followed Samuel and it turned out to be you two all lit up next to my house."

"You never passed on to Heaven?" Catherine asked.

"I don't think so."

"And you didn't see anyone?" Molly asked.

"Not until Samuel."

The two glowing aura sisters left Jimmy out of the look they shared.

"It was bound to happen sometime," Catherine said.

Molly wrung her hands together. "I didn't expect it to be this quick. I just woke up. I barely know what's going on around here much less the rest of the world. Why did He do this to me?"

"He wouldn't have kept you in the dark if it didn't serve His purpose. Trust in the Lord. Isn't that what the Bible says?"

"Proverbs 3, verse 5," Margaret said.

Catherine smiled.

If Jimmy could grasp solid objects, he would have shaken both of them out of their skins. "What is happening?"

They both turned their heads toward him with troubling, sad expressions.

Catherine answered. "Heaven's closed."

Jimmy's gaze darted from the little one to the big one, hoping Molly would be more specific. "What does that mean?"

"It means..." Molly glanced at Catherine, who nodded, and Molly sighed. "It means that the End Times are here and the outcome will depend on us. It means there won't be anymore help from above, and whoever dies will have to wait until everything is resolved."

"Close your mouth, silly," Catherine said.

Jimmy clapped his mouth shut for the second time with a definite clapping sound. Then he opened it again. "Why am I back here?"

Kids started yelling outside and the three of them were distracted for a moment. The shouts grew louder. Catherine shrugged. "You probably have a job to do."

And then she headed for the door. Molly smiled at Jimmy and followed Catherine. Jimmy glided after them because he'd been on his own for a long time. It was nice to have someone to talk too.

Outside, the sunshine blinded him. Jimmy adjusted his hat to shade his eyes, which did absolutely nothing. Now he understood why ghosts only spooked at night. He thought about closing his eyes but didn't want to accidentally float through anybody. He opted to tough it out until he discovered who was making the ruckus. Then he would hurry back to be with his family.

"You son of a bitch, I'll kill you!"

Jimmy's head snapped up. He couldn't believe his ears. Sure, he'd heard Scout curse before, just not in the middle of Main Street in front of all the younger kids.

Mark carted his brother-in-law off like a duffle bag with twelve angry cats inside. Samuel bent over and helped Raven to her feet. Blood trickled down her face.

"This has got to be Billy's doing," Catherine said. "He's been avoiding me like the plague."

"Billy?" Jimmy said. "You mean that little kid that Hunter found in Denver."

"He's been skipping his therapy sessions with me lately," Molly said. "Hunter's been worried about him ever since he started hanging around Dylan."

"Hunter worried?" Jimmy smiled at that. Paybacks were sweet, even in the afterlife.

"Let's find out what's going on?" Catherine said. "Raven looked like she needed some medical attention, and Luis has his hands full."

"Did you want to go back to your family, Jimmy?" Molly asked him.

Jimmy thought about it and shook his head. "I think I'll tag along with you guys."

"Yeah," Catherine said. "Ginger probably has her shirt closed up by now anyways." She ran across the street, hooting with laughter.

"She's something else," Jimmy said, watching the little girl go.

Molly stepped off the curb to follow. "You have no idea."

16.

HUNTER

Hunter awoke and shot off the ground with fists clenched. He looked around for someone to punch. A dozen skinny kids stared at him like he was crazy, and then they looked at each other like maybe they should run away.

Barbie raced over and grabbed Hunter's hands. "It's okay. It's over."

"What? Where's Tommy?"

Barbie smiled and motioned her hand at all the Cozad kids. "The cavalry came and your Tommy decided to lick his wounds elsewhere. You really took it to him with that broomstick. Where did you learn to fight like that?"

Hunter searched up and down the street, making sure it really was okay to drop his guard. Even the six little cannibals were gone.

"Well?" Barbie asked.

"I play lightsaber with the younger kids back home."

Barbie narrowed her eyes. "You hit little kids like that?"

Hunter smiled, and then noticed the tiny mob of pale skeletons standing around in the sunshine. The Cozad kids watched him with sunken eyes like he held all the answers.

"Where did Tommy's group go?"

"We locked them up behind bars in the police station for now," Barbie said. "It's the only way to stay safe. I don't know if I can save any of them. They're too far gone."

"Are you sure?" Henry asked. "My... my sister is one of them."

Barbie took his hand. "I'm sorry, Henry. We'll wait until they wake up. Maybe I can undo whatever that boy did to her." Tenderly, she kissed his cheek.

Hunter expected to see him breakdown. Instead, Henry nodded and looked to Hunter. "I can't believe you're still alive."

"I can't either," Hunter said. "I'll let you know when I find out how that's possible. Thanks for coming to my rescue. That was very brave."

Henry's smile reflected the sunlight. "We got braver as the fight went on. After Barbie knocked out all the little kids, we knew something big was happening so we came outside and watched you whack that guy over and over with your stick. Then when he stabbed you in the stomach, we just sort of knew it was up to us."

Henry looked back at his group and they stood taller and some shook their tiny fists. Combined, all forty-one of them weighed less than a ton, but they had numbers on their side and anger in their hungry stares. And now something else—pride.

Barbie gripped Hunter by the arm and squeezed. "We need to get everyone out of here before Tommy recoups. He'll try and free his group first. We probably have until nightfall, but I can't guarantee that."

"All right, Henry, I can take you guys to Independents. We have food, shelter and no demons. But we have to find transportation. The town is a hundred and sixty miles from here."

Henry scuffed his shoe back and forth on the pavement. "What about the school bus?"

"Does it run?"

"The last time we drove it was about a month ago before all this started. We use it to go on scavenging field trips. We'll have to charge the battery with the generator. There should be enough fuel in the tank to get us to Lexington. We can fill up there."

"Take me to the bus."

They walked in a dense herd, following Henry through Cozad. The children moved faster when the big yellow bus came into sight. Hunter knew the bumpy ride ahead would be terrible, but whatever. They needed to get everyone out of town and this was their only option.

Henry and another kid named Brandon grabbed a generator and a battery charger out of a nearby shed. Hunter noticed the oil-stained coveralls draped over Brandon. His hands were smeared with grit and grime from time spent working on the bus. Brandon popped open the hood like he knew what needed to be done.

Hunter stayed out of the way. He looked around for teeth gnashing monsters and figured they were safe for the moment. "I'll be right back," he said to Barbie. "I have to get my stuff."

He ran, blowing past the 100th Meridian sign, and circled the grain elevator until he found the busted rifle on the pavement, ruined by the long drop. He continued to the stand of trees by Interstate 80 where he'd left his KTM. His side cramping from the hard pace, he slowed before the deep shade of trees, not wanting to go blindly into trouble. He walked under the leafy canopy, his boots crunching over fallen brushwood. His eye adjusted, and there was his orange and black KTM motorbike, right where he'd left it.

Hunter caught his breath and untied his backpack from the seat. He broke out his water bottle, took a couple of deep swallows, and saved the rest. He stripped off his jacket and held it out for inspection. There were holes in the shoulder and chest. It had been a rough twelve hours on his brand new apparel. Hopefully Molly would be willing to patch the holes.

He dug out a clean shirt that wasn't in shreds and tossed the ruined one to the ground. He looked down at his bare chest and shoulders, expecting to see scars, but none were found. Packing the jacket and water away, he slipped on the blue shirt.

He started the bike and gave the throttle a couple turns, revving up the engine and thinking about going home. Scanning the sun's position in the clear sky, he noted there might be seven hours of daylight left. He popped the clutch and headed back to Cozad.

* * *

When Hunter rode up, everybody who wasn't helping with the automotive repairs was huddled inside the bus with the windows partway down. He stopped next to Barbie and cut the engine. The noise was replaced by the quieter hum of the generator. He propped the bike against the bus and Barbie gave him funny look.

"What?"

"They thought you'd left. Most of them didn't blame you."

"I'm not leaving unless it's with everyone." He said it loud enough for all to hear. "How is the bus coming along?"

Brandon tapped the gauge on the battery charger like the needle would give him the desired answer. His shoulders slumped as he looked back to Hunter. "We still have about an hour, give or take."

Hunter nodded, trying to stay positive even though sitting around waiting for the boogey man to return was not ideal. "That's okay. We're going to make it out of here. We'll take the generator and charger with us, just in case."

Barbie grabbed hold and hugged him like they'd been apart for over a year instead of ten minutes. Hunter liked her hugs. Not as back breaking as Catherine's and a little more... grown up. He enjoyed this one very much, until he remembered Molly.

"I'm glad you didn't leave us," she whispered. Her warm breath tickled his neck.

Hunter moved out of her embrace and backed away. "We need to make sure everyone is ready to go."

Barbie tilted her head and smiled. "I'm sorry if I make you nervous."

A howl sounded from inside a nearby building. The tortuous wail traveled the length of his spine and tingled across his scalp. Gritting his teeth, he eyed the building as another howl joined the chorus. The battery couldn't charge quick enough.

"You don't make me nervous, Barbie." Hunter nodded toward the sounds. "They do."

17.

HUNTER

He couldn't ignore it any longer. The noise had to stop. The possessed cannibal kids continued wailing like they smelled fresh meat. The other kids—the normal but famished kids— stayed in the bus, trying not to listen to their former friends. It was tough, even if you weren't half starved and about to pass out.

Hunter took to a knee and opened his backpack to inventory his essentials. He pulled out his clothes and left the food hidden in the bottom. Peering inside, he found an apple and some dried meat and some flatbread. Not enough to share with the group without a fight breaking out.

Barbie grabbed his briefs from the pile of clothes. She held both ends of the waistband and gave them a shake. They were bright red.

"Oh, I like these. Here, try them on for me."

Hunter ripped them from her hands and buried them in the pile.

"Why are you so boring?" Barbie leaned over and gazed at Hunter.

Her eyes didn't catch his attention, but her drooping shirt collar did. He quickly averted his gaze to the pile of clothes and ignored the urge to look back. "Why do you have to make this whole situation harder than it already is?"

"What situation? Am I a situation?"

"No. This town and all the kids are the situation. You're the distraction."

She leaned against the bus and arched her back. "Am I? Oh, I like that."

"Yeah, well, I don't. There's too much going on here for you to keep messing with me. Plus, I have a girlfriend."

"You sound like a broken record."

"What's that?"

"It's an expression." Barbie shrugged and held out her hand. "Let me see your backpack."

"There's no more underwear in there if that's what you're hoping to find."

"Good. I really don't want it rubbing up against the food more than it already has." Her face scrunched up with disgust. "You really should separate your edible items from the nonedible ones."

Hunter pulled his pack close to his chest and looked to see if the starving kids on the bus had overheard Barbie. With all the howling, most had pushed their windows back up. "I don't have enough for everyone."

"Leave that to me." Barbie took possession of his bag and moved to the door of the bus. Hunter followed her out of curiosity and also to provide protection in case she was mobbed by ravenous skeletons. She stopped at the steps and bowed her head.

Hunter thought he heard thunder roll overhead in the sunny blue Nebraska sky.

Barbie climbed into the bus and moved to the back. She slowly walked backwards up the aisle and excited murmurs followed as she handed out the contents of Hunter's bag. Kids brightened as she moved past, and then the bus fell silent except for the chomps and chewing of thirty-nine happy mouths.

She passed Hunter, who stood stunned by the big round steering wheel. Every kid on the bus had an apple, a stick of dried meat, and a whole piece of flatbread. He stumbled down the steps after her. Barbie had given a grateful Henry and Brandon some of the fare before handing Hunter back his bag. She bit into her bright red apple. Juice ran across her chin, and Hunter quickly looked into the bottom of his bag. There was the apple, dried meat and flatbread for him left to eat.

He didn't have the appetite at the moment. "How did you do that?"

"Do you really have to ask?" Barbie said. "I thought you were used to miracles by now."

Hunter rubbed his brow like he could clear the fuzziness from his thoughts. It didn't really accomplish anything. He focused on the broomstick lying on the ground nearby. One of the kids must have brought it along. The dried blood on the pointy end made him uncomfortable.

First bullets and then the stick shoved into his guts—would a nuclear bomb stop him? Did Catherine bringing him back to life cause this invincibility? That had to be it, because this kind of thing just didn't happen on its own. Hunter broke his arm a year ago and that hadn't magically healed. Well, not until Catherine magically healed it. What about the pain in his shoulder that never healed or the blind eye and missing teeth? He wasn't regenerating new parts.

"Don't worry so much." Barbie patted his hand. "The answers will come."

"How about you just tell me what I need to know?"

"I can't. It's against the rules." She nodded in the direction of the howling coming from the police station. "Let's check the prisoners."

Hunter shuddered at the idea. Going to see those crazy kids had all the appeal of spending a day plucking chickens. "I'd rather bite off my tongue and eat it."

"I just want to make sure there really isn't anything I can do for them before we leave. I mean, if I could save one then I have to try."

The other kids were milling around outside of the bus now, looking for water. Their nervous behavior floated around like a contagion. Wes and Carissa were the closest, and although Wes appeared healthy after his possession, he still seemed a little shaken ever since Tommy and his gang had appeared.

Hunter rotated his bad shoulder, feeling the dull ache that would not quit. "Why do you need me there?"

"Backup."

"Backup for what?"

"If I can save one, then I need you to hold off the others while I work to reverse whatever that kid did to them."

Hunter considered the task before him and wished he'd left when he had the chance. His hand trembled as he gripped the broomstick. He patted his pocket for the reassuring weight of his lock blade knife. He wanted to be prepared for last resorts.

"Why can't you just zap them all and then check them out?"

Barbie rolled her eyes like he was stupid. "They have to be awake. That's why I couldn't do it when we dragged them into the jail. Any more questions?"

Hunter shouldered the stick and headed for the screams. "Will I make it home alive?"

Barbie followed. "Sure, if you remember to say your prayers."

They hit the street and were halfway across when they noticed the shuffling of a crowd following. Hunter turned to find every kid out of the bus and on their heels.

The horrible howling continued without pause, like an angry wolf pack caged in an undersized kennel. Hunter imagined how terrifying it would be inside and his knees jittered.

"Uh, you guys don't have to come in there with us," Hunter told the crowd.

Carissa took a step forward. "We feel safer with you guys. Is it okay if we wait in the lobby?" She nodded her head toward the rest of her group to find out if that would be okay with them as well. They seemed pretty happy with the idea.

Hunter waved them on. "Let's go. The more the merrier, right?"

"They're not a very merry crowd," Barbie said to him.

"It's an expression."

Hunter pushed open the door, stepping onto the tile flooring. Light flowed through the glass doors and front windows. The place had been gutted, leaving the counter and a dark entrance where the noise continued to grow like a cold wind.

"How the heck did you see to get them back there?" Hunter asked.

From the counter, Wes retrieved a Coleman lantern that burned white gas. He pumped the primer before igniting the mantles with a disposable lighter. "I'll hold the lamp for you guys."

Carissa stood next to her brother. "Then I'm coming too." She held his free hand and together they walked toward the darkness.

Hunter tapped the broomstick on the ground to make sure it wouldn't break, and then he followed the light. "Let's go play with the crazy kids."

Darkness fell on top of them as they moved farther away from the comfort of daylight. The lantern only worked to draw their eyes into a tight circle. What might lay beyond that circle made Hunter nervous. The howling grew louder until they stood in front of a closed door that separated the hallway from the nightmare. Wes walked past the door and held up the light.

"Are you going in?" Hunter shouted the question over the cacophony and Wes flinched. Hunter tried to smile but the screaming was working on his nerves, making simple facial expressions tricky. He held out his hand. "Give me the lamp. You follow."

Handing the lantern to Hunter, Wes produced a shaky, but grateful, smile. Carissa cowered behind her brother, but at least she'd come this far. If Wes went through the door, Hunter knew she'd be right with him.

Barbie stared at the entrance, her face strained at the rising tone from the hungry, flesh-eating children beyond.

Hunter nudged her. "Are you all set?"

Still staring at the door, she held up a handful of crackling electricity. At least Hunter thought it crackled. It certainly sparkled. The white light enhanced the illumination from the yellow glow of the lantern.

Hunter stretched out trembling fingers and pulled on the door handle. The wailing stopped. The lantern shook in his other hand, bouncing crazy shadows around the walls. Hunter tried to decide which he preferred—the howling or the silence.

Barbie stepped past him with more determination than Hunter was willing to muster. Wes surprised him by going next, with Carissa so close they could have been attached at the hip.

Hunter waited a heartbeat, took a deep breath, and then he brought in the light.

Four cells stretched down another corridor, with the wall on the right and bars on the left. Six sets of dark pupils stared back. Hands gripped the bars and every one of the cannibal children's mouths glistened with saliva. They panted like caged animals, and the sound became the next level of terror as Hunter's feet glued themselves to the floor. The only direction he wanted to go was back. Nothing could be saved in here, especially these tiny creatures of death.

Barbie moved to the first cell, both hands dripping tendrils of white fire, and faced the little girl locked inside. The girl hissed, swatting between the bars at Barbie, who remained unflinchingly out of reach. The girl grew more frantic in her attempts to rip into Barbie, becoming a blur of motion as she raked her black nails through the air and screeched. The others chattered in shrieks and snarls, anxious to be free.

Like a lightning strike, Barbie caught the girl by her wrists. She pulled the child's arms down and drew her near now that she had control, staring into her face.

Fear broke through the fierceness of the girl's features, her dark eyes looking around desperately. She buried her teeth into her bottom lip and bright blood trickled down her chin. Barbie's energy channeled through the child's arms with a jolt. The girl straightened like a rod and the light shined in her eyes.

Hunter watched, unable to do anything but hold the lantern and the broomstick. Wes and Carissa pressed their bodies against the wall like they were trying to pass through to the other side.

Barbie released the little girl and stepped away. The child hissed and retreated to the shadows at the back of her cell. The others down the corridor screeched defiance.

"What happened?" Hunter asked over the noise.

Barbie shook her head. "She cannot be helped."

Barbie stepped over to the next cell where two girls had been contained together. They hissed and snarled and swatted out towards her like the first one, but they also frequently traded places, pacing and stalking back and forth in their cage like two young tigers learning how to use their claws.

"This is where I need your help," Barbie said.

"What? You're crazy. I'm not going anywhere near those girls."

"Don't be scared. I just need you to hold one off while I test the first."

"I'm not scared." Hunter's knees shook so bad he figured she heard them knocking. "I just don't want to be eaten."

"I'll be real quick this time—"

Hunter didn't catch the last part because the howling rose again. "What'd you say?"

"I know what I'm looking for now." Barbie turned to finish testing the others.

18.

HUNTER

Barbie held the second girl's wrists through the bars. Hunter concentrated on the free girl in the cell who kept trying to come over the top and around the sides at Barbie. Each time the girl did, she got poked in the face with the stick. Hunter used the blunt end—he wasn't cruel—but he didn't discriminate where the stick whacked her either. Her right eye took a beating, which probably made her even with Hunter's depth perception.

Barbie's lightning power transferred into the captured girl's eyes then she released her. The girl whimpered and ran to the back of the cell. Hunter allowed the one with the bad eye into the spot at the bars. Barbie clasped on like before and after thirty seconds the process was over; the girl screeched, running away to join the other.

"Can we save one of them?" Hunter asked.

Barbie tilted her head and peered into the darkened cell at the cowering pair. "Let's check the boys first."

The boys were just as feisty, clawing, hissing and screaming guttural nonsense. Two boys were caged together in the third cell. Luckily it was the smaller boys, but they were quick. Hunter worked hard to keep the one off Barbie while she inspected the first. The child ducked and weaved, having learned something from what he could see of Hunter's treatment of the girl. Instead of a poke, Hunter smacked the kid's hands every time one crossed the bars.

Barbie finished in a hurry then switched partners and inspected the second. They went to the last cell together. Hunter whistled at Wes and motioned him to move closer with the lantern. Wes and Carissa hugged the wall as they came after them. The girls leapt at the bars as they passed, smashing against the iron. Wes and Carissa focused on Hunter. When the light rounded the corner of the last cell, they found a solitary boy sitting peacefully on the bench in the back.

He gazed up at them with signature large pupils, pointy teeth and spittle. His hands rested on his knees.

"He doesn't seem that bad." Hunter knocked on the bar of the cell like he was delivering a pizza. "Think he's worth saving?"

Barbie punched him in the shoulder and Hunter winced. "'They're all worth saving. The question is can we save him?" She gazed into the cell.

The boy smiled.

"No. He's too far gone to be saved." She stepped up to the bars and hung her hands over the center rail, tempting the child to come try a bite.

He didn't move.

"Let's get the hell out of here," Hunter said.

Barbie stood back and dug her hand in her pocket. She pulled out the keys to the cell. She selected one and nodded. "Follow me and be ready." Without further discussion, Barbie stepped down the cell corridor.

Hunter jumped after her. "Wait a minute! What are we doing?"

"I have to make a choice and I've made it. I can only save one of these kids."

They stopped in front of the cell with the two girls. The girls rushed forward and hissed a warning at them, but they didn't cross the bars this time.

"Which one?" Hunter asked.

"I'll grab the one I'm going to save. You hold the other one back until I'm done." Barbie bowed her head for a brief moment then she brought up her fist with a ball of circling electricity. The two girls backed away, staring at the white energy.

"That's not much of a fucking plan," Hunter said.

The girls fell silent inside the cell. Barbie jammed the key in the lock and there was an audible click when she turned. "I told you to stop using that word." She slid the cell door aside and entered the tiger den. Both girls leapt at her, but she quickly selected the one she wanted, grabbing her wrists, and spun away.

Hunter charged through the door with his stick and pinned the unoccupied girl to the wall. The small cell exploded with white light and popping energy fused the air, making it hard to breath. The girl Hunter had trapped stared at Barbie, petrified at the display of power. She shifted her non-swollen eye back to Hunter.

"Don't try it," Hunter told her.

"Steven's going after the keys!" Wesley yelled.

One of the smaller cannibal boys in the next cell had squeezed between the bars as far as he could, stretching his fingers toward the keys still hanging in the lock. Wesley swung the lantern back and forth at him.

Hunter's moment of distraction ended with the girl snapping her teeth at him and clawing his arms. He shoved the stick harder and higher. With her bare feet scrambling, she climbed Hunter like a stepladder, but he pushed the stick even higher until it was against her throat. He feared pushing too hard and breaking her neck. Instead he hoped she would choke out.

Now that the stick had moved up, her arms were free to lash out with her claws. She gouged her nails into Hunter's arms then his cheeks. Hunter extended his arms, scared he might lose sight in his remaining eye. The girl's attacks lessened and he stepped back. She flopped to the floor, letting Hunter catch his breath in darkness.

"Where's the light?" he asked with panic rising in his chest.

There was a jangling and Hunter froze.

"They have the keys," Wes said from nearby. "I dropped the lantern."

"We got to go! We got to go!" Carissa said.

"Barbie?"

She did not respond. Barbie's electrical power had winked out, leaving black unknown shapes in the fearful cell block

"Wes, get your sister out of here, now!"

Hunter held his hand out in front and shuffled until he touched Wes's head. The boy yelped and shook with terror. He grabbed Wes and found Carissa shivering next to him. Hunter guided them from the cell and faced them toward the hall. "Run, and get everyone out of here. I'll hold them off as long as I can."

A pair of howls rang out like they were inside Hunter's ears, and the door to the next cell crashed open. Hunter turned, swinging his broomstick wildly, determined to buy Wes and his sister some time.

A solid body flew into him, and he shoved it back then jabbed the air with one end of the stick, hoping it was the pointy end. He slid his right foot forward as keys jangled, followed by the heavy breathing of the three cannibal boys. Two for sure were out, but Hunter wanted to keep the third locked up. One more slide of his feet and he kicked the lantern. He bent over and his hand wrapped around the base of the lamp, on top of the fuel cap. The keys jingled at the end of the cell block. He unscrewed the cap and found a full tank of white gas sloshing over his nervous hand.

Hunter hurled the lantern down the corridor. A shriek followed as it smashed into someone then clattered to the ground. Hunter hustled forward, swinging the broomstick up and down, side to side, with big sweeping chops, trying to make contact. He didn't want any of them getting past him.

His stick met resistance and was turned away. He pulled it back hard and made a series of quick jabs, hoping to stab something soft. His boot kicked a lumpy shape lying on the floor— the lantern had taken out one of the boys. The fumes burned his nose and made him dizzy.

An attack came from the side, ramming him against the bars of the last cell. The caged boy reached through and held him tight with his nails piercing his chest.

"We're going to kill you for our master," the boy said close to Hunter's ear.

Hunter gripped the shirt of the child outside in the corridor with him, holding the kid back. The little terror threw a fit trying to break loose: biting, scratching and kicking every accessible part of Hunter like a six-year-old melting down after a very long day.

"Henry?" a small, confused voice drifted in the darkness. "Henry, where are you? I'm scared."

The caged boy hissed at the back of Hunter's neck. "I've got this one. Kill her. She's no longer one of us."

Hunter's boots slipped on the wet floor as he struggled to hold the boy from running off. The caged one squeezed harder, tearing into Hunter. The other struck him in the face, trying to pull free. Hunter's stick was gone. He had both hands tied up in the kid's shirt. He worked one loose and dug into his pocket. He pulled out his lock blade that he kept oiled, polished and sharp. He flicked his wrist and the blade sprung open. One swing and he stabbed the side of the boy with him in the hall. The child screamed and swiveled away. Hunter swung once more, but the kid twisted out of the way and tripped, then smacked hard against the wall.

Hunter raised the knife. His shoulder protesting in agony, he arched down, bringing the knife towards the last boy, who released him and jumped out of the way.

Quickly, Hunter stepped out of the gas on the floor. He closed his knife, still unable to penetrate the thick darkness, and unnerved by the harsh breathing of the last boy.

"My master and I will hunt you down and everyone you try to save," the boy said from behind bars.

Hunter slipped the knife into his pocket and pulled out his Zippo. He flicked the starter and found the end of the puddle of gas, making sure he wasn't standing in it. The two boys who had shared a cell lay silent and still on the wet floor at the end. The last boy squinted hard at Hunter through the cell bars. Then realization struck and he rattled the cage in desperation.

Hunter released a long steady breath, determined to do what was necessary, and hating it. "Tommy can bring it anytime. I'm sorry about this, but you're not going to be there."

Hunter ignited the white gas and a blue flame curled across the floor and quickly climbed the wall to the ceiling. He turned around, now able to see the little girl with her normal eyes staring at him in fear, as if he were the bad guy. Hunter smiled, unsure of what it really looked like, considering the screams and spreading fire.

"It's all right. I know your brother, Henry."

Hunter ran past her into the cell and found Barbie unconscious. He kept his sight from straying to the body of the girl he grappled with while Barbie performed her magic. Hunter scooped Barbie up and met Henry's sister by the cell door.

"Let's get out of here," he told her. "That way, but stay close to the wall."

He carried Barbie down the hallway leading to the light outside. All the other kids were still hanging around the lobby until Hunter walked in and led them out. The sun was high overhead and the heat hammered him as his energy faded. He stumbled across and down the street to the building where the Cozad kids had been trapped before his arrival.

Hunter laid Barbie in the shade next to the building and dropped beside her. He rested her head in his lap then stared across the street. The fire spread throughout the building then leapt to the next.

His mind numbed to everything. The kids all settled near him and watched the fire consume the building like a giant funeral pyre. Hunter barely noticed Henry's sister. The other kids kept a wary eye on her, as if she would go stark raving mad any second. Quietly, she sat next to Barbie's feet.

Hunter waited and watched. His thoughts turned over the horrible events that took place in the dark cell. Spasms fed through his arms and legs as his body released his terror-filled adrenaline. His good eye blurred with tears because of the violence he'd been forced into using to save Barbie and Henry's sister, and every kid in this town. It was one thing to fight for something. Hunter never wanted to have to kill for it. Even if the ones he had to kill were demonic cannibals, they had been ordinary kids not so long ago. He lowered his head and cried, covering his face so the others couldn't watch his despair.

Hunter jumped when someone touched his neck. Barbie stared up at him.

"It's not your fault."

Hunter looked away. The bus turned down the street and came roaring toward them, followed by Henry pushing Hunter's motorbike. Barbie sat up and Hunter wiped his face with rough swipes. He stood and helped her to her feet.

"Let's get out of here."

19.

SCOUT

Scout barged into his apartment, crossed the living room, and punched his bedroom door. Pain shot through his wrist. He punched the door again with the other fist.

Mark followed inside. "Stop it, Scout. You're just going to hurt the door."

"Where were you, man? Raven and I were attacked in the middle of town and the sheriff was nowhere to be found."

Samuel guided Raven through the door. Her hand was pressed to her forehead trying to stanch the bleeding. Scout hurried to the kitchen and wet a washcloth from their clean water bucket. He wrung out the excess and brought it over to her. She took it from him without meeting his eyes and held it against her wound.

"Look what Billy did."

"Billy?" Samuel and Mark said together.

"He's the one telling everybody I got Jimmy killed. I'm sure of it."

Mark shook his head. "But Billy is a nice little kid. Why would he do that?"

"Why don't you ask him? He's been feeding Dylan with that story, getting him all fired up, and half the town too. Then he threw that rock at Raven. Where were you, Mark?"

Mark looked at Samuel then back at Scout. "We were having lunch. It's been a long morning with the delivery and all. Not to mention the demon dogs."

"Hellhounds," Samuel said.

Mark frowned, agitated. "Whatever."

Catherine knocked on the open door. "May we come in?"

Scout waved her inside. "Come over here and take a look at Raven. She got hit in the head with a rock."

Molly followed Catherine inside. Catherine grabbed a wooden chair as she passed the table and scooted it over next to Raven. "Have a seat so I can examine the damage."

Raven removed the towel. Molly came up beside Catherine and they both inspected the small cut like they were about to perform major surgery.

"Doesn't look that bad," Molly told Catherine. "Closing the wound shouldn't take too much out of you."

Catherine focused on Raven. "Do you want me to take care of it for you, Raven? Otherwise, you'll probably have a little scar."

Raven returned the damp washcloth to her forehead and reapplied pressure. "No, I'll just put a Band-Aid on it."

Catherine patted her knee. "It will be just fine. The scar will be tiny anyways, and that's only if it does scar." She shifted her gaze over to Scout. "So what's going on around here? You had the whole town in an uproar. Why on earth were you screaming obscenities?"

Scout opened his mouth. He closed it again and stared at Catherine until her return stare made him uncomfortable. "Everybody thinks I got Jimmy killed."

"Where would anyone get that idea?" Molly laid a hand on Scout's arm. "You did everything you could." Her eyes shifted and she nodded to an empty space in the apartment. "Jimmy made the choice. No one could have stopped him."

"Billy is telling Dylan that Jimmy died because I snuck off to save Raven."

"Billy wasn't even there when that happened," Molly said. "Where would he have heard about that?"

Mark cleared his throat. "This might be my fault." He looked at Scout. "Remember when you told me about regretting the way things went down that last morning in Denver. I talked about it with Billy, trying to get a bigger picture."

"Why?" Scout asked.

"I don't know. I didn't think it was a big deal or that he would twist it like this. Vanessa is always saying what a little angel he is in school."

"Great," Scout said. "So how do we fix this mess?" He grabbed his backpack and rummaged through his first aid kit, setting out his bottle of iodine, a cotton ball and a Band-Aid.

"I'll go talk to Billy," Catherine said. "We have a relationship."

Scout stopped fiddling with the medical supplies and turned. Everyone's eyebrows were raised in response to the little girl's statement. Samuel chuckled like he'd just formulated an evil plot to take over the world.

Catherine folded her arms. "You people need to get your minds out of the gutter."

Scout squirted some red iodine on the cotton ball. He gently removed Raven's hand that held the washcloth and looked over the cut. "This will sting for a sec." Scout pressed the cotton against her wound and she didn't even blink. "Are you okay?"

Raven glanced at him quickly and nodded.

"I'm sorry about all this," he said.

Raven snatched the Band-Aid out of his hand. "I want to take a look before I cover it up." She left for their bedroom and closed the door.

"I'll talk with her," Molly said. She knocked and asked to enter. Raven's reply was muffled and Molly stepped inside.

"Have a seat," Scout offered the group left standing.

"We should get out of here and give you guys some peace," Mark said. "I'll go with Catherine to talk to Billy. I want to see if he's using what I told him to cause all this trouble."

"But you have your pants on now," Catherine said with a look of pure innocence. "That's no fun at all."

Mark's face blazed the color of the setting sun. His ears burned even brighter. Catherine giggled and reached for his hand, pulling him out the door and down the stairs.

Samuel drummed his fingers on top of the table. "I'll go find Dylan so we can talk about how tough he thinks he is."

Scout shook his head. "You don't have to do that, man. I can handle myself."

"Yeah, I know, but this isn't good for the town. Jimmy would want me to put a stop to all this nonsense. Besides, Dylan's a punk. He might need a bit more persuasion."

"I'm coming with you," Molly said, exiting the bedroom. "I don't want you doing anything stupid."

"Like stand on the porch until five huge dogs are within snapping distance before finally making a move? You mean stupid like that?"

Molly placed her hands on her hips and stuck out her tongue.

"You're alive aren't you?"

"More like back from the dead. And you've also ruined my Nirvana concert shirt."

"I didn't ruin it. It's just fine."

"It's not fine! You're wearing it. I was saving it for a special occasion and now you've gone and ruined it."

"And everyone tells me I used to be a drama queen. Let's go." Molly pushed him towards the door.

Scout walked them out. "How is she?" he asked Molly.

"She wanted to take a nap. She's really upset. Let her get some rest and then just listen to what she has to say. I'll come back later and talk with her some more. I didn't realize how isolated she'd been feeling here."

Scout leaned against the doorjamb and shoved his hands into his pockets. "I didn't either until today."

"Yes, well, Raven has been sensitive to the differences a lot longer than any of us, but she would, being from the outside."

"All right, Oprah, let's hit the road," Samuel said and ran down to the street.

"Who's Oprah?" Scout asked Molly.

She shrugged and followed Samuel.

Scout winced when he pulled his hands back out of his pockets. His swollen, red knuckles hurt but he didn't know if that happened in the scuffle or when he punched the door. Inside, he filled a bowl with water to soak his hands. He considered joining Raven, but his nerves were too frayed to sleep. He carried the bowl to the couch and stared at nothing.

His friends had left to smooth everything out, like anything could ever be smoothed out again. Scout kept picturing the crowd of faces on Main Street. Some of them believed Dylan and Billy and that hurt Scout more than any physical force. They thought he was capable of something so terrible that they were willing to stand by and let Dylan and his friends beat him up. These were the kids Scout had grown up with over the past seven years. This was his family—his fellow Independents. How could everything be falling apart?

Scout set the bowl on the coffee table and dried his hands on his shorts. He dug out the Boy Scout shirt and held it to his face, smelling the fabric. He ran his arms through the sleeves and pulled on the uniform. Then he sat back down on the couch. Afternoon sunlight crept across the wall and onto the bedroom door.

The door opened and Raven hauled her backpack into the living room. She called it her bug out bag and packed it with essentials just in case some world ending threat ever happened again.

"What are you doing?" Scout asked.

She dropped the bag by the front door. "I'm out of here."

20.

SCOUT

It was like getting sucker punched in the chest. The initial shock knocked the air from his lungs. Scout rose from the couch and took a faltering step toward Raven.

She held up her hand. "Don't, Scout. Don't make this harder than it has to be. I don't belong here. I'll never be able to fit in. I have to go before someone else gets hurt."

"What are you talking about? You're the one who got hurt. We'll fix this. Mark and Samuel are already out talking to Billy and Dylan. This will be behind us before you know it. You'll see."

"No, I won't. I'm not going to be here."

Scout wanted to hold her, grab her, tell her that he loved her and wanted her to stay with him. She didn't have to run away. Scout would take care of the problem before it grew out of control. He dropped his head and closed his eyes. The rushing of his emotions roared in his mind.

"Did you hear me, Scout?"

He jerked his head up. "No, I'm sorry. What did you say?"

"I'm leaving, Scout."

"Yeah, I heard that, but..."

"And I'm breaking up with you."

Scout's knees dipped as his plans for the future shattered along with what he supposed was his heart. He tried to think of something to say that would keep her here.

"Why?"

"I'm just not ready to settle down and be the preacher's wife. I want to be out in the world, not stuck in some little town doing nothing but working to survive. I want to live. I want to experience the world and that isn't going to happen in the middle of Nebraska."

"But," he added nothing. He had nothing to say—and everything at once. *I want you to stay. I need you to be with me. I love you.* None of it sounded right. None of his words would be anything more than pleading. He knew Raven would never respect him if he came off weak.

"Can't we try and fix this? Can we give it just a bit more time? I can do something else. I don't have to stay here."

The way Raven stared at him made him want to crawl under the sofa and hide. She never looked at him like that before. She was already gone. All that was left was for her to haul her stuff out the door, down the stairs, and across the edge of town. He couldn't stop her. Not with all the words in the world.

"Where will you go?"

She sighed. "I don't know yet. I'm going east or south. I'm not going anywhere near Denver if that's what you're thinking."

He did think that. The ugly thought climbed from his gut, stepped over the pieces of his heart, and clung like black cancer in his mind. She was leaving Scout to go back to Chase. The guy still infected her like the plague he was. Like the plague he set upon the world—the plague that killed Jimmy.

Raven lifted her backpack and swung the straps over her shoulders.

Scout stood still. "Do you want me to come with you?"

The silence that followed crushed every ounce of his spirit. She sighed again and opened the door. Scout had never heard anything as loud as the knob turning to withdraw the bolt.

"No, Scout." She stepped outside and closed the door.

Scout listened to her heavy steps fade all the way down the stairs. He thought he heard her crying. Hoped she was crying. He stood in the middle of their apartment staring at nothing, wearing his new Boy Scout shirt. He should run after her, should make her stay until she started thinking straight again. He should find Catherine and have her make sure that Chase's influence was gone and that this was truly Raven's choice.

His breathing sounded heavy and harsh, like he'd fought a ten round title match and got his butt kicked by someone who threw all the right punches. Any moment Raven would walk back in and apologize. She'd tell him she was being crazy—she didn't mean it. She loved him more than anything. The door would open—any moment.

The light outside dimmed, casting deep shadows into the apartment as if that was the way things would appear to Scout from now on—dim and dismal, without any hope.

He spun around and jumped up on the sofa, pressing his hands to the window. A dark cloud had moved in on the sunshine. A breeze blew through the screen, chasing around the room before flowing to another open window in the bedroom. He couldn't see her. She wasn't on Main Street. He had to watch her go. He couldn't just let her walk away forever without seeing her one last time.

Scout ran out the door and flew down the stairs, skipping three or four steps at a time. He hit the brick cobbles and looked in both directions. Scout decided she was being honest and was going east or south—not west, to *him*.

He headed toward the eastern side of town, sprinting so fast he could feel the push in his toes. Houses, trees and kids blurred as he passed. Kids waved or tried to say something, neither of which he paid attention to. He had to find her.

He made it to the edge of town without running into her. She had just left the apartment. Surely she hadn't gotten this far yet. The cloud broke past the sun like a lazy giant, returning the heat. Breathing deep, Scout tried to figure out where to run to next.

South, she said either east or south. Maybe she headed southeast, back to their hometown of St. Louis. Raven would go somewhere familiar. She'd go back to the Lou.

Scout rounded the outskirts of town toward south, watching the whole time for Raven. He stumbled into things as he ran: a bush, a bucket, a water hand pump. He ran into a tree and bruised his elbow. These were only minor distractions compared to his desperation to find Raven and convince her to stay.

The road that led south was a pothole bonanza. No sign of Raven—only flat, treeless, open prairie. He stumbled off toward the west with a lot less enthusiasm, convincing himself that she had left to go back to Denver. His energy spent chasing Raven's ghost trail, he staggered to the western edge and fell to his knees. The road out west was worse than the south. After three hundred yards of rubble, the small road turned into prairie where it led to another smaller town fifteen miles away.

He felt relieved because Raven wasn't there either. A sprig of hope blossomed in his broken heart. Scout hurried back to his apartment, pressing a hand to his side where a nasty cramp threatened to make him crawl. Scout dragged tired legs up the stairs and his step lightened when he saw the open door. He took a deep breath and walked across the threshold, ready to do anything to make Raven happy.

Vanessa smiled at him. She held a stack of Boy's Life magazines in her hands and placed them carefully back on the table. Little David sat on a blanket spread out on the floor, playing with Scout's alphabet blocks. He squealed with excitement when he saw Scout and threw the letter B at him.

"What are you doing here?" Scout asked his sister.

"I came by to see if you were all right."

He took several deep breaths, recovering from his run around town. All he wanted to do was fall on the floor in a heap of exhaustion and tears. "I'm fine."

Vanessa stepped closer. "Raven stopped by to get her motorcycle." Vanessa stepped again. "I'm so sorry, Scout."

He couldn't breathe as he silently cursed his stupidity. Of course Raven rode off on her motorcycle. The room spun like a cyclone with his sister anchoring the middle. She took a final step and caught him as the tears fell. He squeezed his eyes shut, trying to stem his sorrow, not wanting to look like a complete mess in front of Vanessa. She held her hand against the back of his head and whispered soft words. He didn't comprehend because his thoughts were chasing after Raven as she drove farther away.

Now she was gone. Scout didn't know why. It happened so fast. Everything today had been like that. Hellhounds, Dylan, Billy, the box of Boy Scout stuff, Raven, Ginger and the baby—everything happened so fast. Scout was along for the ride with neither the choice of direction nor the capability to stop.

Now he just wanted off.

What was happening today? Why had everything gone wrong? How could he return to the way things were this morning before he woke up?

"I like the uniform." Vanessa had moved back and was giving his shirt the up and down. "You finally found one. It looks good on you."

A smile crept across his face like it was ashamed to be there, but he was too happy about the Boy Scout stuff to ignore her compliment. "I found it this morning in the same house where we salvaged all the baby furniture. It was just in a box sitting in the kid's closet."

"Why'd you go out there?"

His smile slipped away like a distant memory. "I went for a ride to clear my head." He sat on the couch and unlaced his shoes, his feet sore after the pounding run. "It's been a rough day."

Little David squawked, holding onto a table leg and reaching for something up on Scout's shelf. Vanessa lifted him off the ground and after a series of grunts and pointing; he came away with a baseball. Vanessa set him on his feet again and patted him on the bottom. Little David threw the baseball across the room and followed.

Vanessa took a seat across from Scout. "I've heard some of it, especially about the altercation on Main Street. Did you really yell obscenities?"

Scout looked away from her penetrating brown eyes. He removed his Boy Scout shirt, folding it neatly then placing it on the sofa beside him. "It's been a really rough day. I'm sorry."

He had excuses for the way things had gone, but in reality he was too blind to see the way things were going and that had cost him his reputation and his girlfriend.

Was it pride? Did he enjoy the attention of preaching? How was he going to preach to these kids now? Sunday was in two days. How would he patch things up before then? Maybe he needed a break. Maybe Independents needed a break from him.

His sister sat quietly watching his internal struggle without comment. She would never stand for anything less than his absolute best. She demanded it of him—made him tougher and kept him alive through her guidance. Not only had he embarrassed himself, but her as well, and that was worse than anything—even losing Raven. He looked up at Vanessa.

"What are you going to do about it?" she asked.

"I'm going to be better."

She smiled. "I'm sure you will be."

21.

MARGARET

The late Friday afternoon sunshine burned at a bright angle across Margaret and Samuel as they walked over to Dylan's house. Not even a breeze rippled through the lines of hanging laundry. School had been cancelled with the birth of baby James. Chores were finished early and now all the younger kids flittered past trying to find that one good hiding spot in a massive game of hide and seek. The group of "its" roamed in a wild pack, kicking bushes and looking under porches. Those that were uncovered were quickly tagged and sulked back to base in shame.

"But I've already been tagged," Emma argued.

"Then why are you hiding?" Reese said. Reese had graduated from Vanessa's school last spring. Now she was the official babysitter of Independents; today her responsibilities had doubled with baby James. Hands on her hips, she wasn't listening to any of Emma's excuses. "This time go back to base."

"All right, all right, sheesh! I was just sitting in the shade. It's so hot out here. You don't have to be so bossy."

"Follow the rules if you want to keep playing."

Emma stalked off in a huff and the group of "its" continued their search. Margaret liked watching them play. Besides little David and now James, everyone else was older than nine. After all the trials and strife fighting to survive, it was good that kids still knew how to enjoy their childhood.

Margaret couldn't believe these things were happening now.

The plague had come and hopefully gone. Hellhounds were on the loose, and she and Catherine were moving among mankind again. She had slept through the past seventeen years totally unaware. Now she felt disoriented in the apocalyptic chaos.

She tried processing everything in that seventeen year blank space where all her choices were made by someone else. That's the only way she could think about it. It wasn't her, but this other person called Molly. And Molly had made a couple major choices for the both of them.

First and foremost was Hunter. Their relationship was very... Margaret's cheeks warmed. She tugged the hem of her shirt down as if she were walking around exposed.

Beside her, apparently lost in his thoughts, Samuel's lips were pressed into a tight frown,. They were getting closer to Dylan's house after checking the weight room on Main Street first. If Dylan wasn't home, they'd have to search the nearby lake where he fished for the Brittanys.

"What are you thinking about?" Margaret asked.

Samuel smiled and put his arm around her shoulders. "Are we going to have one of your famous chats? Because I have a lot on my mind."

"And which of your issues would you like to start with?"

Samuel laughed. "How about we start with the one where I'm not getting any?"

Margaret gulped but allowed herself to remain calm. Talking about these types of things appeared to be popular in the present. She guessed she'd have to adjust to it. "Maybe you shouldn't think about sex so much."

Samuel dropped his arm and his smile. "Um, I'm just playing. I really don't want to talk about my issues."

"Maybe we should talk about what happened this morning."

"You mean how we narrowly escaped the hellhounds because you froze up?"

Margaret frowned at him. "No, I want to talk about the couple of minutes you were no longer with us."

"Oh. You don't like to beat around the bush."

"We're not little kids playing hide and seek with our feelings. We need to let them out or they will fester and drive us crazy."

Samuel stopped. They were a block from Dylan's house. He turned to Margaret with an open face, but his hands slid into his pockets like they held the really good secrets. "All right, what do you want to know?"

"Do you remember anything?"

"From when I died?"

Margaret nodded.

"I remember Jimmy."

"Jimmy?"

"Yeah, he was lying in an open grave and then there was this bright light and I followed him back to my body. He told me everything was going to be all right. I asked him if he'd talked to Greg. He shook his head and then I woke up to find you lying topless next to me." Samuel smiled a wide, toothy grin at her that quickly turned sad. "Of course, somebody had already covered you with my blanket."

Heat raced back into Margaret's face, and this time she couldn't quell her discomfort. "We better go find Dylan before dinner."

"That's a great idea." Samuel grabbed her hand and pulled her, chuckling along the way.

They knocked on Dylan's door and stood waiting around until too much time had passed.

"Let's check out back," Samuel said.

There were two outbuildings behind the house. The smell of burning wood that made the mouth water passed through the roof of the smokehouse Dylan operated for Chef Brittany. They found Dylan in the smaller wooden shed, fixing up his fishing gear for the evening. Samuel walked though the door after pounding on the side. Margaret followed, noticing a sudden switch in Samuel's personality. Gone was the easygoing, lopsided grin and slouching. Samuel's eyes fixed on Dylan with a fierce, dangerous glint.

"What's the word, Dylan? Picked anymore fights since lunchtime?"

Dylan looked up from his seat at the work bench where he sharpened barbs on a fishing hook. Dark splotches circled his eyes like a raccoon, and a white strip of tape crossed the bridge of his nose as if to keep it from falling off. Dylan turned back to his work.

"Are you here to beat the shit out of me?"

Samuel leaned against the other end of the counter, next to stacks of plastic trays containing a rainbow collection of rubber worms. "Look, I just want all this stuff you've been stirring up to stop. Scout didn't get Jimmy killed no matter what you heard."

Dylan laid down his whetstone and the hook on the table. "You don't know that for sure. You weren't there."

"I was," Margaret said. "And it hurts me to know that

everything we went through in Denver has led to so much anger and animosity. We lost a lot back there. Jimmy made the choice to save Hunter. No one made that choice for him. Scout fought to keep Jimmy there, but Jimmy knocked him down and took off. Whoever told you differently read the situation wrong. And if that someone was Billy, he arrived right when everything happened."

Dylan swiveled on his stool and faced them with unconvinced eyes. "What about when Scout and Raven left the night before and Raven hooked up with her old pals?"

"You mean when she was captured by someone she trusted, who had been her best friend before she decided to make Independents her home?" Margaret didn't wait for the obvious response building on Dylan's tongue. "Raven gave up a lot to join us. She made a mistake and misjudged someone she cared about."

"And then Scout disobeyed Jimmy and went to save Raven on his own," Dylan said, like he'd been there.

"Dylan, have you ever been in love with someone?" Margaret asked.

Dylan looked away.

"Because one day when you find someone, I hope they never get stripped away from you. It's not an easy thing to live with. I was awake when Scout returned after losing Raven. He was tearing himself apart inside worrying about her. And he alone saved Raven and Catherine. He even took out Patrick in the process. And Raven? She held out under terrible torture only to reveal a small piece of information when she could have told them everything."

Anger surged into Margaret as she defended actions by people she considered heroes. Certainly more heroic than her, because when you added everything together all the blame fell solely on her. That ugly thought cast about in her mind, sending hot tears down her cheeks.

Samuel moved and curled his arm around her. "Hey, Molly, are you all right?"

Molly. She had done so many terrible things before Catherine had healed her mind. Why did God do this to her? Margaret was one of His faithful followers. She had been there doing His Will from the beginning. What possible benefit could have been gained from the seventeen years without knowledge of her true identity? What purpose did she serve until this morning when Catherine brought it all back?

Margaret pressed her face into Samuel's chest and cried out

her frustrations. Samuel rubbed her back and stroked her hair. She wept for a while and then backed awkwardly into a folding chair that Dylan held for her. She accepted the seat and wiped her eyes.

"I'm sorry," Margaret said.

Samuel shrugged it off. "Don't be. Your day started earlier than usual. You should see how emotional I get after picking beets all day. And yes, I think we're having beets tonight."

Margaret took a deep breath, smiling at Samuel's attempt to make her do just that. She refocused on Dylan. "Look, Scout didn't make the perfect choice running after Raven, but he was doing what he thought was right, unlike when I led Chase to Catherine and then hit Jimmy over the head so Patrick could win the fight."

Both Dylan and Samuel looked away.

"You could say that everything leading up to Jimmy's death happened because of me. That's something I have to live with, just like Hunter living with Jimmy's sacrifice. But blaming Scout for any of it is just plain wrong."

Dylan spun back and forth on his stool. "Billy made it sound like Scout and Raven were responsible for everything. Why would he do that?"

"Billy left everything he knew to join us. He was probably trying to fit in. Judging from what Ginger and Raven told me about Denver, he probably had to fight everyday just to stay alive. It's different here. We take care of each other."

"I guess so," Dylan said.

"Plus, when we first met Billy, he had just killed Patrick to save Hunter. Billy still refuses to talk about it. Has he ever spoken to you about that?"

Dylan shook his head. "Hunter told me about it. I never bring it up with Billy."

"Killing somebody like that when you're barely nine has got to mess with your head," Samuel said.

Dylan winced, closing his eyes in apparent discomfort.

Margaret scooted to the edge of her chair. "Are you okay?"

"I've got a bad headache. I guess I didn't count on Scout being so tough."

"Are you kidding? Scout's scrappy. I bet you think twice next time."

"That's not helping right now." Margaret slid off the chair towards Dylan. "Do you mind." She held up her hands.

His eyes widened in alarm. "What are you about to do?"

"I'm not sure yet. I may be able to help."

"All right, just watch the nose. It's tender as hell."

Margaret laid her hand on Dylan's forehead. She prayed, asking for God to help ease Dylan's pain and to allow her to mend his broken nose. Upon thinking amen, a light flooded into her spirit like molten grace—pure, alive and energizing. Margaret allowed the light to flow over Dylan and felt the healing begin.

Samuel stumbled into the wall and several items clattered to the floor, but Margaret couldn't break the process now that her healing was in motion. The light pulsed then fled back into her, tainted by the pain and the wounds that had been lifted from Dylan's body. This was the unpleasant part. She brought all of that hurt inside of her and channeled it through. Then she lifted her head, opened her eyes, and all of the badness fled from her in a throbbing flash. She felt nauseated and extremely worn out. It had been a long time since she had performed a healing. Her legs refused her weight as she slipped from Dylan.

Samuel caught her before she hit the ground. "My God, Molly, how did you do that?"

Margaret wanted to answer, wanted to tell Samuel her real name, but the world dimmed around her and then she slept.

22.

JIMMY

Yesterday, Jimmy enjoyed digging his grave, without all the hassle and responsibility of feeding a whole town. He'd come to accept his fate of being dead. Like he had a choice, but death was no big deal. At least he found more across mortality's threshold than simple oblivion. He was glad to be back among the living, even in his ghostly state. He had missed other people, so it was nice seeing all his friends again—especially Ginger.

He followed after Catherine and Mark, careful not to float through anything and especially anyone. The handful of accidental times he'd shared space with a living person had really freaked him out. There was this sticky sensation, like he might actually become glued inside them if he didn't pull away fast enough.

He wanted time alone with Catherine to ask her about this whole being dead business. Maybe she could explain exactly what he could and could not do. All that depended on whether she knew the answers and if she was willing to share. She'd have to be straight with him now, right? Who was he going to tell in his present, intangible state?

Jimmy was happy to see that Independents hadn't changed after he left for Denver. This place was paradise compared to conditions there. He was proud of the society he helped build for kids to grow up in. Now they were growing up with Catherine's help.

Jimmy was so excited to see that Vanessa had made it past her eighteenth birthday. Did that end the plague? Catherine said she needed to cure Jimmy to save the world because Chase had started the plague by infecting Jimmy's parents. He didn't understand that. Why had his family become such a focal point for so much misery?

"Hey, where are you wandering off to?" Catherine called.

Jimmy had drifted away from the path without noticing. Mark was knocking on somebody's front door, while Catherine hung back in the street, smiling at Jimmy.

He shrugged, or at least thought he'd performed the action. He didn't know how he appeared to Catherine when he couldn't even see his own hand. He floated over next to her.

"What's Mark doing?"

"Billy plays with some of the boys who live here. We're just checking it on the way to Billy's house."

"Who does Billy live with?"

"He and Preston took over a house together a couple months ago. Before that he'd been living with me and Ginger, but I guess he found that too constraining. I always made him pour the tea and play Barbie dream house with me. He was a pretty decent Ken."

Jimmy smiled, remembering the day when he and Ginger discovered their mutual affection for one another. Somehow Catherine had known all along.

"Remind me who Preston is?"

"He's about the same age as Billy. Another one of Hunter's motorcycle gang recruits. Hunter is teaching them survival skills. I think your brother is ready to settle down."

Jimmy laughed at that. "How long have I been dead?"

"Everybody settles down eventually, silly," Catherine told him.

Mark walked up, closing the conversation. "He's not here. Let's go try Billy's house."

They started off again with Jimmy floating behind. He expected to feel something from the intense afternoon sunshine, but instead it was nothing as usual. Jimmy wanted time to walk the fields on the southern outskirts of town—his old stomping ground. Samuel probably had all the crops under control, but he wanted to check just to make sure.

They walked to a ranch house that had the typical facial look with two windows for eyes and a door in the middle that made the nose. The porch was the mouth. This one smiled with neglect and Jimmy knew that, soon, somebody would have to replace the support beams underneath the sagging wooden planks. Mark stepped up and rapped three sharp knocks on the wooden frame of the screen door, which rattled on rusty hinges. No wonder Preston and Billy found this house vacant. Jimmy couldn't wait to see the inside.

The door swung open and he recognized the little kid that had protected Hunter in Denver. Jimmy would never forget the sight of Patrick lying in a pool of blood with a hatchet in his back. He could still hear the chickens clucking. Where had Patrick gone when he died? Jimmy had only been an hour behind him. Maybe Patrick was the last soul to enter Heaven, unless the other alternative was still open for business and had first dibs.

"Hello, Billy," Mark said. "We need to talk."

Billy's eyes darted back and forth like he wanted to bolt and needed to figure out which direction to start running. Then his gaze settled on Jimmy for a moment. Billy's mouth dropped open and he retreated from the door, moving into the shadowy interior.

Mark and Catherine shared a look with one another. Catherine glanced back at Jimmy with a puzzled frown that he found troubling.

"May we come in?" Mark asked.

"Sure," Billy said without enthusiasm.

Mark opened the screen door that screeched in protest. Catherine walked in and Jimmy panicked, trying to rush up the porch and through the door before Mark, but Mark stepped in his way and Jimmy drifted to a stop before he passed through his old friend. The screen door banged shut, leaving Jimmy outside. Mark left the front door open so Jimmy decided to hang out on the porch and listen in.

"Kind of dark, isn't it, Billy?"

"I like it that way."

"Yeah, well, I'm going to open the curtains so I don't trip over anything, okay?"

"Okay."

"What is that smell?" Mark asked, pushing the curtains aside. "I think you got something rotting away in here."

"It came with the house. We haven't been able to find where it's coming from."

Jimmy stared in through the screen door. The open curtains brought needed sunlight into the sparse living room of Billy's house. The little boy sat on a battered sofa with his hands tucked between his knees and his head down. The sun's rays snuck past the dusty streaks in the window to rest on Billy. Catherine stood just inside the door and Jimmy couldn't see anything of Mark except for his large shadow on the wall like some looming judge invading Billy's privacy.

"Billy, did you throw a rock at Raven?" Mark asked.

The boy sat perfectly still. "Yes."

"Why would you do something like that? That's not like you."

He shrugged.

"What's going on, Billy? Are you the one telling Dylan that Jimmy died because of something Scout did?"

Billy lifted his head and looked at the door where Jimmy waited to hear the answer. He looked right at Jimmy and then dropped his head again. Something about the lack of color in Billy's eyes was disturbing.

Catherine turned her head and spotted Jimmy on the other side of the screen door. Then she took two quick steps at Billy. "You see him, don't you?"

Billy didn't move. He didn't say a word.

Mark's shadow on the wall shrank until Jimmy saw Mark's broad back come up behind Catherine. "See who, Catherine? Who did Billy see? What's going on?"

Catherine ignored him. Everything about her had tensed. She stood an inch taller and her tone grew harsh. Catherine was worried. That made Jimmy nervous as hell.

"Billy, look at me."

Slowly, Billy lifted his gaze and met Catherine's. She sucked in a breath at the same time Jimmy simulated the same action. Billy's eyes were white orbs. He curled back his lips in a smile and his teeth had changed into little points, like a farm cat.

"What the...?"

"Mark, watch out!"

Billy sprang to his feet, grabbing Catherine by the arm and yanking her behind him with inhuman force. She flew headfirst over the sofa into the wall with a loud wham and dropped onto the cushions.

Mark balled his fists, ready to pummel some sense into the little kid.

Jimmy moved through the screen right as Billy swiped Mark across the chest. Mark's agonized scream rang out in the small living room. He stumbled away from Billy with stripes of red blood spotting through his torn orange T-shirt.

Billy pressed Mark with a flurry of razor clawed swipes,

backing the bigger boy into the wall. Mark held his hands out to protect himself. Billy worked his way closer and buried his teeth into Mark's hip. Again Mark screamed and hammered down on top of Billy's back. The little boy fell, but just as quickly pushed back up. Mark scrambled around the wall to escape.

His mouth dripping with Mark's blood, Billy stalked after him, licking his lips like he wanted more.

"Billy!" Jimmy said.

The boy turned, and Mark disappeared into the hallway. The tiny monster gazed at Jimmy with cloudy eyes and cocked his head. "Why are you here? You're not supposed to be here anymore."

"What are you doing, Billy?"

"I'm about to have dinner."

"Who are you?"

"I was Billy." His awful smile spread wider, showing off the red maw. "The plague was the start. Now there will be famine and those of us who deserve to live will eat the fattened cattle of this world, and none are fatter than the inhabitants here." Billy stepped closer to Jimmy. "I'm told we have you to thank for that."

Jimmy floated back a step and Billy chuckled, cold and unconcerned. Mark made a retching sound from the back of the house.

"Ah, my roommate has been discovered. Too bad Preston's flesh has already turned. At least now I have fresh meat to satisfy my hunger."

Billy returned to the sofa and looked down on the unconscious Catherine. A red bruise covered her forehead that would be purple by morning if she was still alive. Her chest rose with a breath and Jimmy felt grateful for a brief moment.

"I guess I should rip her throat out before she wakes up." Billy almost looked sad when he said it. "Otherwise she might get the upper hand since I don't have any more surprises left. I really wanted to take my time with this one. Well, that's the way little saints crumble."

Jimmy reached out. His hand slowly passed into Billy's shoulder with a cold shock so intense that Jimmy thought he was back among the living again.

Billy arched his body and jumped away from Jimmy's touch. He stared in horror. "What did you do to me?"

Mark charged into the room with a baseball bat and swung for the fences. The aluminum ripped across Jimmy's chest, sending his ethereal body into motion. Billy ducked the swing and came up with one of his own, catching Mark on the back of his rotation. Mark screamed and kept spinning, but missed him for the second strike. Billy clawed Mark again and then shoved the unbalanced kid in the back. Mark sprawled on the floor and the bat flew out of his grip. Billy pounced on top of him.

Without another thought, Jimmy dropped into Billy. It was like sinking into a frozen pond after breaking through the ice. The uninviting experience left him numb and shivering.

Jimmy blinked and found himself staring down through Billy's eyes at the back of Mark's neck. He tasted the warm saltiness of Mark's blood in his mouth. His stomach rolled and he threw up, emptying the contents on the worn carpet in the living room. He tried not to think about the ingredients as the room began to spin faster and faster.

Mark bucked him off, throwing Jimmy face first into the floor. His nose burst in bright sparkles of pain. He hoped Mark wouldn't smash the baseball bat into his skull as his thoughts switched off and his mind blanked out.

23.

HUNTER

Tommy the Cannibal Perv watched them on their way out of Cozad. He stood at the edge of town, waving goodbye while the kids in the school bus shut their windows and buried themselves below the seats. Hunter stopped his motorbike a safe distance away and shot Tommy a good double-dose of middle fingers before revving his engine and speeding after the yellow bus.

The ride back to Independents was slow. Hunter led the way on his bike as the stationary sun hung in the sky. He felt sorry for the poor kids riding in that bouncing metal can because the roads they would follow were buckled in stretches or pocked with potholes. Buses weren't designed for off-roading, and whenever Hunter traveled too far ahead he would stop and watch the kids being jostled like dried beans in a maraca. He tried to find a smooth path for Henry to follow, but every once in a while they just had to suffer or be stuck. No one wanted to be stuck when nighttime arrived.

Hunter tried to outride the stench of horror covering him as he sped across the land. His mind kept playing the scenes from the fight in the jail. The lamp's light going out. The sounds of cannibals moving in for the kill. The smell of the white gas on the floor. The knife stabbing into a little kid and the flick of his Zippo. Heat from the bright orange fire, and the screams that followed.

There was no other way to put it. Hunter just murdered a bunch of kids. No matter how twisted they had become, Hunter killed them. Now he was going to have to live with that.

Part of him wanted to return to Cozad and take care of Tommy once and for all, but his first priority was these kids in the bouncing yellow bus. They required a good meal and a decent night's rest in a warm bed without the nightmares of cannibal children gazing through their windows. Hunter gripped his handlebar tighter. He would deliver those kids to safety, and then he would return and finish Tommy.

He slowed to another stop and waited for the bus to close the gap. A couple miles farther and they would be near a clean water source he often used. The afternoon sun brought down bright, stifling heat. Even with the bus windows open, the kids had to be melting in there. The air conditioning was inoperable. Brandon had been lucky just to turn over the engine.

Behind the lumbering bus, a dark cloud of smoke rose into the sky. Hunter's fire was probably burning all of Cozad to the ground. He felt two ways about that. First, it reminded him of the horrible events and second, at least the tragic evidence of Cozad's previous inhabitants would be destroyed along with his part in it.

Normally Hunter would have headed southeast by now, but the bus wouldn't make his usual route, so following I-80 was the best option. They refueled the bus at one of the gigantic truck stops that dotted the interstate. The founders of Independents may not have considered the availability of gasoline when they chose to settle in Nebraska, but they lucked out because of all the truck stops. They hadn't even touched the reserves left in this state, not to mention the farmers who kept their own supply tucked away to operate their tractors and combines.

Hunter led them off the interstate to the pond near a farmhouse and barn. All the kids unloaded from the bus, carrying their water bottles or plastic jugs to refill them along the shore. Hunter tapped drops of iodine in every bottle and, after a good shake to kill lingering parasites, they gulped their water down and the process was repeated.

A silver tail splashed upon the surface, and excitement rippled through everyone in a wave of pointing fingers and shouts. Quickly Hunter retrieved his fishing supplies out of his backpack and huddled the group together.

"I've got four hooks, so I need four of you to cut some branches for fishing poles. You can use the saw on my army knife. Make sure the branch is green inside so the pole will bend a little without snapping."

Four kids took off at a trot toward a stand of trees on the other side of the pond.

"I need a couple more of you to find some bait." He noticed a boy quivering with untapped energy. He handed the kid his small plastic spade. "See if you can dig us up some worms."

The boy glowed. "Where should I dig?"

Hunter smiled and pointed down. "Start at your feet and work outwards."

Two girls wearing identical pink shirts stepped up expectantly. "What can we do?" they asked, as if they shared a brain.

"Do you guys know how to catch grasshoppers?"

Their eyes lit up. "We sure do."

"Good! Catch a lot of them, okay?"

They sprinted for the high grass and the hunt was on.

"The rest of you guys gather wood and build a fire." Hunter handed Brandon his Zippo. A brief image of the last time it was struck threatened to destroy his rising spirits, but he swallowed it down. "Make sure I get this back."

Brandon nodded and led another group of wood gatherers toward the trees as the first four returned with their fishing poles. Hunter helped string up their lines with hooks and a sinker. He broke up one of the extra sticks to use for bobbers.

"I found one! I found one!" the boy with the shovel hollered, pulling a fat wiggling earthworm out of a hole.

Hunter received the slimy invertebrate. "Great job! Keep digging."

The boy dropped where he stood and made another hole.

Hunter pinched off a segment of the worm and handed it to one of the girls. She gave the piece of worm a puzzled look.

"Just run the hook through the middle of the worm."

She made a yucky face, but did a good job hooking the worm. Hunter dumped the other half of the worm in one of the boys's hands and the two baited hooks plunked and settled into the water. The boy and the girl watched the floating sticks intently for bobbing action.

One of the two girls ran over with a couple grasshoppers. The agitated bugs stirred in Hunter's grip. He told the girl to catch more and she scampered off after her hunting buddy, who was still busy in the field.

Hunter showed the other boy and girl how to hook the hoppers, and then four lines were in the water. Nervous chatter rose on the bank, but Hunter shushed them all.

"We have to be quiet or we'll scare the fish away."

Everyone looked at him and nodded in agreement.

When the first stick bobbed under the water, the boy holding the line almost dropped his fishing pole. He quickly regrouped and hauled the fighting crappie to shore. All the Cozad kids huddled around the flopping silver-green fish like it was a miracle from Heaven.

"All right, all right," Hunter said, using his best 'settle-down' voice. "That's one. I'll clean it and we'll keep fishing. How's the fire coming, Brandon?"

Brandon smiled by the growing flames and smoke. "It's getting hotter, sir."

Hunter shook his head with embarrassment. "Please don't call me, sir. My name's Hunter. I'm just a kid like you."

"Yes, sir," Brandon said, and continued feeding sticks into the fire.

With a resigned sigh, Hunter retrieved the panicky fish from the ground. He unhooked it, whacked its head on a rock, and flipped open his lock blade.

Hunter stopped cold. Dried red flakes stained the blade. He closed his eye to block out the tainted blade. After several deep breaths, Hunter opened his eye and stepped to the pond's edge to wash his knife. He uncapped his iodine, dousing the cleansing red liquid over the knife, and returned to the unconscious fish.

Holding the crappie, he looked at the multitude of expressions on the faces around him—ranging from horrified to hungry. He grinned and gutted the fish.

*　　*　　*

A full belly later, Hunter sat on the grass at the edge of the pond, feeling amazingly better. Eight different kids caught over twenty fish, from white bass, to crappie, to sunfish, and three nice sized catfish. Everyone was happy, evident from the smiles and the pile of fish bones.

The brutal sun left its perch high in the sky, heading toward late afternoon. Gentler rays warmed Hunter's skin and danced along the water. Bees dipped into the surrounding wildflowers and he came close to believing that everything would be all right. His shoulder had other ideas, as the numbness coursed down his bicep and back inside to his shoulder blade. He hunched and tried to pop muscles loose or stretch ligaments without success.

Barbie dropped to her knees behind him. She placed firm hands on his shoulders and started rubbing.

Hunter ducked his head and groaned with relief.

"Is that doing any good?" Barbie asked.

"You have no idea." A string of drool dropped into his lap. He quickly sucked in the excess before looking like an idiot.

Barbie rubbed deeper, tougher, with her grip as more of the tightness in Hunter's shoulder released its hold. "You keep a lot in here."

Hunter moaned as his eye closed. "I got beat up pretty bad five months ago. The pain's been there ever since, probably always will be, just like I'll never see out of this eye again."

"Losing the sight in your eye and the pain in your shoulder are different things." Barbie sat and hooked her legs around him. The shoulder massage continued. "You're keeping this pain in your shoulder. It's up to you to let it go."

"That's bullshit."

Barbie dug her nails in and squeezed. Hunter winced and cried out, trying to scoot away from her grasp, but she held on. He stopped squirming and she wrapped her arms around his chest and pulled him back—pressing her soft body against him. All of his concerns melted away in an instant.

"You're blaming yourself for something and you're too important to let it weigh you down. We have a lot to do before the fight is finished."

Hunter shook his head like he was waking from a dream. "What are you telling me?"

"I'm telling you to hang on. Don't be discouraged. I'm here for you."

"But... I have a girlfriend." He moved her arms from around him and stood. The guilt he felt replaced the pain in his shoulder. He turned and regarded her smiling up at him, but it wasn't a mocking smile. The sadness in her eyes made the smile sincere.

"I'm sorry," he said.

"Don't be. I'm not." Barbie stood and wiped the grass from her jeans. She headed towards the shore of the pond.

Hunter watched her walk away, wondering why she kept hitting on him.

A loud buzzing broke his thoughts. The cloud of smoke from Cozad now filled the sky, moving in impossible, swarming patterns. Then the first grasshopper hit his face. Startled, he brushed his cheek. He looked up and a hundred more rained down on him.

This was not smoke.

24.

HUNTER

The enormous cloud filling the eerie sky transformed into a buzzing roar, thrumming with billions and billions of insects. From a distance, the long tendrils that fell from above could have been mistaken for rain, but they raked at the ground. Vegetation was reduced to chaff where the insects touched. With haunting realization, Hunter scanned the area for cover. The bus had all those windows and the size of the swarm made Hunter believe they needed something more solid. The farmhouse or barn that lay beyond the windbreak of giant evergreens was their best option. They would have to run for it.

The grasshoppers crashed from above like a hailstorm. Kids batted at their hair and the sky as insects pelted them. Henry sheltered his little sister, waving his arms with his eyes closed.

"Everyone run to the barn!" Hunter pointed in that direction and a group of kids broke ahead of the crowd. Others were more preoccupied, struggling under the assault. Hunter ran to where he was needed. He stomped and slapped his way to two kids that swatted the air.

"You have to run to the barn."

"They're all over me," the girl said.

The boy pinched his face tight with his eyes barely open to keep the bugs out.

"It's going to get worse," Hunter said. "There's a lot more coming. You have to follow the others to the barn." He grabbed their hands and put them together. The boy chanced a look in the direction everyone was running. Hunter squeezed his shoulder. "You have to get her there."

The boy nodded and dragged the girl. They picked up speed as they broke into a grasshopper-free pocket. Hunter searched for more stragglers.

Barbie prodded and pushed other kids toward the barn. Hunter locked eyes with her, seeing they shared similar fears, and then they rounded the rest of the kids together and trailed the group while the thunderous buzz from the swarming cloud bore down. Running for their lives through the eerie darkness made everything that much bleaker.

"What's going on, Barbie? This isn't natural is it?"

Barbie narrowed her eyes, mouth pressed in a firm line. She kept her legs and arms churning in the direction of supposed safety. "Are you always the master of understatement?"

"Why? Does that turn you on?"

"Now? You want to flirt with me now? You have terrible timing."

"I like to think of it as a rhythm."

One of the boys they were following tripped and took out two other kids on his way down. Barely slowing, Hunter grabbed two of the skinny kids as Barbie scooped up the third. Everybody regained their feet and continued running. Hunter took a second to check the cloud's progress and his stomach dropped. The black mass crested like an enormous crashing wave.

They hit the windbreak and Hunter cut through, breathing hard. He paused to help the others between the heavy boughs. The swarm rose in a crescendo of incessant humming as billions of wings strummed together. The final five kids broke through the giant hedge, showing scratches for their efforts. Barbie was the last one when the swarm bounded into the evergreens. For an instant they had shelter from the storm, and then the insects broke over the top and tumbled down.

"Run for it!" Hunter urged them on, waving his hands to herd them along. Something bit his back underneath his shirt and he swiped at a grasshopper, squishing it in his palm and throwing it to the ground. Dozens of insects twitched in his hair and more fell onto him. The others had their share of grasshoppers going for the same ride, but at least everyone still moved towards the barn.

Another fifty feet and they slid into the giant doors. Hunter pulled on the handles, but they wouldn't open because the others had locked them out. He pounded on the wooden boards. "Open the door!" He hoped that someone inside could hear him over the swarm. He pounded harder and the others joined in. Panic showed in their wide eyes and more of the bugs rained down on them. One boy turned to fight, slapping and stomping everything around him. One of his wild slaps caught Barbie in the side of the head and knocked her to the ground. Hunter threw the kid against the door where he fell next to Barbie, struggling to regain her feet. The barn door opened and Hunter hurled kids inside. Barbie slipped in next and then he pulled the door shut and slammed the board down to keep it locked.

The smell of smoke caught Hunter's boggled senses first. Someone had decided to light a fire inside a steel drum filled with trash. It provided some light, but that wouldn't last long. The smoke had nowhere to go except for small cracks in the walls and roof of the barn. Hopefully they wouldn't asphyxiate waiting for the killer bug storm to blow over.

Hunter turned on the kids huddled around the burning barrel in the middle of the barn and erupted. "What dumb ass locked the door? You nearly got us killed!"

Henry held up his hand—the other cradled his sister. "I thought everybody had made it."

Hunter bowed his head, hit by a wave of shame. Barbie glaring at him didn't help. Outside, the raucous noise rose now that all the bugs had finally made it to the party. Hunter breathed deeply then released it in a long hiss. Another grasshopper bit into his back. He ripped off his shirt, swiped all the hoppers off, and stomped them into the dirt floor.

"Okay, everybody look around and see if we're missing anyone else." Hunter finished shaking the bugs out of his hair.

Everyone started counting and looking for friends among the forty-two kids that formed the final census of Cozad. Barbie took charge of the headcount.

Hunter walked over to Henry. "Sorry about yelling like that. It was a little messed up out there. Is she okay?"

Henry nodded, working a strand of blonde hair from his sister's brow. "She's been through a lot today. She just needs rest."

"I'm all for that. I think we're safe here for a while."

Henry bent down and wrapped his other arm under his sister's knees, lifting her up. "You think it's safe by the walls?"

The roof rattled and popped from the intensive onslaught, but the barn was holding. The incredible noise of angry insects had everyone watching the walls in fear. Mold and stale air mixed with smoke as dust shook out of the rafters and drifted slowly down, switching places with the rising smoke. Anyone with asthma was screwed.

Stalls lined the sides of the barn: one filled with lumber, old rusted tools hung in another, while horse tack and other farm implements occupied other areas.

"I wouldn't sit right next to the walls. Maybe next to these support beams would be best. That way, if these bugs bring the barn down you'll probably be all right."

Henry's jaw dropped. His sister's eyes popped open.

"I'm just teasing. Sorry, that was kind of dumb to say. We're safe in here."

Henry shook his head and kissed his sister's before guiding her away from Hunter. He slid down one of the structure beams and held his sister protectively while they watched the ceiling rattle.

Hunter mentally punched himself in the face and told himself that once everyone was safe, he'd do it for real.

Barbie walked up, her face muscles tight. Hunter waited for the bad news.

"Brandon isn't here. He's the only one. He was working on the bus when the bugs hit."

"Nobody saw him running for the barn?" he asked.

"The bus was too far away. He probably didn't even know we were running before they were on top of him. Hopefully he's safe inside the bus."

"Hopefully the windows will hold."

The trash in the barrel burned down along with the light. The kids held one another as the approaching darkness threatened to strip away the last of their bravery. Hunter grabbed some lumber out of one of the stalls and laid an eight-foot, two-by-four over a cinderblock. He jumped, snapping the board in half and he handed the pieces to Barbie.

"Put those in the barrel."

She smiled at him, patting him on the bottom. He jerked with embarrassment. "You're so handy to have around."

He regained his composure and smiled as he dropped another board on the block. "You have no idea. Better hurry before the fire burns out."

"Why? Are you afraid to be with me in the dark?"

"Yes," he said, and cracked another board in half. "Here, two more." He placed them lengthwise into her arms on top of the first set.

She plopped them into the barrel, sending sparks of ash up from the trash. They lazily floated in the air. Hunter held his breath, hoping they would settle on something nonflammable.

Once the fire raged harmlessly in the steel drum, and the smoke found the high ceiling of the barn where it filtered out, Hunter leaned on the beam across the stall from Henry and his sister. They had relaxed some after the blunt dose of Hunter's honesty. She slept peacefully with her head in Henry's lap. He stroked her hair and Hunter smiled.

Henry looked up. "Thanks again for saving her."

"Thank Barbie. I just went along for the ride."

Barbie turned her head from the fire and came over. "Thank me for what?"

"For saving Sophie. I hope one day I can repay you."

Barbie leaned down and kissed Henry's forehead. When she stood up, Henry's eyes were closed, and a huge smile stretched to the corners of his lean face.

"You just take care of her," Barbie said. "She's very special."

"I know." Henry returned to admiring his sleeping little sister.

Barbie leaned on Hunter. Her softness weighed upon his body and his thoughts. Both were heavy in a way that Hunter did not want to admit. Too tired to fight, he allowed her to share his space.

"What are we dealing with out there? It's not everyday a cloud of bugs fall from the sky. This has something to do with Cozad, doesn't it?"

"They are part of Famine's tools. A plague of a different sort. The bugs didn't start off in one giant cloud, but grew with each passing field, building in numbers, and they will keep building."

She paused and Hunter grasped at what she was saying, but his mind had trouble reeling in the last bit. "Why? What are they doing?"

"They feed. They will strip the land and feed until there is nothing left."

The information was too heavy combined with everything else. He dropped his foot back for leverage and gently pushed her off.

"The direction that cloud was headed..." he couldn't finish. His mind refused to allow the thought to blossom any further than it already had. But the idea had mushroomed and the spores were spreading fear throughout his limbs, numbing with deadly poison.

"Yes," Barbie said it for him. "It's heading for Independents."

The noise of the grasshoppers outside subsided gradually and sunlight pushed through the cracks of the barn. Hunter rushed to the door, flipping up the board that had locked them in and kept the bugs out. He hurried into the late afternoon sun and then around the side of the barn to look southeast where the cloud progressed in a wispy, buzzing trail. The awesome bulk filled the horizon, carrying disaster toward Hunter's home.

On a nearby hilltop, Hunter saw Tommy the Perv with both arms stretching toward the sky, displaying his middle fingers. Famine smiled at Hunter. Then he descended down the other side and disappeared after his cloud.

25.

SCOUT

After a while, Vanessa left Scout alone. He sat on the couch in the dim aftermath of his breakup, wishing he had something better to do than wait for supper.

Raven didn't need to leave town. They could have worked their problems out together like couples did, not bolt when the first sign of trouble popped up. But Raven chose the easy way out. She was riding into the sunset while Scout sat in their apartment and stewed.

It sucked.

Shadows stretched into the living room as evening approached. He thought about rehearsing Sunday's sermon, but the idea left him feeling cold. Raven said she was leaving him because of the way she was treated by everyone else. He was left with a congregation that drove his girlfriend away. How was he going to bring those kids the Good News?

Standing up, Scout noticed the early birds milling around Main Street, waiting for the Brittanys to open their doors. He looked at the orange sky in the west and then picked up his spiral notebook.

He read his sermon out loud. The topic was about loving thy neighbor. Scout didn't miss the irony and his presentation sounded hollow. How could he continue to preach to these kids after the way they treated Raven? He stopped and tossed the notebook on the couch and looked out the window again.

A black storm cloud swelled over the horizon, rolling and

breaking apart before closing back in on itself unlike any other cloud he'd ever seen. Scout sunk his knees into the back of the couch and leaned forward for a better look. A grasshopper twitched outside on his window sill and then hopped into the sky, wings buzzing.

"Do you hear that?" someone said on the street below the open window.

"Yeah," said another boy. "Sounds like a car."

"Sounds like a really big car. Let's check it out."

The boys raced across the street, and Scout leaned closer, cocking his ear. The loud drone sounded like a tractor engine running full bore inside a barn. Scout looked back at the cloud as the massive shadow from its approach blocked the late afternoon sun, creating an eerie kind of twilight. His window screen rattled from the sound and he jumped back. Then the screams started and Scout shot out the door and ran down the stairs to the street.

He slid to a stop on the brick cobbles as something struck him in the face, and then another and another until he threw up his arms, wondering if Billy had returned with more rocks. Twenty or so grasshoppers hummed and twitched at his feet. He picked one up. Several more bounced off his back. Scout looked toward the sky that was falling like a giant hand intending to crush everything underneath.

Across the street, candles were being lit inside Brittany's. Kids plastered their faces against the large pane windows to see what the deal was and a few began trickling out beneath the awnings, staring up at the creepy darkness.

"Get back inside and get everybody away from the windows now!" Scout ran across the street, waving his arms frantically. "They're grasshoppers! It's a whole cloud of grasshoppers!"

"What's the problem?" one of the kids said. "Get the Raid, right?"

The first wave dropped on top of Scout and knocked him flat. He rolled with the flow, scrambling to his feet. Jason, the smart kid with the jokes, looked on in horror. Scout grabbed him by the arm and another kid by the shirt collar and flung them both through the door.

Scout charged inside after the two stumbling boys. "Everyone get away from the windows! Blow out those candles!"

"But we won't be able to see," a girl said.

"Bugs are attracted to light."

Candles were instantly snuffed.

"Move to the back. Don't panic," Scout said. "Take the tables with you as you go."

"Why?"

"We'll need to hide under them."

The sound of moving tables scraping across the hardwood floor barely registered over the loud din of grasshoppers outside. Scout didn't know if the windows would hold. The swarm that fell on him had felt like a sandbag dropping from a hot air balloon. If that much weight pushed against the windows, they'd have flying glass everywhere—followed by a massive bug swarm.

Scout pushed a table to the back. "Is that all the tables?"

"Yes, I think so."

"Luis?"

"This isn't normal."

"Who's with Ginger?"

"No one's with her right now. I was getting us some food."

Scout pictured Luis's clinic with the same large windowpanes facing Main Street. Sure, metallic blinds covered them, but they wouldn't hold back squat.

Scout grabbed Luis by the shoulders as the light outside grew dimmer by the second. "Get everyone under the tables and flip the front ones sideways, facing the windows."

"Why?"

"In case those windows shatter and the grasshoppers rush inside."

Scout released Luis and moved toward the door, tripping over the chairs that had been left behind. The noise outside scared the hell out of him. Luis's clinic was to the left, past Mark's police station and the thrift shop where Hunter and Scout dumped off the usable stuff they found. Scout had to reach Ginger and little James.

He pulled the door open to the giant buzzing cloud of grasshoppers swarming down. He'd read the stories of Moses in the Bible. Was this like the plague of locust that God unleashed on the Egyptians to convince their rulers to free their Hebrew slaves? Someone other than God had sent this plague. Scout was certain.

Now the dark mass totally blocked the sunlight. He skimmed the storefronts, running his hand over windows and doors as bug after bug struck him and landed in his hair, working their way under his shirt. Most disturbing were the stinging bites once they found his skin. Scout smashed and flicked, while shuffling through the grasshopper piles on the walkway, stomping now and then with satisfying crunches. He passed Mark's and then the thrift shop. Finally he crossed the window of Luis's waiting room and found the door. Scout turned the knob and slipped inside, shutting the noisy insects out.

"Ginger!"

He stood on shaky legs, swiping away the bugs who'd ridden him inside. He stumbled through the darkness and found the doorway that led to the delivery room.

"Ginger?"

He barely heard the crying baby over the incessant roar outside. Scout blindly walked with small steps, his arms stretched out in front until he bumped into Luis's desk.

"Ginger! Where are you?"

"Scout? We're under the desk. Is that a tornado outside? "

"No. There's a billion grasshoppers dropping out of the sky. I need to get you someplace safe."

"What? We're not safe here?"

Scout regarded the direction where the sound reverberated off the windows. "No."

"How big are the bugs?"

"There are a lot of them out there. Are you and the baby all right?"

"Yes, thank you for coming."

"No problem." Scout searched his memory and found the hallway to the back nearby, where two separate doors led to a storeroom and a restroom. He opened one of the doors to a dark windowless area.

"Scout?" Ginger called after him in a shaky voice.

"Here, I'll take James." Scout held the squirming bundle and helped Ginger to her feet. He cooed at James and the baby quieted. Scout supported the baby's head, covered by a little stocking cap. In spite of his growing fear, Scout managed a smile. Of course Jimmy's kid would be wearing a hat. The baby cried some more.

"He must really be scared," Scout said.

"I think he's hungry."

"Oh? Well, I'll let you take care of that once we're settled."

Ginger laughed and laid her head on Scout's shoulder just as a giant crack sounded behind them. The crack traveled straight up Scout's spine. His fear became reality after an enormous crash. Glass and a gust of wind blasted inside Luis's clinic, pitching them forward with concussive force. Scout covered James and caught his balance inside the open doorway. A tidal wave of insects roared into the delivery room. The door slammed closed, leaving Scout with a hysterical baby James alone in the small room.

Ginger screamed from the other side.

26.

MARGARET

She awoke on a strange couch inside an unfamiliar house. Margaret sat up and held herself steady as blood rushed to her head, making her dizzy. It had been a while since she'd performed a healing, even one as small as a broken nose. Being the conductor of God's light and the transference of His divinity to the person being healed was no easy task, but people needed miracles so they could be saved and their faith restored.

Her head buzzed. That was something new. She stuck a finger in one ear, trying to pop it. The front door was open to an unnatural darkness waiting outside.

Margaret rocked forward and stood, checking her balance before venturing on. She crossed the room and gripped the doorframe for support. She felt better after a couple deep breaths. The feeling ended quickly.

Samuel and Dylan stood silently in the front yard, stunned. A massive cloud, buzzing with swarming insects, descended in a dark, rolling blanket on top of Main Street. She was in Dylan's house, which had been built on a highpoint at the edge of town. The slight elevation provided a scary view.

Margaret walked up behind the boys and stopped beside Samuel.

He looked at her then directed his attention back to town before bringing it once again to rest on her. His face showed complete incomprehension. "Are you okay?"

Margaret nodded. "When did this start?"

"About five minutes ago. I've never seen anything like it."

"No one alive ever has."

"What can we do?" Dylan asked, mirroring Samuel's dumbfounded expression. The tape had been removed from his nose and the black eyes were gone. "Everyone is down there."

Margaret nodded again and gripped Samuel's hand for needed support to keep her grounded. The sight of that massive cloud and the fear for the people trapped indoors was overwhelming. "Nothing can be done against that. All we can do is pray for the safety of our friends..."

"Is that it, Molly?" Samuel searched her face.

"What do you mean?"

"You," he paused, watching her. "You healed Dylan, just like Catherine. How is that possible?"

Margaret gazed back at the town, wishing she could do something. She knew the concentration of bugs was not a normal occurrence. A large amount of focused power had gathered those insects together then pointed them like a loaded weapon straight at Independents. Margaret was sure that Main Street wasn't the only destination of the swarm, but rather a brief stop. Chase was the plague. This was the work of Famine.

"Molly?" Samuel shook her hand. "Are you sure you're okay?"

"Yes," she said. "I've had a realization today, thanks to Catherine. I'm still adjusting. Can we talk about it later?"

"Sure, if there is a later."

"I need to pray," Margaret told them.

"I didn't know you were so religious," Samuel said, letting go as she pulled away.

"I used to be a long time ago. That's part of the realization."

Margaret walked over and knelt beside a large tree with a full view of the town, under siege from the roaring wings of a billion insects. She bowed her head and spoke to God.

He immediately answered, as if waiting for someone to ask for His help and eager to give it. Margaret's earlier fatigue was stripped away. A jolt of energy filled her and she clenched her fists to contain the swell that His light provided and listened for the instructions of His message.

Margaret opened her eyes, aware of His will.

She stood and turned to find Samuel and Dylan staring at her. Their mouths hung open like they had their own plans on how to trap the flying insects.

"You're... you are..." Dylan tried to say.

"You're glowing, Molly," Samuel said.

Margaret smiled and opened her hands. She held twin circles of light. "I need you to take these. We're going down there and this will protect you."

Samuel stared at the light she offered, but made no move to touch it. "That's crazy. This is crazy. What is that?" He stepped back. "Who are you?"

"Samuel," she snapped. "I am your friend and I'm telling you to take the light. It's a gift that has been given to us to help everyone trapped down there. It won't hurt. Take it. Or I will rip your shirt to shreds."

His mouth dropped open again. He narrowed his eyes at her. "You wouldn't dare."

She smiled and stepped toward him. "Please, we don't have time to waste."

"Just don't hurt my shirt." Samuel reached out and grabbed the light from her hand. It seeped into his palm and shot through his body. Margaret knew he felt the same euphoric transformation from the power of the Lord's holy light. Samuel now glowed as brightly as her, wrapped in a cocoon of power and protection. His smile gleamed with magnificence.

"Okay, Dylan. We need your help too."

Dylan stepped up and took the light without a word. His skin blazed, and together the three of them appeared as stars sent down to walk the Earth.

"Now," Margaret said. "Follow me."

She spun towards town and sprinted down the hill with abandon. Her feet barely touching the ground, she felt like she was leaping the whole way there. Houses and trees blurred as they crossed the half mile from Dylan's house to Main Street in seconds. Margaret and the two boys drove into the center of town, and as their lights pierced the heart of the storm, the bugs fell in lifeless piles. The swarm of insects curled away to avoid them, hovering near the two story rooftops, unwilling to come down any farther.

"They're afraid of us," Dylan said.

Samuel laughed like he'd had a little too much of his homemade wine. "I always thought bug zappers were cool. I just never thought I'd be one."

Margaret took in the situation. Every window on Main Street had shattered. Tendrils filled with grasshoppers dipped down into some of the buildings, like festering streams running in and out. The sight sickened Margaret. She prayed they were not too late.

Margaret pointed to Brittany's. "Everybody's in the cafeteria. You guys get in there and drive the remaining bugs out."

Samuel nodded. "What are you going to do?"

"Ginger," Margaret said and ran to Luis's, where a long tongue of the swarming cloud streamed into the broken window of the clinic. Margaret jumped through the window frame, right into the thick, swirling chaos that had nowhere to hide from the Lord's light. The place exploded with bugs dropping, followed by screeching and movement as the panicky insects struggled away from Margaret's path to the safety outside.

A naked bloody lump lay by the far wall. Margaret's rage surged. And then sorrow threatened to take her out of action when she recognized what was left of the tawny hair on the head of her best friend, but the Lord's light kept her strong.

The baby's crying came from behind a closed door down the small hallway in back. The door swept open and a wild-eyed Scout burst through, brandishing a mop.

He shaded his eyes from Margaret's light. "Molly, is that you? Where's Ginger?" But then he saw her on the floor and stumbled into the wall. "Oh, sweet Jesus!"

Margaret rushed forward and gripped his wrists. A small amount of her light seeped into him and he calmed. The baby screamed from where Scout had left little James safely in the restroom.

"Go tend to the baby while I see about Ginger," she said.

He nodded like that was the most reasonable thing he'd heard all day. Scout turned down the hallway, dimly lit by the glowing light he now carried. She knew the light would be enough for Scout to soothe James as well.

Margaret knelt next to Ginger and gently held her bloody hand. She still lived, but the mass of bugs had gnawed at her skin. The pain and the crush of their numbers must have knocked her unconscious. Margaret touched Ginger's head and confirmed the concussion.

The baby stopped crying and Margaret heard Scout gently singing to little James. She thought her heart might burst when she recognized the song, "Jesus Loves Me."

She closed her eyes and blocked everything out except for the need to heal Ginger. The conduit of light the Lord supplied filled her with strength and power. Margaret rested her other hand above Ginger's still beating heart and made the connection between her friend's mind and soul so that the body could be healed. She prayed again and a surge of power from the light covered Ginger's torn flesh. Margaret breathed in the light and held the tension of that pain until she opened her eyes, releasing all of it.

The glow shot from Luis's clinic into the roaring cloud above Main Street where it suffused like lightning rolling in a thunderhead. The flying insects lifted higher and moved away until the natural light of day returned.

Margaret's light was depleted, spent in the service of saving her friend. Ginger lay naked on the floor, her hospital gown in shreds and her wounds healed.

Margaret remained conscious due to the generous help she had received. Still she swayed from the light's absence. Unable to stand, she crawled to the bed and pulled the fitted sheet from the mattress to cover Ginger.

Scout slowly entered the room with James, the expectant look of sorrow creasing his face. He stopped—sorrow swapped with surprise.

"How is he?" Margaret asked.

Scout stared at her, then back to Ginger, then finally down to the little sleeping bundle in his arms. He smiled. "He's perfect."

"That's good," Margaret said, curling up next to Ginger and closing her eyes.

"What happened? How did she get better?"

With her eyes still closed, Margaret wiggled her fingers at him. "Magic."

"You're not funny."

"Yeah, I've been told that before."

Something screeched outside. The sound traveled along Main Street, bouncing off the buildings in echoing waves. Margaret opened her eyes and pushed herself up. Scout handed her baby James. His feet crunching through the dead bugs and broken glass scattered on the floor, he headed toward the empty window frame.

James opened his bright blue eyes that reminded her of Catherine. The smell he carried in his pants reminded her of something else. She searched around for a clean diaper and found one under an upturned table.

"You're not going to believe this," Scout said from the window.

She quickly changed little James and wrapped him up in his blanket like she'd done for thousands of babies in other lifetimes.

She had already guessed what was walking the streets outside and it made her heart sink. All that was left was the description.

"Some tall, creepy dude is standing out there. He's looking for something."

Margaret held James close and kissed his cheek.

"Food," she said, but Scout didn't hear her.

"I bet he's looking for trouble," he said.

27.

JIMMY

Jimmy's head throbbed and he thought that was really weird, considering. He tried lifting his hands to check out the situation and found his arms restricted, as well as his legs, and realized he was tied up.

That was totally weird, considering.

He opened his eyes and took a deep breath of carpet fibers where his face was currently planted. He knew that was absolutely weird, considering he was supposed to be dead.

Jimmy rolled his head to the side and coughed out the dust and stray hair from the carpet. His mouth already held many other disgusting flavors. What he wouldn't give for a glass of water and some toothpaste.

"What's it doing now?" Catherine asked.

Mark looked back into the front door. "The cloud is heading out towards the fields."

"That's what I thought it would do," Catherine said, sounding like this cloud was the worst thing to ever happen in the world, or at least in Independents.

The events before he passed out rushed back to Jimmy all at once, and now he knew he was lying on Billy's carpet, but everything beyond that got really weird. He remembered the confrontation with Billy. How Billy had obviously lost his mind, with all the talk about eating Mark and Catherine, and then he remembered sinking into Billy to try and stop him.

Mark was staring at him. "He's awake now."

"He is?" Catherine came around so Jimmy could see her. Her forehead was bruised and a frown crossed her lips. Her eyes grew wide when she looked at Jimmy. "Oh!"

"What's happening? How can I be all tied up?"

Mark quickly stepped back into the house, carrying an aluminum bat and looking absolutely terrifying with the way he held it. "You're tied because you're some kind of sick, twisted freak. You're lucky I don't brain you right now and be done with it."

Catherine placed her hand on Mark's arm, the one holding the bat. "Mark, will you give me a moment to speak with him, please?"

"Sure, speak away, and then I'll brain him."

Jimmy squirmed in his bonds but quickly stopped when Mark took a menacing step forward. He tried to shrink or melt into the carpet fibers. Neither amazing feat happened. He held his breath and prayed he wasn't brained on the spot.

"I need to speak with him alone," Catherine told Mark.

"I don't think so. This crazy bastard might try and chew through the ropes."

"He won't do that, silly. I can handle this, trust me. Just stay outside the door and I'll scream real loud if I need you." She emphasized her request by placing her hands on her hips like she meant business and Mark was delaying progress.

Mark looked at her then at Jimmy. He pointed the bat and the tip of the barrel swung an inch from Jimmy's nose. "I'll be right outside, Billy. If she even makes a peep loud enough to be considered a scream, I'm running in here and putting this in the center of your skull. You got me, right? Shake your head once for yes."

Jimmy shook his head once even though Mark had called him Billy. Something was totally wrong and Jimmy needed answers now.

Mark walked out into the fading sunset. Jimmy realized he must have been unconscious for a while since it had been mid-afternoon when they confronted Billy.

"I was wondering where you were." Catherine kneeled next to him.

"What is happening? Am I who I think I am?"

Catherine cocked her head and smiled. "That didn't make any sense, silly."

"You know it's me and not Billy, right?" Jimmy said.

"Of course. I knew the moment I saw your eyes. They are the gateways to the soul, you know. You can't hide a soul as big as yours anyways."

"But how is this possible?"

Catherine shrugged. "Possession would be my first guess. But I'll have to investigate before I can say for sure. Do you mind?" She raised her hands and held them above Jimmy, ready to do something miraculous.

"Go ahead. Knock yourself out." Jimmy's voice sounded nothing like him. "This is the most excitement I've had in months."

Catherine laid her hands on his head and bowed her own. A wind tore through the front door, blasting dust around the room. Jimmy felt a strange stirring in his chest like a giant fish swimming in a small bowl. Catherine's hands started glowing and the fish grew agitated and thrashed wildly. Jimmy was unable to do anything but wiggle because of his bonds. His stomach rippled and his arms strained against the rope cutting into his wrists. He felt a scream ripping him apart from his toes to the top of his head and fire burned in every nerve, melting his skin and setting his bones ablaze. He searched, but only saw light, and wanted nothing more than to tear away and scurry into darkness.

The light continued pulsing through him, chasing the big fish until it gripped the creature in both hands and yanked it out, freeing Jimmy's borrowed body from the entity's powerful presence. A terrible apparition writhed in the air above him, trapped by Catherine's light. Another gust of wind blew in through the door and the creature's form shattered into a thousand fragments.

Jimmy watched the light dissipate with nervous tension still holding him rigid. Catherine knelt above him, panting like she ran a race and smiling because she won first place.

Mark stood in the doorway, tightening his grip on the baseball bat. "What happened?"

Catherine, still breathing hard, turned her head. "Had to... chase away ... a demon."

Mark narrowed his eyes. "So what do we do with him now?"

Catherine winked at Jimmy. "You can untie Billy. He's going to be fine."

Mark walked over, looking unconvinced. He tapped the bat against Billy's chest. "Is that right, Billy? Are you okay?"

Catherine pushed the bat away. "Would you stop, silly? You're scaring him. I told you he was okay."

"Yeah, but I want to hear him tell me."

Jimmy swallowed. "I'm okay, Mark, really."

He said it, but he didn't believe it. How can you call possession being okay? Sure Catherine had chased something away, but what was Jimmy? He was another something. And where the heck had Billy gone? Jimmy had questions, but Catherine was up to her secretive routine and he figured it best to play along until they had a private moment together when he could make her tell him everything.

Mark tapped the bat in his free hand.

Jimmy returned to the task of self-preservation. "I mean it, Mark. I'm okay." He sounded scared; it wasn't difficult. "I don't even know why I'm tied up. I don't remember anything."

"I'll tell you what happened. In fact I'll show you what happened, what you did to Preston." Mark bent over and picked Jimmy up by one of his tied arms like he was a Samsonite suitcase packed for Grandma's house.

"Mark, put him down!" Catherine snapped. "What happened in the other room has nothing to do with Billy. He wasn't responsible." She slapped the bat out of his other hand and poked him in the chest.

Mark dropped Jimmy to the ground, knocking the wind out of him.

"Billy was possessed. That means he had no knowledge of what the creature in charge was doing, so just drop it."

"He already did," Jimmy said at their feet. He gasped from the lack of oxygen combined with the pain that jarred every one of his joints.

Catherine bent down and untied his hands then his feet. Jimmy rubbed the feeling back into his small wrists and marveled at how different they were from his old set of long arms. This definitely moved to the top of the "weirdest things that ever happen to him" list.

Mark stooped over to retrieve his bat again. He walked to the door, staring at Jimmy the whole time, and leaned the bat against the doorjamb. Then Mark looked outside. His jaw fell open from whatever sight he viewed. "The cloud has created some type of giant dust storm out over the fields. What is that thing, Catherine?"

She joined him at the door. "My guess is it's a cloud of bugs and they're eating up all the crops."

"What!" Jimmy leapt to his feet. He ran past Catherine out to the front lawn and stared off toward the fields where the giant swarm tore into the earth like a tornado. He staggered like he was intoxicated from spending time with Samuel's barrel of wine.

Catherine wrapped her arm around his waist for support. With Jimmy inside Billy's smaller body, they now stood eye to eye.

"What is happening?"

She stared at him then nodded. "Famine's coming. This is just the start. I'm not sure what type of entity is responsible for this, but we should expect the worst. Like Chase and his plague."

"What can we do?"

She pointed to the cloud. "There really isn't anything we can do against that swarm of bugs. We'll wait it out and see what's left." Catherine turned to Mark. "We should go to Main Street and assess the damages."

Jimmy watched, afraid to move, as the cloud of bugs continued churning dust and debris over his fields. All of Independents's food was being obliterated. All of Jimmy's hard work over the years was being destroyed by something like Chase's plague.

This late in the season, there would be no time to grow enough food to make it through the winter. They would be lucky if half their population survived. He remembered something about hellhounds killing all the chickens and hogs this morning, but at the time he was too excited to see everyone again to consider the implications.

"Billy?" Catherine said like she had repeated it a couple of times and was now worried. "Mark and I need to go check if everyone's all right. You should come with us."

Jimmy broke out of his spiral of thoughts leading him deeper into something he had no control over at the moment. "Why do we need to check on everybody?"

"Because before that cloud of bugs hit the fields, it sat over Main Street for a time. We need to make sure no one is injured."

Jimmy started moving towards Main Street. Ginger was there with his newborn son. Jimmy sped up.

"Hey, wait for us," Mark called.

He pretended not to hear and pumped his legs faster, no longer afraid of Mark and his bat now that something threatened his family.

He rapidly approached the center of town and noticed the debris first. Gravel from the roofs of the buildings was scattered everywhere like gray pieces of hail after a storm. Sparkling edges of jagged glass were interspersed as well, and Jimmy was thankful that Billy had chosen to wear shoes today.

He turned the corner at the edge of the building that was Ginger's Clothing Center. He hit the cobbles of Main Street and skidded to his butt right in front of a tall kid with black hair and clothes that didn't fit. Jimmy noticed the boy's long fingernails, splayed out like he intended to use them. Then he looked up into the kid's dark, dilated eyes. Eyes like Chase's.

The kid smiled down at him. "Ah, there you are at last. I have arrived."

Jimmy crab-walked backwards until he sliced his hand open on a piece of broken glass. He stopped and pulled the sliver out, releasing a warm stream of blood that trickled down his arm to his elbow. Jimmy pressed his hand to his shirt.

"That looks delicious," the boy said, looming over him. "Why do you move away from me? You do remember your master?" He narrowed his dark eyes as his long oily hair swung away from his face. A look of shock replaced suspicion. "You! But you're supposed to be dead."

Jimmy stood as Catherine and Mark ran up beside him.

"I know," Jimmy said. "I've been thinking the same thing all day."

28.

HUNTER

Late afternoon was slipping away when Hunter led the Cozad kids back to their bus. The knotted group stumbled along looking at the sky. They found Brandon in a bloody heap underneath bus seats, amidst the broken glass from shattered windows. His skin had been torn away and death followed. Hunter hated being right about the safety of the bus. Nobody wanted to ride in it again. Hunter's motorbike had fallen over, but was otherwise unharmed.

"What are we going to do?" Henry asked.

"Let's go back to the truck stop and see what we can start up. Hopefully we'll find a couple of vans or SUVs."

Hunter and Henry rolled the generator and battery charger the half mile distance to the truck stop on I-80 and located a Winnebago suitable for the trip home. They searched inside the store for supplies, swapping out the old battery, and while the new one charged they changed the oil, filled the gas tank, inflated the tires, and wiped down the dash with Armor All. Henry drove the RV back to the pond where everyone waited, still searching the sky for more bug clouds.

In their absence, the others had debated about what to do with Brandon's body. No one had the stomach to pull him out of the bus. Instead they had siphoned gas out of the tank and splashed it inside the empty window frames. Wesley held a makeshift torch with cloth wrapped and doused in gasoline around one end. Hunter didn't want to know where the cloth came from or why it was dotted red. He handed his Zippo lighter over and walked away, not really in the mood for another fire today.

Wesley lit the fabric and a rush of flames and black smoke followed.

"Thank you for everything, Brandon. We'll miss you," Carissa said, and her brother tossed the fire through a busted window. The bus ignited and everyone scurried for the Winnebago parked a hundred yards away.

Barbie walked over as Hunter started his bike. "Can I ride with you for a while?"

"Are you sure? It might be more comfortable in the RV."

The line waiting to board the Winnebago had dwindled to Carissa and Wesley. There was a couch and a couple beds for the forty-two remaining Cozad kids.

He shrugged. "Yeah, that's fine. Go ahead and get on." He made room for her by unhooking the bungee cords around his backpack on the end of the seat. "Do you mind wearing this for me?"

"Not at all." Barbie looped the straps over her shoulders. She threw her leg across the seat and scooted up close to Hunter.

He resisted the urge to slide up or push her back. Any movement might provoke a comment from his new riding companion that he didn't want to deal with at the moment. They only had a two hour drive before reaching Independents; he could handle the closeness.

Henry pulled the Winnebago forward, giving Hunter the thumbs up. Hunter returned the gesture and clicked into first, second and then third as the bike picked up speed. They traveled into the falling dusk of nighttime, past the farm that had been their refuge during the grasshopper storm. Hunter turned his single headlight on and Henry painted his back with bright light.

They followed an easy path toward Independents, created by the insects. An enormous swath of dirt, two football fields wide, headed straight south. Hunter wanted to ride fast and catch up with his imagination that had already arrived in Independents, flashing him all the gory details it could conjure. Brandon's death had twisted into a town full of Hunter's friends, hacked and chewed into pieces by the terrible power of Tommy the Perv's storm. Hunter shook his head in agitation, trying to clear his thoughts, but the images had taken root.

Barbie leaned into him and tightened her grip around his waist. At least it took Hunter's mind away from things he had no control over.

"Why do you keep coming on to me?" he asked over the engine noise.

"Well, somebody has a high opinion of himself," Barbie said loudly in his ear. "Can't a girl flirt a little?"

"It's just making me uncomfortable. That's all."

"Oh, sugar, why would it make you uncomfortable? I'm only out for a bit of fun. You can play along if you want. I won't bite much and only in the places you want me to."

"I have a girlfriend."

"Yes, I know already. Please. You don't have to tell me every time. She's not here."

"She will be soon," Hunter whispered.

"What was that?" She clawed his belly.

Hunter fought to keep from crashing his bike, with the lights from the Winnebago sending their crazy shadow wobbling ahead.

"I said she will be here soon. I mean, we will be there where she is... soon."

The conversation broke, and they rode in silence except for the engine whine and the whoosh of their speed. Hunter didn't think about the fate of his home and the people there anymore. He thought about Barbie's hands wrapped around him and her body pressing against his back.

She shouted, "Maybe we should stop for the night."

Exhausted, Hunter wanted nothing more than to pull over and rest. But he rolled on the acceleration and sped for home.

Barbie eased off his back and settled her hands lightly on his hips.

They traveled for an hour after leaving the burning bus, surrounded by darkness and the stars above, with another hour left before reaching Independents. The RV rode over the new super highway created by insects. It made the trip so much easier, but the churned up, scattered prairie grass also made it much more disturbing.

With help from the Winnebago lights, Hunter spotted large mounds lying in their path. He slowed to a stop before riding into their midst, holding his hand up to keep Henry from running them over. The big RV pulled up to their right.

"What is it?" Henry asked out the window.

"I'm not sure. We'll go check. Wait here." Hunter stretched to peek inside the window. "What's everybody doing?"

Wesley leaned over from the front passenger seat. "They're all asleep. Henry won't let me drive."

Hunter observed the red rims around Henry's eyes. "You look pretty beat."

"I'm all right."

"Are you sure? Why not let Wesley take the wheel a while so you can get some rest?"

Henry looked back inside then leaned out the window. "I don't think he can reach the pedals."

"I can too," Wesley cried.

Henry shushed him. He pointed back to the interior of the Winnebago.

"I can too reach the pedals," Wesley said, softer. "You just like being in charge."

Henry faced the windshield and blew out a giant sigh.

Hunter smiled. "Just give him a chance. He can't hit anything out here except for me."

Henry pointed toward the dark mounds ahead. "What about those?"

"Yeah, hold on a sec. We'll see what it is and be right back." Hunter released the clutch and throttled forward at a cautious pace. He was not taking any chances in the dark this close to home. Who knew what Tommy had left along the way to block their progress?

Riding up close, Hunter realized the mounds were gruesome, bloody corpses of cattle lying in heaps strewn across the now barren prairie. The grasshopper storm had caught the slow moving beasts unawares. Hunter knew the herd. Comprised of two hundred head, they roamed this part of the state and the survivors in Independents had taken what they needed in years past for their meat supply.

Last spring Hunter, Samuel and some of the newly elected ranchers rounded up a dozen cows and a bull to start their own stockyard. Bull wrangling took some ingenuity on Samuel's part, who dressed as a rodeo clown and ran flat out for the open cattle trailer.

Now the cattle left behind lay stripped of their hides and chunks of their meat. The sight renewed Hunter's fear for what awaited him at home. Frantic with nervous energy, he dropped the kickstand. "Can you get off?" he asked Barbie, as horror-filled spasms traveled along his arms.

She slid off the rear of the seat and Hunter quickly dismounted, walking tight circles around his bike as she worked her way out of the straps of his backpack.

He stopped, looked at the dead cattle, and then redirected the look at Barbie. "What is happening here?"

"I'd say our enemy is drastically decreasing the food supply." She folded her arms and rubbed her biceps against the chill in the air. "There's a reason he's called Famine."

Hunter wished sleep was possible, but wouldn't entertain the thought a moment more until he reached home and found Molly safe. His body was stiff from 24 hours of action and little rest. He rotated his arm, trying to relieve his aching shoulder.

"So this is his plan? Kill the cattle and what?"

"Look at the ground, Michael. Now imagine what those bugs will do to whatever crops you have back at your town. This is what Famine does, and he's doing it right at the end of the growing season. Nothing grows in the snow."

"How do we stop him?"

"That's what we have to figure out."

Hunter walked toward one of the cattle. By midday tomorrow the meat would be buzzing with flies and ruined underneath the blazing sun. Hunter searched the darkness, lit only by the Winnebago headlights, for signs of surviving cattle. Motionless mounds lay everywhere.

A dark shadow rose from behind one of the cattle, too small to be anything other than a calf, only calves didn't move like this shadow. Three other shadows rose from behind three different carcasses, and that's when Hunter noticed the shining red eyes. Whatever the menacing shapes were weaved towards them around the mutilated cattle.

"Barbie?"

"Find something to defend yourself with, quickly."

Hunter had no idea what kind of weapon he was going to find out here on the stripped Nebraskan plain. He scanned the barren ground and saw a couple sticks lying around in the dirt. "What are they?"

Barbie's hands crackled with lightning. "Hellhounds."

"Great! I don't suppose they like to play fetch."

29.

HUNTER

The dogs emitted a low growl from deep in their chests. Probably meant to put fear in a person. It did a super-efficient job, along with the teeth and red eyes.

Barbie looked scary enough with blue electrical sparks dripping from her tightening fists. Hunter turned away so he didn't blind his night vision in his one good eye. He dug out his pocketknife and wrapped his coat around his left arm for padding and protection. He never needed a gun out in the Big Bad, but the danger level had elevated in the past 24 hours. He'd have to bring up the subject at the next town council meeting—if he made it back home.

"Here they come," Barbie said.

Hunter turned back to see. There were more than just the original four he'd counted. The Winnebago was too far to make a run for it and play hit the hellhound.

"Get on the bike," Hunter said.

"They're all around us."

Hunter swung his head, careful not to look at the bright light around Barbie's hands. Twenty big, black dogs, forty pinpoints of red, converged on them from all sides. The math was too high to add up all the sharp teeth. Two dogs closed within ten feet and crouched low.

"Then what's the plan?"

"Stay alive," Barbie said, and shot an arch of lightning from her outstretched hands, cooking the nearest dog.

"Okay, do that nineteen more times and we're—"

The other dog darted straight for Hunter, who raised his protected arm and rolled with the impact. He swung his knife into the animal's flank and landed on top, stabbing until the beast lay motionless.

The next attacker came fast, charging in low with its teeth snapping and spit flying. Hunter dodged and feinted with the knife. The dog bolted into a gap and nipped Hunter's hand through the coat. He sunk his knife in the hellhound's neck, twisted and pulled out. The beast rolled over and bled.

His chest heaving with adrenaline, Hunter swerved and another two hellhounds were on him. He stabbed one while the other bit into his ankle, yanking to drag him down. Hunter grabbed a fistful of coarse fur on the one beast he was stabbing and brought his knife down over the hellhound's back. The other hellhound bit deep and Hunter screamed, agony firing through nerve and tendon. A lightning bolt fried the stupid thing.

He hobbled on his injured leg as his newfound healing process asserted itself. Barbie ran over to his side. "How many have we gotten so far?"

"It doesn't matter." She looked around.

"Are you giving up?"

"No, it doesn't matter because there's an infinite supply of these hellhounds."

"Infinite?"

"Michael, I need you. Now is the time. What are you waiting for?"

"You're kidding, right?"

"Michael, please!"

"Look, I told you. I have a girlfriend. Watch out!"

Barbie whirled around to the approach of gnashing teeth. She zapped the dog to the ground and wobbled from the effort. "I can't do this much longer. You know this, Michael."

Hunter couldn't respond. Three dogs took turns moving in and out of range, trying to break through his guard. He slashed back and forth, knowing sooner or later he'd be overwhelmed. One of the hellhounds stumbled and Hunter knifed it. The dog reared, ripping the weapon's handle out of Hunter's sweaty palm.

Everything slowed—Hunter was dead without the knife. The other two dogs attacked with a fury that scared him to his core. He found a feral place buried inside and fought back, roaring with rage. Punching and kicking, he attacked the hellhounds, never surrendering his flesh to more bites. The beasts peeled away and regrouped. More dogs were filling in the ranks.

Barbie yelled something about the Winnebago. Hunter sought out the RV in the darkness with his good eye. Hellhounds swarmed the vehicle. He imagined the terror of the kids from Cozad—like they needed more. Where were the good guys in all this? Did Heaven really believe they could overcome everything Hell was throwing at them with two little girls? Catherine and Barbie had some pretty amazing talents, but they had limits. Barbie's electricity flickered, like her generator was about to run out of gas.

As if she could read his thoughts, Barbie looked up, bent over from exhaustion. The sweat on her face glistened under the moonlight. Her eyes were twin pools of pleading desire. "Michael, you must help or we die!"

"I am helping! What the hell are you talking about?"

Barbie shook her head and addressed the sky. "Lord, show me what must I do?"

And then she smiled in what looked like grim determination. Hunter didn't like it. Barbie walked over and grabbed Hunter's head and kissed him hard on the lips. He struggled to break free of her clear insanity.

Hellhounds were circling them and she wanted to make out.

He pushed her off, but before he could scold her, his shoulder erupted with a fresh pain unlike anything he had ever experienced, including the time he was kicked in the mouth as he laid on the cement floor of the stinking chicken shack. This pain was a thousand times more horrible. It was a throbbing ache that built wave upon wave, spreading from his shoulder into his upper back.

Hunter fell to his knees, reaching back to find what was wrong. That's when he noticed that he was glowing. His whole body shined like the Christmas tree when the Brittanys went overboard with lights. The hellhounds retreated a safe distance, frightened of the brilliance for some reason.

Barbie stood nearby wearing a satisfied grin. She seemed eager and expectant and totally unconcerned about his suffering.

The bright light flooded over the dead cattle, all the way to the Winnebago, where the dogs scattered like cockroaches, scurrying for the darkness. They stalked the edges of the light, noticeable only by their glowing red eyes. The hellhounds howled from their position. The sound traveled around the open prairie with a promise that when the light faded the hunt would renew.

Unlike the healing light of Catherine, this light served absolutely no purpose, or at least it wasn't making the pain cease. Hunter screamed, hunched over with his forehead pressed to the ground, and his fingernails clawing the earth.

"What the fuck is happening to me?"

"Watch your language, Hunter!"

"Fuck you!" he yelled, and although it didn't ease the pain, telling Barbie off felt really good. The flesh on his back ripped open and he feared a hellhound had attacked.

Hunter pushed up to his knees. There was no dog, only the excruciating pain that escalated higher than he could mentally handle. He shouted and cursed in a rambling fit. Then Barbie fell on the ground before him and wrapped her arms around his waist.

Hunter struggled. "What did you do to me?"

"This was meant to happen since the day you died. You are being reborn."

Hunter wanted to throw her off. Instead, he gripped her tightly. She squeezed him back and buried her face in his chest. Then the pain tore him in half and he hit the ground face first. Barbie reached for his hand and kissed it, but Hunter no longer cared. He closed his eye and allowed unconsciousness to swallow him whole.

30.
SCOUT

All the bugs flew off into the setting sun at the creepy dude's arrival. He looked like a stick figure with his jeans stopping at his calves and his shirt hanging just above his belly button. If the guy started trouble, Scout would have to take him out.

"What's he doing?" Molly asked.

"He's just walking down the middle of the street." Scout turned back.

Molly rocked little James in her arms and Ginger slept on the floor beneath a bed sheet. Scout couldn't shake the image of Ginger's skin stripped from her body. He also couldn't explain how Molly was able to heal her. A lot of stuff was happening and Scout was slowly catching up. He looked back to the street again right as Billy came around the corner and slid to his butt in front of the creepy dude.

Scout stepped through the busted window frame. Billy might have been bad mouthing him all over town for who knew how long, but that didn't mean Scout was going to let something bad happen to the kid. This new guy oozed badness like an infected wound.

He moved into the street as Catherine and Mark ran up behind Billy. Scout was too far away to hear the exchange, but whatever was being said, Catherine appeared to have a lot on her mind. She helped Billy to his feet and Mark stood protectively with his aluminum bat ready to tee off on the creepy dude's skull.

Scout hurried, but was too late.

The tall kid moved so fast he shimmered, and he sliced open Mark's throat. A spray of blood pumped out everywhere. Mark fell to his knees and stared into the distance like something better was over that way.

Billy screamed, "You son of a bitch, I'll kill you!" He charged underneath the first swipe and wrapped his arms around the creepy dude's knees. Billy squeezed and lifted. The tall kid crashed over like a skinny tree and Billy scrambled on top, swinging his little fists with no regard for his own life.

Catherine stripped off her shirt and pressed it against Mark's throat. Mark slid backwards with Catherine guiding him down. The unused bat rolled over the cobbles.

Scout ran towards the bat. Two forms of light popped out of the shattered window of Brittany's In the falling dusk, the glow appeared to be giant lightning bugs that didn't blink. Scout's eyes adjusted.

Samuel and Dylan streaked past to help Billy in the scuffle. The creepy dude shoved Billy off and regained his feet before the lights arrived. Billy stumbled headfirst into Catherine, knocking her away from Mark.

Scout sped up.

Dylan came in low as Samuel flew into the startled dude's chest. They hit the ground in a big pile of light and dark. Punches were exchanged on both sides. Samuel concentrated on the creepy dude's face, while Dylan was kicked off and flew backwards. The guy rolled over on top of Samuel, raking down with his nails. Sparks flickered from the light, leaving Samuel protected.

Dylan jumped to his feet and shot into the tall kid like a laser beam, knocking him off Samuel, and they tumbled. When the motion stopped, everybody was separated.

Scout dropped beside Mark and reapplied pressure on his torn throat. Mark gripped Scout's wrist with panic reaching his eyes. His mouth gaped open like a fish out of water. Catherine lay unconscious as Billy groaned and pushed himself off of her.

Back on the street, the fight had resumed after a brief pause. Scout couldn't watch that now. He had to find help for Mark. Catherine wasn't able to help anyone at the moment.

"How is he?"

Scout looked up, startled to find Billy addressing him. "He's bleeding badly."

Billy looked back to the fight and then gently rolled Catherine over. "She's hit her head twice today. I hope she's okay."

"What happed the first time?" Scout asked, finding the change in Billy curious.

"Billy threw her into a wall," Billy said.

"Uh, you mean you... right?"

Billy frowned, brushed a stray strand away from Catherine's eyes, and nodded. "Yeah I guess I do mean me." He looked back at the fight briefly. "Where's Luis?"

Mark's grip had lessened. The shirt underneath Scout's hand was drenched. "He was in Brittany's when the bug cloud hit."

Billy jumped to his feet, eyes wide with fear. "He left Ginger alone!"

"He was getting them dinner. Molly's with Ginger and the baby now. They're all safe."

"Molly! She can heal Mark!" Billy took off running. He poked his head into the window at Brittany's. A second later Luis stepped out the door and followed Billy to the clinic.

"Wait!" Scout yelled. "We need Luis over here!"

Luis turned and started for Scout, but Billy grabbed the young doctor's arm and dragged him to the clinic. Scout didn't want to believe it.

"Catherine! Catherine, wake up! Mark needs you!"

Catherine lay silent on the cobbles. Scout saw the purple bruise on her forehead even in the growing darkness.

Mark coughed and kicked, his life sputtering out beneath Scout's useless hands. And then Mark's struggles ceased, his eyes open to the night sky. Scout couldn't look down, but refused to release the man that loved his sister.

Dylan had been knocked around pretty good by the tall kid. He lay on the ground dazed. The light covering him dimmed.

Samuel glowed like a bonfire, pressing the tall kid hard with shots to the body and face. Scout never realized Samuel was this good in a fight. Samuel the clown was wailing on the tall kid, hammering his head, knocking him sideways. Then he followed with an uppercut and the kid landed on his back. Samuel dropped, driving both knees into the creepy dude's ribs.

No one could keep struggling after that, but the creepy dude was made from some type of durable steel. He swiped Samuel in the side of the face, flipping him headfirst into the pavement. Samuel's light flickered and died.

Dylan lay quietly. The loss of light left Scout blind. He hoped the creepy dude wasn't making the rounds, finishing everybody off. Scout wanted to help his friends, but he still believed that pressing the bloody shirt over Mark's motionless throat was saving his life.

Scout heard dragging as someone moved away, one slow step at a time. The noise had receded when Scout's eyes adjusted. Samuel and Dylan still lay where they had fallen. Samuel rolled over and sat up, shaking his head.

"Are you okay?" Scout asked.

"Yeah, I'm fine. I can't believe that dude wouldn't go down."

"Where did you get the light from?"

"Molly. She's been holding out on us."

"What?"

"Never mind, we'll deal with that later." Samuel hobbled over to Dylan and checked his pulse. "Dylan's alive. Is that Mark?"

Scout's sorrow burst wide open. He wept as hard as the day his mother and father died. The pain tore through his body and soul. Nothing in this world would ever heal him. No magic or little girl wielding it.

Samuel dropped next to Mark and placed a hand on Scout's shoulder. "You can let go. You don't have to do that anymore. He's gone."

Scout refused for a moment before his resolve faded into the pain. He swayed in a circle and blubbered nonsensical things.

Samuel removed the shirt and exposed a horrible gash, darkened by a final spurt of blood. He tossed the soaking mess aside and removed his own shirt. Wrapping it around Mark's lifeless throat, Samuel tied off a half-hitch that resembled a bowtie.

For some screwed up reason, Scout laughed. More tears streamed to the forefront of his sanity. He crossed his arms and rocked, closing his eyes against further stimulation that would make him laugh or scream.

A hand gently touched his head. "What's wrong, brother?" Molly asked.

Instant clarity fired and he knew. He knew that everything would be all right. He had forgotten in his pain and struggle what he should never forget. The Lord works in mysterious ways, but He's always working, and Scout had forgotten to pray and ask for His help.

Scout looked up through tears at Molly's smiling face. She showed no concern over her twin brother's death. He blinked away the rest of his sorrow and pain. "What do we do?"

"We do His will, always." Molly knelt beside him.

She laid her hands on her brother. One on his forehead and the other over the knot. "Guys, I need your help. Please lend me your strength by laying your hands on Mark."

Scout and Samuel did as required and Molly bowed her head and prayed aloud. "Dear Heavenly Father, please return Mark's spirit to us. Amen."

A bright pink light flowed from her hands, encompassing Mark's body like a pulsing field of vibrant energy, crackling with new life. The light tingled up Scout and Samuel's arms. Mark bucked and his chest began to rise. The light pulsed and Scout knew underneath the bowtie the gash across Mark's throat was healing, and his soul was returning. Miracles happened every day, and Scout thanked the Lord for every one He blessed them with.

The light flowed from their arms and Mark's body into Molly. Darkness came again and then she released the light through her eyes with a solid burst. One by one, Scout, Samuel and Molly fell on the bloodstained cobbles beside Mark's breathing form.

31.

JIMMY

After Molly left, Jimmy went about the business of seeing to his family. Luis had their medical needs covered, so Jimmy righted the bed and swept all the broken glass and dead bugs away from Ginger and his son. James nestled in Ginger's arms, latched onto his favorite spot. Jimmy did his best to focus on the work.

With the windows broken, Jimmy worried the baby might catch cold, but the August night clung to the leftover afternoon heat. Luis restarted the generator. He found light bulbs in a cabinet to replace the busted ones. Luis stored trash bins in the back. Jimmy quickly filled the first and was halfway on the second when the baby started crying.

"Billy," Luis said.

Jimmy kept sweeping up the last bit of debris.

"Billy!"

Jimmy turned to find Luis staring at him. It took him a second to realize he was being called. He set the broom in the corner and hustled over.

"Can you hold the baby for a minute? I need to run some tests on Ginger."

Jimmy shrugged like it was no big deal. Inside, his emotions performed back flips. It was all he could do to keep himself from cart wheeling around the clinic. He reached out with shaky hands.

Luis mistook Jimmy's excitement. "You don't have to be nervous. Just make sure you support the baby's head. The muscles in his neck aren't strong enough."

Jimmy crooked his arms and received the handoff. There was life, warm sweet smelling life. Little James looked up at his father and cooed.

"Oh," Ginger said from her clean sheeted hospital bed. "I haven't heard him make that sound. He must really like you, Billy."

Fresh tears swam into Jimmy's eyes. His son *liked* him.

He wanted to tell Ginger who and what he was to her and little baby James. But he didn't know exactly who or what he was yet, or how long his current arrangement would remain. The last thing he wanted was to cause her more distress. He would have to straighten this out with Catherine first.

Jimmy knew he should go out and see what was happening and who needed help, but right at that moment everything that was important to him was in his arms, and as long as this moment could be extended, Jimmy wanted it to continue forever.

James rolled his head, closed his eyes, and farted.

Jimmy cradled his little angel and hummed a lullaby from memory.

Luis asked Ginger all kinds of questions concerning pain and discomfort, moving around her bed and checking her temperature, pulse and blood pressure.

"I feel perfectly fine."

"So I'm noticing. Everything checks normal."

"I am kind of hungry."

Luis pulled the blood pressure cuff off Ginger's arm. "I know. I'll go over in a bit and see if Brittany has some food for us. The inside of their building was worse than this one."

"Was anybody hurt?"

"No. Thankfully Scout showed up. Everybody was just standing around gawking. He made us move to the back of the place and use the tables as a protective barrier. That right there saved us when the glass broke and the bugs came pouring in."

"What's wrong?" Luis asked.

Jimmy glanced up from his inspection of James's face. Ginger's face was pinched in what looked like anguish.

"Are you in pain?" Luis placed his hand on her forehead.

She brushed his concern away. "No, I didn't have a table when the bugs broke in. Scout barely had time to save James. I didn't make it."

"But you look fine," Luis said.

"Yes, thanks to Molly."

"What?"

"Molly healed me just like Catherine. That, and the way she helped with James's delivery. She's not the same Molly."

"She's not mean again, is she?" Luis asked.

Jimmy smiled. No, Molly hadn't reverted back to being the self absorbed person she was a year ago. Thank goodness. Jimmy barely survived the old Molly.

The thought of surviving seemed very odd now. He lived inside another kid's body, but living was probably not the best description. Haunting spirit might be more accurate.

Jimmy felt a rumble underneath his son's bottom. James squirmed in obvious discomfort.

"I think James just pooped. Where are the diapers?"

Luis's unhinged expression crossed the gap between horror and shock. Ginger's smile lit the room brighter than sunshine.

"Would you like to change his diaper, Billy?" she asked.

"Yes, please."

Luis pointed to the changing table with a confused look. Ginger giggled.

Jimmy laid his son on the changing mat and unfastened the disposable diaper, noting how everything fit together so he could put the puzzle back correctly. "What do I use to clean his bottom?"

Luis fanned his nose. "Use the wipes in that plastic container next to the clean diapers and drop everything in that blue bin. Make sure the lid goes back on quickly."

Jimmy held his son still with one hand. James watched his father with large round eyes, earning the little guy a smile. Jimmy made quick work of the mess and dropped the soiled diaper in the blue bin, grateful that he didn't have trash duty tomorrow. Jimmy didn't know what Billy did around Independents. Maybe he was still in school. Another dose of Vanessa lecturing about compound fractions was worrisome. Maybe he could graduate early if he revealed his true identity to her. And maybe she'd think he was crazy and have Mark lock him up.

"You're really good at that," Ginger said, leaning on a metal walker. Even hunched over, his girlfriend was taller than him now. Jimmy still thought of Ginger as his girlfriend, even if she didn't know he was back. "I might need your help until I'm on my feet again."

"I would love that." Jimmy smiled. "You're on your feet now, you know?"

"I meant more on my feet. Luis wants me to get my circulation flowing. I don't really need this." She picked up the walker and shook it. "He feels better if he thinks I'm safe."

"You're recovering fast," Jimmy said, and finished putting James's clean diaper back together. He wrapped the baby in his blanket and cradled his son close to his chest once again. "Should you be messing around like that?"

Ginger smirked at him and he wondered if she'd been hanging around his little brother too much. "I believe I have Molly to thank for that. It seems her intervention took care of all my aches and pains."

"That's enough walking, Ginger," Luis said. "Get back in bed."

"Is that the doctor's orders?" she asked.

"What?"

Jimmy laughed as Ginger hobbled back like an old woman. James fell asleep in his arms. Each little breath puffed in and out. Jimmy would have held his son forever, but Ginger beckoned for her baby to be returned. Grudgingly, Jimmy complied.

Ginger brought James in close for a kiss then she laid back. "Can you raise the head of the bed for me, Billy? This lying down is driving me crazy."

"Sure," Jimmy said and turned the wheel, slowly raising Ginger into a sitting position. "I hated lying in this bed."

"Oh, what happened?"

Jimmy looked up and remembered that he was about to mention the time his ribs were kicked in by that monster, Patrick. That was before he died and became somebody else. He shoved his hands in his pockets and tried to come up with something good, but found himself against the blank wall of his imagination. "I got a splinter once."

Ginger nodded slowly. "I hope Luis didn't make you stay overnight for that."

Luis returned from tinkering around his desk. "I'm going to see if there's any food and check on the others. Will you stay with Ginger?"

"Not a problem. You better check on Mark and Catherine first. And be careful. There's some crazy kid wandering around out there. Hopefully Samuel took care of him. We're going to have to wait until morning to figure this mess out. I don't like the way those bugs went after the fields. I don't want to speculate, but it can't be good."

Luis stared at Jimmy funny.

"What?"

"You seem different."

"I'm noticing that too," Ginger said.

Jimmy didn't know how to reply. The kid they knew as Billy was different. So he just shrugged instead.

Luis left, moving into the still night air. Jimmy guessed it to be around nine o'clock but he didn't know for sure. The sun had lowered out of sight about an hour ago and everything turned quiet on Main Street. He grabbed a chair and scooted close to the bed next to Ginger and little James. He turned the chair around and sat, leaning his arms up on the back. It was an uncomfortable stretch because his new body didn't quite fit.

Ginger wouldn't stop staring.

"What?"

"You remind me of someone."

"Who's that?" Jimmy said, guessing at the answer and feeling nervous about it.

"James's father," Ginger said, and brought up her hand to wipe a stray tear from her beautiful eyes. "You barely met him before everything happened."

"He seemed like a great guy."

"He was the best person I've ever known. I loved him so much. I miss him every day. I'm just thankful he left me little James before he passed on. It's a blessing. I only hope I can raise him to be as good a man as his father."

Jimmy rested his hand on her arm. "You aren't alone in this, Ginger. I'll help."

"I will too."

Scout had entered through the door with Catherine leaning on him. She was wearing a khaki buttoned shirt with patches on the sleeves. The shirt hung past her knees. Her forehead had seen better colors in the past. The current purple blotch wasn't one of them.

"I mean if that's okay?" Scout said.

"Of course it is," Ginger said.

Jimmy hurried over to help with Catherine. He wrapped his arm around her waist and she did the same around his shoulder for support.

"You don't look so hurt," Jimmy said.

Catherine lolled her head sideways at him. "Shouldn't you be dead?"

Jimmy's eyes widened. He looked at Ginger and laughed

nervously. "You're such a kidder, Catherine. I think you hang around with Samuel too much."

"There's nothing wrong with that," Samuel said, carrying a sleeping Molly. "Where do you want me to put her, Luis?" He looked around the clinic for the missing doctor. "Never mind, I'll take her out to the couch. We need more beds in here so I can take a nap later." Samuel disappeared back through the door.

Jimmy helped Catherine into the chair next to the bed. The little girl smiled at the baby before resting her head on the edge of the mattress. Jimmy worried about her injury and all the stuff she'd been through today.

Scout moved to the other side. He was giving Jimmy a funny look. Jimmy wondered how many funny looks he was going to rack up before the day ended. Maybe he should've worn a mask to give everyone a reason to look at him so funny.

"What?"

"You really messed things up for me. I didn't kill Jimmy."

"Of course you didn't. That's dumb. Who was saying that?"

"You were, Billy," Scout said.

It was Jimmy's turn to hand out a funny look. "I was?"

"Raven left me because of all the trash talk you were spreading."

"She did?"

Scout's strange expression dropped. Jimmy didn't care for the new one, because it appeared like Scout wanted to pound him in the face.

"I'm sorry, Scout. I haven't been myself lately."

"What does that mean?" Scout's voice grew louder.

Catherine lifted her head off the mattress. "It means he was possessed by a demon. He's all right now and he's sorry. Can we keep the shouting down? My head hurts."

Scout stared at Billy for a long uncomfortable minute. "Is that true?"

"Yes," Jimmy said. "I don't remember anything. I apologize if that caused Raven to leave you. I never would have wanted that."

Ginger took Scout's hand. "I'm sorry she left."

Scout smiled down at her. "I don't think she was very happy here with me."

"Oh, I don't believe that." Ginger kissed the back of his hand. "Thank you for saving my baby, Scout."

Scout's smile grew across his face like a row of Nebraskan corn.

Jimmy shifted his feet. Jealousy crept up his unfamiliar spine and festered in his mind. This wasn't the homecoming he wanted. How could he be this close to his family yet so far away?

32.

HUNTER

Birds whistled from somewhere above. Hunter felt warm, and he rested with Molly lying in his arms. Nothing else mattered. Birdsong, sunshine and the girl he loved—he couldn't start the day off any better. He opened his eyes and looked up into the deep green boughs of a cottonwood tree. A robin hopped from branch to branch. Hunter had no idea where he was and, at the moment, he didn't care. The horrible nightmare he'd had about the dogs was a fuzzy memory. He closed his eyes and listened to the chirp of the robin.

Something tingled in his mind. Some weirdness he couldn't quite shake. He opened his eyes again—both of them.

He bolted straight up, shedding Molly, and touched his left eye. He waved and saw his hand clearly. How did he get his sight back?

He looked down at Molly, only it wasn't Molly.

Barbie lay on her elbows, arching her eyebrow at him. "Well?"

"Well what? What happed last night? Did we...?"

"Did we what?"

"You know?"

"I know what?"

Hunter walked over to the tree, rubbing his head. He noticed the large knobby bark first. Then he spun around and realized where he was. "This is Catherine's tree. Why did you bring me here?"

"I didn't bring you anywhere. It was the other way around."

"How did I bring you here? I can't remember a thing."

"What do you remember?"

Hunter stared off into the distance and noticed the huge swath of dirt that cut through the prairie and he recognized the path of destruction the grasshoppers had left. He tried to figure out where he last was in relationship to Catherine's tree. Yesterday had been the longest day of his life. This one was shaping up the same, except that he was better rested and could see out of both eyes again. All he needed now were some straight answers.

"What the hell happened last night? I remember the dogs then my back felt like it was ripping apart." Hunter reached and touched his naked shoulder blade. "Where's my shirt?"

"I don't know. Maybe you lost it somewhere in the fight."

He looked at the open prairie as if expecting a pack of black salivating dogs to come rushing out of the tall grass and launch for his throat. "I guess we won."

"Yes, we won," she said. "Then we came here."

This time, Hunter arched his eyebrow. "And then?"

Barbie stood and wiped her jeans free of dirt and grass. "You don't remember?"

"No," Hunter said. "I blacked out. How would I remember?" He pointed to his eye. "Did you do this?"

She folded her arms and looked away. Hunter knew his tone was a little rough, but really, she had no right to do whatever she did to him. He was unsure how to feel, but mostly he was upset for having lost control if he and Barbie had... He loved Molly. How could he hook up with the first girl who threw herself at him?

"There are things here you don't understand."

Hunter walked over, grabbed her hands, and held them firmly. "So tell me. I've got nowhere to be."

That wasn't true. If the bugs headed to Independents, Hunter couldn't hang around talking about the forgettable sex he may or may not have had with Barbie. Not to mention the whereabouts of the Winnebago full of Cozad kids.

Hunter lowered his head. "Maybe we should go see if the others are okay?"

Barbie shook his hands. "It's okay, you know? Not to understand everything. I don't get it all myself, but I know His will guides us."

"Who's will?"

She gripped his hands tighter. "When you figure that out,

everything else will be easier."

Hunter nodded. He had a good idea who "He" was, or at least who she meant. Hunter never gave God or religion much thought. He attended church service because his girlfriend made him wake up for it every Sunday morning. Scout was good at the whole preaching thing, but to be honest, Hunter would rather sleep in.

The return of his eyesight bothered him the most. He didn't deserve to see out of that eye. He lost it after Patrick had beaten him to death. Hunter received the miracle that should have saved his brother. The least Hunter could do was walk around blind in one eye for the rest of his life.

"Why did you heal my eye?"

"I didn't. You did, when you transformed."

He blinked both eyes. "Transformed? What, did I become a robot or a jet plane?"

Her eyes watered like she was about to spill a big bag of emotions. Instead she drew in a deep breath and released a long sigh. "You transformed into an angel."

Hunter stared at her as if marbles had tumbled out of her ears. "You're shitting me."

She pulled her hands away and reared back with the right, bringing it around quickly. Hunter blocked the punch with his left arm, thankful he could see them coming now. He grabbed hold of her hands again.

"I told you to quit using that bad language."

"Why? What do you care?"

"Because you're beautiful," Barbie said. Then she lowered her voice. "Talking like that makes you ugly and taints the gift inside you."

Hunter wanted to pursue this topic and give her a few more choice phrases, but then the sound of a motorbike broke across the prairie and his big KTM came rolling their way, followed by the Winnebago. Henry handled the big motorbike cautiously over the flatland. Wesley drove the Winnebago, steering back and forth over every bump he could find, wearing a bright smile that reflected the morning sun. Henry killed the engine. He regarded Hunter with his head down, searching through the length of his bangs like he was afraid to look Hunter directly in the eyes.

"You guys made it out all right?" Hunter asked.

When Henry's head came up his mouth dropped open, but he remained silent. He looked at Hunter and then at Barbie.

"He doesn't remember," she said.

"I don't remember what?"

"What we were just talking about."

"My cussing? I really don't understand the big deal."

Barbie shook her head. "Not that. The other thing."

Before Hunter could remember what the other topic was, Wesley shot out of the Winnebago. None of the other kids followed but they did crowd up to the front windshield, staring out at Hunter like he was a lion on safari.

"Let me see them!" Wesley shouted with excitement. "Where are they? Folded down behind your back?"

"What are you yelling about?" Hunter asked.

Wesley circled him. He came to the end of his search and frowned. "Where are your wings? I wanted to see them up close in the daylight. I couldn't believe when you flew over and killed all those dogs trying to get at us. That was awesome! Are you really an angel? How does that whole flying thing work? Is it scary up there? I heard about planes, but I never got to fly in one before the plague. Can you take me flying sometime?"

Hunter was still working through Wesley's ramble when the talking stopped and he realized it was his turn. How could he respond to that? "I have no idea what you're talking about. What wings? I can't fly."

"See, he doesn't remember," Barbie said with a hitch in her voice. She turned and faced the opposite direction.

"You had these giant, brown, feathery wings shooting out your back. How can you not remember?" Henry asked. "It's not like you were flying around dropping dogs in your sleep. I even heard you talking to Barbie, but you sounded different."

The dull ache pulsed in his shoulder, reminding him that it was still there. Henry and Wesley had clearly lost their minds. "Look guys, I don't know what you saw last night, but I'm no angel. Shit, I'm the farthest thing there is from an angel."

"Please, don't," Barbie said softly without looking back.

Hunter sighed and placed his hands on her shoulders, squeezing them to offer some type of comfort even though he had no idea why she was upset. Her mood swings were frighteningly similar to Molly's before Catherine healed her mind. Hunter didn't want any part of that craziness, but this was different. Barbie was upset about something Hunter couldn't remember.

"Look, the last thing I saw was a bunch of those dogs going after the RV. Then I had this incredible pain in my shoulder and back and I blacked out. Next thing I know, I woke up next to you under Catherine's tree with my shirt off. So you're telling me that I was flying around with wings, dropping dogs out of the sky. Am I the only one who thinks that sounds crazy?"

Henry walked back to Hunter's bike and unzipped his backpack. He brought out the shirt Hunter was wearing the night before and threw it at him. Hunter caught it in one hand.

"I didn't lose it after all." He flapped the shirt out, tucked his arms inside, and then he noticed the two holes evenly spaced in the back. "What happened to my shirt?"

"That's where your wings popped through. After you finished up with all the dogs, you asked me to help take it off because you said it was restricting your movement. Then you flew off with Barbie. We may be scared, hungry and tired, but we're not crazy. You grew wings and flew around up there in the sky. I'm sorry you don't believe us or remember. It was pretty cool."

Wesley stood in the morning sunshine with a mixture of excitement and depression fighting for the right to exist on his face. The keys to the Winnebago jingled in his hands.

The rest of the gang watched from behind the safety of the windshield. All eyes bored into Hunter like he was about to perform a neat trick. Sprouting wings and flying in the sky would certainly qualify.

Barbie was still turned away.

Hunter walked over to his bike. Wesley and Henry stepped back. Hunter sighed and opened his backpack. He dug out a dirty shirt that didn't have any holes in it and slipped it over his wingless back. The torn shirt he tossed on the ground. He returned for Barbie and grabbed her elbow, guiding her into motion.

"Hey, what are you doing?" she asked.

"You and I are going to have a little question and answer time." Over his shoulder, Hunter yelled back to Henry and Wesley. "We're going to be leaving in a couple minutes. I want you guys ready to go when we return."

"Who gets to drive the Winnebago?" Wesley called after, but Hunter decided they could figure out that one on their own.

He led Barbie away from the others, thinking that all the stupid secrecy stopped here. This was where he found out what's going on. First, he needed to know who was crazy in the group. For some reason, he thought it might be him.

He turned around the one person who should have had all the answers. At least the ones he needed. She was just like Catherine, and now he wanted straight talk, or something bad was going to happen.

"Tell me everything."

Barbie searched his eyes. She seemed to be looking for this birdman that everyone claimed roosted somewhere inside his skin. Her face masked something different though. She was sad, and Hunter felt that her sadness was somehow shared by him, only he didn't know what there was to be sad about. The Big Bad was just a sad place now.

Barbie released another slow sigh.

"When you died and Catherine brought you back, someone returned with you. He's needed to fight the war that's coming."

Hunter nodded. "So you're saying an angel came back and is living inside me."

"Not just any angel. He and I have a relationship."

"You have a relationship with an angel?"

"Not just any angel, Hunter. God's archangel, Michael."

That's total bullshit, Hunter thought.

"No, Hunter. It's the Will of God," the angel said. Hunter covered his mouth after he involuntarily spoke.

Barbie smiled at him.

33.

MARGARET

Margaret thought today would be a good one, considering things couldn't get any worse. She looked out her window at the new morning and the debris scattered along Main Street from the grasshopper attack. She rolled over onto her back, trying to remember how she made it to bed. Someone had carried her here after she healed Mark. She thought about how much explaining she'd have to do, and decided that maybe today wouldn't be so great after all.

After kicking the sheet off, she sat on the edge of her soft, wide bed. She felt guilty about sharing it with another person. She knew Molly truly loved Hunter, but Margaret's chastity had been very important. Now she would have to come to terms with having a lover. That word alone made her cringe.

Memories of times spent in the bed with Hunter brought other, unfamiliar sensations, mixing with the guilt like one big stew of confusion. If Hunter returned today then that would ruin all her chances at a good day. She'd rather face horsemen and hellhounds than have a discussion with him about the future of their relationship.

Margaret selected clean clothes out of her closet. She removed Samuel's shirt that looked just fine, except for the dirty splotch on the back that probably happened when she fainted in the middle of the street last night.

Margaret dressed and opened the door to her living room.

Samuel sat on the couch with his chin resting on his chest and a long strand of drool hanging from his lower lip. He should have been in the fields by now, but after yesterday's business, he probably needed the extra rest.

She took one step and his bleary eyes opened. His head popped up and the drool snapped in half, dropping onto his lap. He wiped the leftover off his chin and smiled.

"Sorry, I didn't mean to wake you. What are you doing here?"

"I was assigned to you."

Margaret raised her eyebrows.

He laughed. "When Mark woke up injury free, thanks to you, he wanted to run home and be with Vanessa and his kid, but he also wanted to stay with you. I told him I could handle it. So here I am, handling it."

"Did you sleep at all?"

"Sure. But I wake up early, and since all you have around here are these boring psychology books, I must have drifted off again. How are you doing?"

Margaret considered everything in a flash and shrugged. "I've been better. But that probably can be said for everyone in town."

"You got that right. We have some major problems, including that freak that almost killed Mark. I need to check out the damage to the crops. Billy said that the bugs left Main Street and went straight to the fields. We could be in a lot of trouble if he was right."

"Do you want to go now? I was on my way out to see Mark and Vanessa."

Samuel stood and stretched, his shirt lifted, exposing his flat stomach. Margaret quickly regarded the street outside, where kids now milled around cleaning up debris. Since Jimmy's death, the kids of Independents had grown more responsible in the upkeep of their town. His legacy inspired that.

"Well, do you mind looking at the fields with me real quick? I'm sort of your personal guard until I'm told otherwise. Plus, I want to be there when the sheriff questions you." Samuel's smile stretched across his face, wide and toothy.

Margaret's shoulders tightened with tension. A lot of people would be lining up for answers. It was one thing for Catherine to be so secretive, but these people had known Margaret, or rather Molly, for the better part of six years, and in her twin's case, all of her life.

"Why do you want to be there when I see Mark?"

Samuel's eyes twinkled like he knew a good joke and was trying to figure out if it was age appropriate for the audience. Normally he didn't stop to consider. "You turned Dylan and me into electric bug zappers and then you healed your brother's slit throat. I'd say you're quite the miracle worker and I'd like to know how that is and if I can borrow the textbook. What you did to me last night—it was incredible."

Margaret nodded. "Yes, it was." She looked out the window once more. Emma had taken up position in the middle of the street, directing the others with a lot of pointing and shouting.

"So do we have a deal? You're coming with me to the fields first?"

"Do I have a choice?"

"Sure, you can walk on your own freewill or be dragged. I'd offer you a piggyback ride but that might send the wrong message to everyone we pass."

Margaret laughed. "What, that you're a big dork? I'm pretty sure that message has been received loud and clear."

They left, walking down the stairs to ground level. Emma caught their attention and waved them over. Margaret followed Samuel.

"Great, we could use the extra hands," Emma said as they arrived. "I've got all this glass to clean up along with this sticky roof gravel and there are some ripped awnings that will need to be mended. I'm counting on you to pick up the slack there, Molly, since Ginger is still recovering. The Jenson sisters are already disassembling the old material. You'll probably need to make all new awnings. Maybe instead of stripes we can go with a bolder color that will really set off our Main Street area?"

"We're headed out to check the fields," Samuel told her. "Molly has to stick with me, but it looks like you have everything under control."

"Well of course I do, but my people are getting hungry and we haven't seen any of the Brittanys."

"They were still cleaning up the mess inside when I carried Molly home late last night. They're probably still sleeping. Go on in and set out some bread and fruit for everyone."

Emma's eyes bulged out. "Do you know what would happen if Chef Brittany found me messing around in her kitchen?"

"As a matter of fact, I do." Samuel leaned over and spoke quietly so no one else but Margaret could overhear. "My advice: don't get caught and make sure you have someone else around to blame if you do."

He left quickly. Margaret offered Emma a reassuring pat on the shoulder in passing.

When Margaret caught up, she prodded an elbow into Samuel's side. "You're kind of a troublemaker."

Samuel cocked an eyebrow with a self righteous smile. "I'm a full fledged troublemaker. We all have our hidden talents. You can heal people and I can cause great strife with a few well placed suggestions. I call it my master plan."

"I call it a bunch of grief."

The walk to the edge of town left them feeling less anxious about their destination. As they moved from Main Street, the debris of broken glass and roofing materials lessened and converted into green leaves and broken branches. The grasshoppers appeared to have ignored the houses completely.

The optimism vanished as soon as they crested the hill overlooking the fields. Total devastation was the word that sprung to Margaret's mind.

"We are so dead," Samuel said.

What lay before them looked like a giant lawnmower had ridden right over their food supply and torn it to shreds, scattering the chaff on the ground as far as their eyes could see. The orchard was stripped bare. Trees stood with their naked branches reaching towards the sky, robbed of their leaves and fruit.

"Should we get help and gather what we can?" Margaret asked.

Samuel stared out across the horizon of his hard labors these past many months. His face darkened with emotion. "I don't know. It doesn't look like anything is edible down there now."

He stumbled down the hill in a trance, as if his feet were dragging him somewhere he didn't want to visit. Margaret walked behind him with the same type of dread. She saw past the torn field into the future comprised of a long winter without enough food for everyone, a winter full of hardships and sacrifices. Fear crept over her for the inevitable season ahead, and the destruction of the crops was only the start. The monster that attacked her brother would be around all winter long, picking off the weak. This was Famine's doing, and he was just warming up.

She spent the next half-hour following Samuel as he assessed the situation without hope of finding anything salvageable. By the end of the fruitless tour, neither Samuel nor Margaret felt like doing anything other than lying down and giving up. Margaret knew she should be stronger. That she should be the one sharing

God's light, starting with Samuel, but overwhelming despair left her hollow and scared.

"We better go see your brother now," Samuel said. "He and Vanessa should be the first to know that we probably won't survive the winter."

Margaret shook her head, wanting to say something, but nothing came to mind. Samuel took off at a fast pace, walking up the hill to Independents. Margaret ran to catch him. "There's a reason this is happening, Samuel," she said at last, not knowing the reason, but wanting to encourage him. "He has a purpose for all of this."

Samuel stopped short, and Margaret bowled into his back, knocking him down in the dirt road. Samuel pushed up slowly to his knees. Margaret grabbed his arm and aided him to his feet.

"He who?" Samuel said, brushing off his knees. "And don't tell me Scout has you believing too. We're on our own. The only purpose out there is the one we make for ourselves."

"That's not true. What about the miracles you've witnessed? What about the light last night that gave you power to fight your enemies? Where do you think that came from?"

Samuel kicked at a divot in the road and looked up at Margaret. "I don't know. But what purpose could *He* possibly have in allowing our crops to be destroyed? How do we know *His* purpose is the one controlling everything? Maybe something more powerful is calling the shots and *He's* along for the ride like us."

"That's just not possible. There is no one more powerful than God. That's not to say others can't affect the world in which we live."

"If God is so powerful, then why doesn't He just put a stop to this and give us back our lives?"

Molly reached out and took Samuel's hands. "I think He is. That's why Catherine and I are here. He is making a stand and He's doing it in Independents. That's why that creature and his insects came. Everything that will decide the fate of the world is going to happen right here."

Samuel's hands hung loose in hers. He stared into her eyes as if searching for the truth hidden behind them. "Who are you, Molly?"

She squeezed his hands and reached a decision. She would no longer hide the truth from him or the other older kids in town. This was too much for them not to know and understand. They had the right to know.

"My true name is Margaret. I am a holy saint. I have been placed here to fight this evil by your side. We will prevail through this, Samuel, with God's guidance and grace."

34.

SCOUT

Scout woke to bright sunshine streaming through his bedroom window. He tied on his shoes and stepped out with the hope that Brittany's was still serving breakfast. His hunger was second only to his concern that last night's events would carry over into today. He stutter-stepped onto Main Street, expecting to find a mess, but instead the whole place had been miraculously cleaned up. How he slept through the entire street sweeping project mystified him.

The crowd noise from Brittany's flowed outside like a wave of jabbering, excited voices. Scout entered through the doorway instead of jumping through the empty window frame. When the door closed behind him, silence swept over the room in a sea of shushes. Like the beginning of a spring shower, clapping slowly grew to a crushing, tumultuous applause. Everyone rose to their feet and faced Scout. Cheers rained down on him, and the look of joy on everyone's face nearly made Scout weep from the unexpected pleasure of appreciation.

Even more unexpected, Dylan approached him first and shook his hand with a genuine smile and a firm grip, convincing Scout that this was no elaborate hoax. This was real.

"What's going on, Dylan?"

"Word has gotten around, Preach... Sorry, I mean, Scout. You're a hero. That's all everybody's been talking about. How you came in here and told everyone what to do with the tables. The tables, man. If they hadn't set them up like you told them, we'd have lost half the town when the windows blew and the bugs poured inside."

Kids formed a tight circle around Scout, holding out their hands and shaking his, patting him on the back and gripping his arm. The girls gave him hugs and the boys smiled broadly like they were happy to count Scout among them. This was the best moment of his entire life.

After the fiftieth "You're welcome," Scout cut through the remainder of the crowd in search for food. Dylan followed.

"Man, then you fought through that swarm of bugs and saved Ginger and her baby. I'm sorry I doubted you."

Scout finally gave into blushing embarrassment. He waved Dylan off. "I was just here when it happened. You'd have done the same thing. At least you and Samuel were able to fight off that creep."

Dylan leaned against the buffet where Scout was picking out bread and fruit for his breakfast. "Yeah, but we had help. I don't know what's happened to Molly, but she's different. She healed my broken nose last night before the bugs hit town."

Scout was considering the limited options of the buffet and wondered what was up with the Brittanys this morning. They were up late last night cleaning when he'd left Luis's for home. Then he remembered why Dylan needed his nose fixed.

"I'm sorry about the cheap shot. I hope your nose doesn't hurt too much."

"Man, it hurt like a fucker... Sorry, Scout. I don't mean to cuss in front of you."

Scout laughed. "Didn't you hear what I called Billy yesterday? Don't worry about it."

"Well, we both had it coming. I'm sorry I listened to him." Dylan paused, rubbing his arm and looking at the floor. "I'm sorry about Raven."

Scout lowered his head. The apple shook in his hand. He'd been trying to think about something other than her, but the reminder stabbed him in the chest. How could the earlier elation fall away so quickly?

He let the topic drop. Raven left because of Dylan and Billy, plain and simple. There was no reason why he should forgive them, now or ever— but especially not now. Scout needed time to heal and move on.

Dylan nodded like he understood Scout's unspoken feelings on the matter. "Have you seen the fields yet?"

Scout carried his plate to his usual table, now void of his normal dining companions. Luis and Ginger were in the clinic. Mark and Vanessa weren't around either. That left Samuel, Molly and Catherine among the missing. Of course Hunter had yet to return from his ride in the Big Bad, but that was no surprise. Scout sat and Dylan claimed a chair beside him.

"I just got up. What's going on with the fields?"

Dylan scooted his chair closer. "It's bad. The bugs ripped the crops to shreds. I've been waiting on Samuel to find out what he plans on doing." Dylan leaned in and lowered his voice. "I don't know how we're going to make it through the winter."

Scout sat back in his chair. The apple and the slice of bread he'd taken for breakfast sat before him. All he wanted to do was eat. If the fields were as bad as Dylan was letting on, this might be the biggest meal he would enjoy for quite a while. During that first winter after the adults had died from the plague, Scout had gone several days with less food than what he was about to eat.

"I'm sure we'll come up with something." It sounded lame even to him. If the fields were as decimated as Dylan said, then they needed to start making immediate plans for the winter. "Let's go look at the fields. I bet Samuel is already out there. Then we'll go to Mark and Vanessa and start figuring out how we're going to make it. We'll need Brittany there too."

He stood, pocketed the apple, and took small bites of the bread. All eyes turned his way and the noise of the cafeteria wavered. The kids applauded Scout on his way outside. He nodded appreciation, but hoped he wouldn't have to see these same kids starving in the next week or two. He met as many eyes as he could then exited the cafeteria with Dylan in his wake.

The August heat warmed his skin as he finished the bread, feeling better with something in his stomach. By the time they reached the end of Main Street, he heard a familiar sound. Scout wanted it to be Raven riding her motorbike back to him. Maybe she realized the Big Bad wasn't all that great compared to life in Independents.

The bike rounded the corner and Hunter throttled his big KTM up the remaining stretch of road to where Scout and Dylan waited. A dark-haired girl hung on to his waist and Scout shook his head. Here he was hoping Raven was coming back to him, while Hunter rode up with a new hot chick. Like that guy needed more air to inflate his ballooning ego.

Hunter killed the engine and smirked at Scout. "Miss me?"

"Like the plague."

"Wow, you're in a great mood."

"It was a rough night. Who's your girlfriend?"

"She's not my girlfriend," Hunter said a little too quickly. The girl behind him jabbed him in the shoulder and he winced. "At least she's not right now."

"What does that mean?"

"It's complicated. This is Barbie. Barbie, meet Scout and Dylan."

"Hello, boys," Barbie said, dismounting from Hunter's bike. She shook the tangles out of her thick brown hair. "The rest of the gang will be here soon. Do you have some food for them to eat? They're starving."

Scout and Dylan looked at one another.

Dylan spoke first. "The rest of what gang will be here soon?"

"I sort of rescued a bunch of kids from Cozad," Hunter said. "It's a long story, but they had no food and nowhere else to go."

Hunter looked around the street as if he expected to see something that wasn't there. "Um, did you guys have a storm last night?"

Scout narrowed his eyes at his friend. "No. We had a mass of grasshoppers fall from the sky right here on Main Street before they headed out to plunder the crops. We were just going out there to take a look."

"Yeah, we met up with those bugs before you guys. I was afraid they were heading this way. Did anything else happen?"

"Was he tall and creepy?" Scout said.

Hunter dropped his head and was quiet for a moment. A large motorhome pulled up to the corner and stopped before the driver saw them and then drove the rest of the way. The brakes squealed as the big white contraption halted and the engine cut off.

Scout turned around at the sound of murmuring. The kids of Independents had stepped out of Brittany's for a look at the new arrivals.

"We need to gather everyone together, now," Hunter said. "We're in a lot of danger."

Scout looked into the front windshield of the motorhome and saw a bunch of skinny kids staring back. Scout acknowledged Barbie. "You don't appear to be with them."

She placed her hands on her hips and tilted her head. "Why do you say that?"

"You don't look as hungry as the ones in the motorhome."

"She's got her own special talents," Hunter said. "Kind of like our little friend Catherine."

"Then she isn't the only one. Molly has developed some of those same talents."

Barbie bounced with excitement. "Margaret's here too?"

Scout shook his head. "I don't know a Margaret, but his girlfriend, Molly, was very busy yesterday."

"Oh, no," Barbie said.

Hunter looked from Scout to Barbie several times before settling on her. "What?"

Barbie squeezed her forehead like a ball-peen migraine pounded her temple. "Please tell me your girlfriend's name isn't Molly."

"Why does it matter what her name is?" Scout asked first.

Hunter nodded. "What he said."

The crowd from Brittany's grew bolder and scuttled closer for a chance to hear the conversation. As a group, they were amazingly quiet, except for Emma.

"I don't think she's that pretty," Emma said to someone in the crowd.

Barbie shot her a look that could have melted the pavement underneath the young girl. Emma, however, returned the look as coolly as a glacier.

Barbie smiled and the three boys took a step away from her. She ignored their retreat and returned her attention to Hunter. "Molly is short for Margaret. Margaret, Catherine and I are sometimes referred to as the Three Holy Maids, or the Three Virgin Martyrs."

Scout, Hunter and Dylan looked at each other.

Barbie threw up her hands. "Aren't there any Catholics left in the world?"

"I think these kids have enough going on without getting a history lesson from the Church," Catherine said from behind Barbie.

Barbie swiveled on her feet so fast that she nearly fell over. "Hello, Catherine."

"Hello, Barbara. It's about time you showed up."

"I've been locked away in a tower," Barbie said. "I thought you would have been kind enough to come to my rescue."

"I did." Catherine walked over and hugged Hunter. "I sent him to do it."

Hunter returned Catherine's hug. She looked up at him. "You

got your sight back."

Scout slapped his forehead. "I knew there was something different about you."

Hunter smirked at him. "You have no idea."

35.

JIMMY

Jimmy pushed back his hat and wiped the sweat from his brow. It felt fantastic to be alive and digging. The shovel was huge in Billy's hands, but that only took some adjustment and a bit of settling down to business. Jimmy hadn't been tall when he first started farming so many years ago. He didn't know where he stood as far as being alive again because he still needed Catherine to explain everything. For all he knew, he could drop dead any moment and float away. What happened to Billy? His spirit or soul or whatever had gone somewhere.

Jimmy was close to completing his task. He wasn't about to let anyone other than Mark see what Billy had done to his housemate. He had left the bedroom shaken earlier when he went to see why Mark had been so upset. If Jimmy had a baseball bat, he would have bashed his own head in just to keep out the image of Preston torn asunder in his bed.

Jimmy's stomach heaved again. Luckily he skipped breakfast. He probably wouldn't eat for days, but from his earlier viewing of the fields, not eating might be his only choice.

He pondered the situation, glad to think about something else—something he understood. Farming had come naturally in his first life. It only took a cursory view of the devastation for Jimmy to know that nothing had survived the cloud of bugs that descended on the fields. They even tore through the greenhouse, where the more delicate vegetables and winter crops grew. So in the middle of August, what could they do that would provide food for the upcoming winter? Jimmy would have to check Chef Brittany's canned stores, kept in a separate building on Main Street, and hope they'd had a good growing season. They would supplement their diets with protein if there were any livestock left. Jimmy would have to investigate more about the sheep, goats and cattle. Their main source of protein had always been chickens and hogs, but those were gone thanks to the hellhounds.

They needed to repair the greenhouse. Expanding it was something they should have done already—nothing like being forced into action. If Samuel had the seeds, then winter wheat and barley needed planting now.

Jimmy brushed his arm across his face and left a trail of sweat and grime. He wiped it off with the front of his shirt. He removed the hat he found in Billy's house and scratched his head. He fought a fleeting memory about the plague. Feeling stupid, he smiled because Billy was probably around ten years old. Jimmy had plenty of time before he needed to start worrying about the plague again.

He regarded the red Nebraska Cornhusker hat with a black and bold N. Jimmy liked it. Until he had a cap on his head, he never felt fully dressed. He rounded the bill, trying to suit his preference. Good enough. Pulling the hat back on, he tossed the shovel out of the grave. If he had a nickel for every grave he'd dug in his various lifetimes, he'd have a lot of useless nickels because there was nowhere to spend them.

Jimmy climbed out and walked toward the house. The morning sunshine warmed his skin until he stepped into the cool shade of the front porch. He waited a moment, trying to gear himself up for what lay ahead. The longer he waited, the worse Preston's remains were likely to get. The sight and smell was bad enough already. Jimmy tied one of Billy's clean shirts around his head, covering his nose and mouth. Luckily a plastic shower curtain still hung in the bathroom where water no longer ran. Jimmy ripped it down and trudged toward Preston's waiting corpse.

He took several deep breaths then pushed his way inside the dim room, heading straight to the window. He threw it wide open. At the side of Preston's bed, Jimmy laid out the shower curtain on the floor. Being careful not to look at the remains, he unhooked the corners of the fitted sheet then pulled everything over the side onto the shower curtain. The body hit the floor with an ugly flop.

Jimmy wrapped Preston up, tied the loose ends, and dragged the package, slowing only on the drop from the porch. Then he moved quickly out into the sunshine again. He slid Preston next to the open grave and dropped to his knees, rolling the corpse with some respect and dignity until it fell into its final resting spot.

He wasted no time burying the body. Refilled in three minutes, Jimmy smoothed the mound with the back of the shovel, giving it a couple pats to seal it down for eternity.

That's when he heard the heavy breathing behind him. He turned and found the youngest Brittany panting like a thirsty dog. The lines in her face made her look sleepy; her dull gray eyes stared at the mound of dirt. She held her fingers splayed out at her sides.

"Brittany? Are you all right?"

Her eyes snapped up and she hissed through her teeth. Jimmy instinctively held the shovel between them for protection. This was not the sweet little hostess he remembered from the last time he was alive.

"Did you find the sweets?"

The tall, dark-haired kid from the night before rounded the corner of the house, followed by the other three Brittanys. All the Brittanys behaved like the youngest, with the panting, fingers splayed and the same dull gray eyes. Their unnatural manner was equaled by the boy leading them around Independents.

"What did you do to them?" Jimmy asked, even while he considered running for his life. "Who are you?"

The tall boy chewed on a fingernail then spat the fresh clipping to the ground. He licked the front edge of his pointy teeth. "I am Famine and I hunger. As for your friends, they are now my servants, as was the one you now possess."

"You mean, Billy?"

The kid shrugged. "That was his name, wasn't it? I knew him from before." He spread his arms wide to indicate himself. "So now I have a question for you. How were you able to come back from the dead? I thought Plague killed you. He told me so."

The youngest Brittany sniffed at the edge of the grave like she was locating a bone in the backyard. With the other Brittanys watching, Jimmy dropped the shovel blade in front of her.

"Move away. Now."

She hissed, but crawled back on all fours just the same. She stopped at the tall kid's side. He patted her head.

"Doesn't seem right you coming back from the dead and poor

Billy out a body. Although after all he witnessed succumbing to the demon's possession, I'm sure he wouldn't be the same. Some people don't stomach what I do very well. Oh, excuse me. What we do." Famine patted Brittany's head again.

"You're the one responsible for what happened to Preston," Jimmy said.

Famine grinned like he was burning with pride. "I don't know Preston. I can only imagine the horrors he faced if he knew Billy. Demon possession is such a wonderful transformation, just like my enchantments. Take my new pets, for example. They hunger but have yet to dine on human flesh. They recognize the smell of an easy catch. That's what brought us to the foot of your new grave. I think they would love to satisfy their hunger on something other than spoiled meat. Something fresh would be a proper first meal."

Like they knew their turn had arrived, the girls snarled at Jimmy. He held the shovel, but it was one little boy against four stark raving mad Brittanys and Famine—who was the craziest of them all.

"Did Chase send you here?"

"Chase? No, Chase is like me. He's a general."

"What are you fighting for?"

"For the world, my tiny morsel. We're fighting for the whole wide world."

Jimmy didn't like the idea, but he had no choice. He was going to have to hit the first Brittany to rush him and the rest of them too, but he had little hope of escaping alive. The youngest Brittany broke first, succumbing to whatever desire drove her forward. Jimmy swung the shovel, connecting the backside with her shoulder. The impact shivered up his arms, forcing him to hang on. Chef Brittany charged, leaping over the stunned, smaller Brittany. Jimmy jabbed the shovel in the air and she peeled off as the last two Brittany's followed right behind her. He knocked one off course, but the next oldest came in clean and tackled him off his feet. The landing jarred his body. His air whooshed out and he gripped Brittany's head as she snapped and growled at him. Jimmy pulled his feet in and kicked up with all his might. Brittany flew off and landed in the soft turned dirt of the grave.

Jimmy rolled to his feet and ran. Main Street was a good four blocks away, with the pursuing Brittanys panting behind him. He sprinted onto the street, leaping across potholes as they came. One Brittany stretched out to grab him just as a pothole arrived. Jimmy cleared the obstacle, but the Brittany stepped right in and tumbled over the broken pavement.

Jimmy's new body was faster than he thought, but he was running for his life. Feet slapped concrete as another Brittany caught up and he cut to the right. Chef Brittany sped past and Jimmy crossed back to the left, sending her into a conflicting spiral. Her feet tangled and she hit the ground face first with a solid smack.

Jimmy pushed his legs faster when he saw the buildings of Main Street two blocks away. No one else appeared to be around, and he hesitated to call for help for the possibility of getting more kids killed. Knowing his luck, one of the younger kids would answer the call and then he'd be responsible.

He heard a growl and another Brittany took a shortcut through a yard that Jimmy should have thought of himself, except for the chain-link fence that would have slowed him down. Brittany hurdled over the fence like an Olympian. She lowered her shoulder and drove into him. Scraping across the gravel, Jimmy screamed in pain, but fought his crazed attacker from chewing him to bits. He pawed at her with his hands and one strayed too close to her mouth. She bit down hard and tried to rip a chunk of his hand away. Jimmy bucked like a bronco but she held on with her mouth. He drove a thumb into her eye and her jaw loosened enough to pull his hand free. He kicked, clawed and squirmed until he broke loose, but before he could run again she grabbed his ankle and hauled him back.

Despite their various injuries, two more Brittanys hobbled towards them. Famine hadn't appeared, but he would be along to supervise the kill soon enough. Jimmy struggled to kick free.

"Brittany, please! It's me, Jimmy! Lord, help me!"

Brittany stopped for a moment and tilted her head. Her eyes focused and the grayness cleared. "Jimmy? You're not Jimmy. Jimmy's dead."

"You're right. I'm Billy. You know me, right?"

She shook her head as if a fog threatened to cover the situation with layers of doubt. "Yeah, I know you. Why does my head hurt?"

"That doesn't matter. We have to get away."

"Get away from what?"

Jimmy knelt down and turned her head. "The other Brittanys."

Brittany scrambled to her feet. Jimmy tugged her along by the hand. The other Brittanys stumbled after them, and Jimmy was happy that the hits with the shovel and potholes had slowed them down. They rounded the corner to Main Street and ran to a Winnebago. Jimmy barely gave it a look before he dragged Brittany past. He ran toward a small crowd gathered in the middle of the street.

His heart thumped as his little brother's eyes turned on him and went wide.

"Jimmy?" Hunter said.

"Jimmy?" Scout repeated.

Catherine refocused everyone on the immediate problem. "What's wrong?"

"No time," Jimmy said. "The other Brittanys... something's wrong... right behind us."

A horrible scream came from the Winnebago. The Brittanys tore open the side door and rushed inside. The RV rocked like a party had started, and not the good kind.

Hunter swept past Jimmy, heading for the trouble. Jimmy handed Brittany over to Catherine and followed his brother.

36.

HUNTER

Hunter wanted to believe his brother lived, but that wasn't possible. What was possible? A Winnebago full of scared kids under attack by a trio of raving Brittanys turned into cannibals. That's hard enough to swallow without adding his brother's return from the dead. What's more, how did he know Jimmy was alive inside Billy?

Hunter heard the screams and the unexpected defiance. The Brittanys had bit off more than they could chew. Four kids had Chef Brittany pressed into the front windshield; her wild eyes stared at Hunter like he was there to save her. He skidded to a stop. Billy, or rather Jimmy, bumped into him from behind. Hunter looked down at his brother and smiled.

"This isn't the time, Hunter," Billy said, or Jimmy—whoever.

"You don't realize the craziness I went through yesterday. And now this morning's starting out the same way."

"Try being dead for five months, then we can talk about your crazy day."

Scout ran up with Dylan, followed by Catherine and Barbie. Nobody looked ready to go inside the RV. Given enough time, they wouldn't have to worry about it because the Cozad kids were doing pretty well on their own.

"So what's the story?" Hunter asked.

Jimmy pointed to the window where Chef Brittany was squished above the dash. "The guy from last night who calls himself Famine showed up again with the Brittanys this time. He's hypnotized them or something."

"Barbie and I went through this in Cozad. It sounds like they're possessed."

"Billy—I mean—I was possessed. I don't think this is the same thing."

Catherine threw her arm around Jimmy's shoulders. "You're right. It's not the same. Possession takes more effort and there are minor demons involved. The Brittanys are under an enchantment. Leave everything to me and Barbie. As long as they haven't eaten, we should be able to free them all."

"Eaten?" Scout asked. "Eaten what?"

Barbie shook her head. "It's better not to think about it. Just don't get near their mouths and you'll be okay."

A loud crash drew their attention and all eyes watched a Brittany fly through a side window. She hit the ground hard, gulping for air like a perch out of the pond. No one should have to work that hard to eat.

"Scout, go hold Brittany down so Catherine can straighten her out," Hunter said. "The rest of you follow me. I'll help Chef Brittany out of the windshield before they kill her. Billy, you and Dylan get the other Brittany out of the back. Hopefully she's still in one piece." Hunter thought about calling him Jimmy again but decided against it. Maybe his brother wasn't ready to announce his arrival to the whole town, and maybe everyone else wasn't ready to accept it.

"Is it safe for us to go in there?" Dylan asked.

"I'll tell the Cozad kids that you guys are okay. They might listen to me."

"You sure have grown up a lot," Jimmy said.

Hunter smiled at his brother, happy to have him back in whatever form. "I wish I could say the same."

Hunter threw the door open and was met by a Brittany jumping out for her life. Two of the Cozad kids held her by the hair while a third was busy throwing kidney punches. The crazed cannibal look had been replaced by fear. Hunter grabbed Brittany's outstretched hands and yanked her to safety. She popped loose and clawed at him before he tossed her to the ground. Jimmy and Dylan took over, while Barbie crackled electricity from her fingertips.

"Okay, everyone!" Hunter shouted in the doorway. Those closest backed away like he was about to sprout wings and kick ass. "If you're not holding the girl against the windshield, I need you to exit the RV. It's safe. We have all the cannibals accounted for. When everyone is off, except for those of you holding the last one, Catherine or Barbie will come in and fix her, unless you need me to take over and hold her now."

"We have her," Henry said. He was busy pressing Chef Brittany's face into the defrost vent. "She picked the wrong day to mess with us."

"Just don't hurt her too much," Hunter said. "She's a friend and we can probably still save her."

Wesley smiled from his position at Brittany's feet. "She's all right. We're just keeping her warm for you." Carissa and Sophie shoved the middle of Brittany into the window.

Hunter stepped out of the way and the kids evacuated the bus. Many of them sneered at the Brittanys receiving treatments on the ground. Those girls would be serving them food after all of this was over, but those awkward circumstances could be worked out later.

"How are we doing with these two?" Hunter asked.

"I'm all finished," Catherine said, brushing her hands together.

"Me too," Barbie said. "It's a lot easier when they've just been turned."

"Let's take care of the one that's left then we'll go hunt down Tommy the Perv."

"You mean the guy from Denver?" Jimmy asked.

Hunter frowned. Of course Jimmy would remember that guy. He heard the story of how Tommy had groped Ginger at the diner. She had been so upset, and it pissed Jimmy off because he didn't get a chance to pound on the dude. Hunter understood, but Jimmy wasn't exactly all grown up in an eighteen year old body anymore, and Tommy had undergone one seriously extreme makeover.

"Let's finish up here and then we'll deal with Tommy," Hunter said, but Jimmy didn't look like he wanted to wait. "You hear me, right, Billy?"

Jimmy looked up at his brother, anger brimming in his eyes. "Yeah, I hear you, but I want a piece."

Hunter nodded. "Which one of you wants to fix the last one?"

"You better let me," Catherine said. "Barbara looks tired."

Tired or not, Barbie shot Catherine a nasty look. "It's Barbie, and I can do what needs to be done. Maybe it's time for you to have your morning nap."

Catherine placed her hands on her hips. "Barbie, huh. I have a whole collection of Barbies at home. All of them are prettier than you, even the one missing her head."

"I'm locked in a tower for over a year and you're playing with dolls. Nice."

They stared at one another across the short distance.

"Hunter, my arms are getting tired," Henry called.

"Girls?" Hunter said. "One of you needs to come now."

They broke eye contact at the same time. Catherine had the advantage of being closer, but Barbie was speedy and leaped over the fallen Brittany. They arrived together, but Catherine threw her shoulder into Barbie's hip. Barbie spun out of the way with her head pinging off the side of the Winnebago. Catherine hopped inside, glowing with pride.

"What?" she said at Hunter's look of disapproval.

"Let's just get this over with." Hunter met a very perturbed Barbie at the door. He took her arms and led her back to the street before a real fight broke out.

"She can't do that to me!" Barbie cried.

"How long have you known her?" Hunter asked.

Barbie looked up at him. "Centuries. Why? Just because she looks like a little girl doesn't mean she is one." Barbie yelled past Hunter's ear. "She's older than all of us."

"I'm trying to concentrate in here!" Catherine yelled back.

"I really don't like her," Barbie said.

Hunter smiled. "She's been a pain in my butt since I met her."

"Still concentrating."

Scout and the others were helping the newly awakened Brittanys from their shared fog of possession or whatever Tommy the Perv did to make them crazy. The youngest Brittany had a huge gash on her forehead from her flight out the RV window. Jimmy had already removed his shirt and pressed it against the wound. The other Brittany sitting on the ground kept apologizing.

"You didn't do anything wrong," Scout said. "It's not your fault."

"He waited in our house. He came into my room with the others and he put his hands on me. They didn't even try to stop him."

The haunted look in her eyes filled Hunter with regret. He had to stop Tommy now, before more people got hurt. Like Cozad, Independents wasn't prepared for anything as monstrous as Tommy. His presence would terrify the community.

"We have to secure the town and get everyone accounted for,"

Jimmy said. Hunter regarded him. "Now," his brother added.

Hunter nodded and waved off the funny look Scout gave him. "Billy's right. Dylan, get the older guys together and have them do a sweep through town. And find someone to ring the town bell for an emergency so we can get everyone here."

Dylan passed the Cozad kids, who milled about in confusion. Then he ran up to the Independents kids, who were doing a pretty close impersonation of the Cozad kids. He stopped long enough to instruct the older boys about what Hunter wanted and the smaller group split off to perform the sweep. The town bell started ringing and both the Cozad and Independents kids wore startled expressions.

"Scout and Billy, help the Brittanys over to Luis's. He can take care of Brittany's head."

"Couldn't she do it?" Jimmy said, with a look to Barbie.

"She could, but I need her and Catherine fresh when we find Tommy."

"I'm coming with you."

Hunter sighed. "This isn't going to be a fist fight. You've seen him. He's not natural. He's not the same Tommy the Perv from Denver." Jimmy's new face twisted in a familiar frustrated expression, but Hunter continued, "Plus, I've been through some changes after my trip in and out of death."

"What are you talking about?" Scout asked. "And why does Billy here want to go after this Tommy so bad? Who is Tommy?"

"Tommy is the one causing all this mess. I think he's another Chase."

"What was Chase?" Scout asked.

"Seriously, Scout?" Hunter said. "We've been in the middle of this for a year now. Haven't you figured it out?"

"Figured what out?"

Barbie gave Hunter a small shove. "Give him a break. You didn't know anything until I told you this morning."

"What did you tell him?" Catherine asked.

She stood in the open doorway of the RV, looking exhausted. Henry held up Chef Brittany, who looked even worse. They all stepped out in a bunch.

"Maybe we should talk in private," Barbie said.

Catherine looked around at the gathered group. "No, we can talk here. Scout needs to know, as well as some of the others."

Hunter knew she spoke of Jimmy.

Barbie released her hold on Hunter. Scout grinned at him like he knew something was up. Hunter shook his head.

"We were attacked by hellhounds last night," Barbie said.

"You too," Scout said. "Molly and Samuel fought off five of them yesterday morning. They barely made it out alive... but Catherine helped."

Hunter's pulse sped up. "Is Molly okay?"

"She's fine," Catherine said. "Go on, Barbie."

"Thank you," Barbie said, most likely indicating her appreciation for Catherine calling her by her chosen name. "Well, Michael's alter ego finally appeared and saved us all." Apparently chosen names were not as important for others.

Catherine stepped over and placed both of her tiny hands on Hunter's face. She pulled him down. "You got your wings. I wanted to be there with you the first time. Did it hurt?"

"Like a son of a bitch."

Barbie punched him in the shoulder. Hunter bit his lip through the pain.

Catherine smiled at him and kissed his forehead. "I guess you realize how important you are now."

"I was important before being implanted with an angel."

"That was self importance," Catherine said, patting him on top of the head. "This is different."

"Excuse me," Scout said. "What the hell is going on around here?"

Barbie and Catherine shared a look. Catherine released Hunter and took another step into the circle of the small group gathered by the RV. The Brittanys sat in a huddle together, the older ones helping the youngest with her gash. A shirtless Billy stood by their side with his hat tilted back and his thumbs hooked in his belt loops. Hunter was amazed no one else could tell that the little kid was Jimmy. Henry, Wesley and their sisters swayed in the heat with hungry looks in their eyes. Scout stood in front of Catherine with his arms crossed.

Catherine raised her head and stared straight at Scout. "Hell is what's going on. Chase was only the first and now we have to deal with Tommy. He won't be the last, but we have to take them as they come."

"Take who as they come?" Scout asked.

Hunter knew what she was going to say, and he still didn't want to believe it.

"Tommy is Famine, the second horseman of the apocalypse."

"You've got to be shitting me."

Everyone looked at Billy, who shrugged bare shoulders and lowered his hat to block the morning sunshine from his eyes.

Hunter's laughter sounded crazy, even to him.

37.

MARGARET

Independents's greenhouse was now a frame without substance. The cloud of grasshoppers had destroyed the plastic panels that allowed sunlight in and kept the cold out. Samuel's expression worsened every second he scanned over the broken bits of his labors. Margaret knew what it meant—no food and a lot of hard work to regain what they had lost. The problem was time. The growing season was over, and before long kids would get hungry.

"So, uh Margaret, right?"

Margaret looked at Samuel and smiled. "That's right, although I do remember my entire life as just Molly, so don't feel like I'm not the same person you've always known."

"Oh, okay. It's just I want to apologize for all the immoral thoughts I've had about you over the years. I mean, now that you're a saint and all. I just wanted to ask for—"

"Forgiveness," Margaret said. "You're forgiven, but not by me."

"What does that mean?"

"It means I can't grant you forgiveness for thinking dirty thoughts about me." Margaret couldn't keep the warmth of discomfort from rushing into her cheeks. "But since you selflessly gave your life to protect me, and Catherine was able to bring you back, then I'm guessing He forgives you."

They left the ruined greenhouse and walked three blocks to the corner that led to Mark and Vanessa's home. Flowers surrounded the brown house, untouched by last night's bug storm, and two giant trees stood on either side like posted sentries. What worried Margaret was the door standing wide open.

She started to jog, and Samuel stumbled after her before catching up. They crossed the front lawn, heedless of the walkway. Margaret leaped the steps to the porch and tumbled through the threshold, landing on her knees in the living room with a thud. Samuel's clump-clump sounded right behind her. He accidentally stepped on her foot, but hopped off quickly.

"Molly, are you all right?" Mark asked as he bent down and lifted her up. "Most people knock first, but since you're family, I guess its okay for you to charge inside."

Margaret stood with the offered help, feeling too stupid to string words together.

"I think we're all a little jumpy after last night," Samuel said. "Where's momma bear and baby bear."

"They're in the back sleeping," Mark said. "It was a long night for everyone."

"Why was the front door open?" Margaret asked.

"I wanted to take a look around outside the house and came back in to get my sunglasses. Didn't realize leaving the door open was such a big deal."

"You know how it is, Mark," Samuel said. "Some crazy dude rides a hurricane of bugs into town. He slashes your throat and the bugs destroy our food supply. That kind of stuff puts people on edge."

Mark stared at Samuel then switched over to Margaret. "Point taken. So what brings you guys here?"

"I promised to come by and have a talk with you," Margaret said. "And what Samuel just mentioned about the more serious problem with the food. We need to start figuring out what we're going to do."

Mark played his fingers across his throat where not even a scar remained after last night's slashing. "Okay, Molly. How are you able to deliver babies and heal people?"

"Don't forget the lightshow," Samuel said. "She turned Dylan and me into a couple of bug zappers. Speaking of which, can you do that again sometime? That was a blast."

"Samuel, please let me talk to my brother for a minute," Margaret said. Samuel nodded without comment, which was unusual for him. Margaret was thankful since she was stressed out enough already. "Mark, I'm still your sister and have always been, but I've also lived before as someone else."

Mark's face showed the proper skepticism. She'd seen it on Samuel's face a half-hour ago. The only cure was to push on.

"My name is Margaret. I was martyred for my religious beliefs and later canonized as a saint by the Catholic Church. I'm known as the patron saint of pregnancy. Catherine and I, along with Saint Barbara, are the Three Holy Maids."

Mark fell onto the couch and Samuel found a seat on the opposite side. Neither he nor Margaret knew exactly what her brother would do or say once the initial shock wore off.

"You really are crazy," Mark said.

Margaret sighed. "No, Mark. I'm not."

"You sure sound crazy."

"And you had your throat slashed open last night by a tall dude with bad hygiene," Samuel said. "Maybe you should take a moment to reflect about how it felt to lay dying in the street before calling your sister crazy."

Mark flexed his hands, giving a sideways glance at Samuel. Then he touched his throat again. "What was that thing, Molly? Was it the devil?"

"No. That was Famine, the second horseman of the apocalypse."

The town bell rang across Independents and Margaret looked out the open window, seeing only sunshine and green grass. Mark and Samuel stood up from the couch and walked outside. They left the door open, expecting Margaret to follow.

Vanessa came out of the bedroom with a handful of David wrestling in her arms. She held him securely like any loving mother would. "Why is the town bell ringing?"

"Don't know." Margaret waved at her nephew, who smiled back and stretched for her fingers.

Vanessa stared at Margaret. "I heard what you told Mark. I believe you. How can I not? I saw how you helped Ginger deliver her baby. I just don't understand it. There are a lot of things I don't understand these days, but I know miracles are happening. I also know that the Big Bad still has plenty for us all to worry about. Is it really the Four Horsemen of the Apocalypse? Can we stop them?"

Margaret shrugged. "This is only the second one. It's a process we're going through. We have to try." Margaret tickled David's chin and he squirmed, giving a giggle and a bigger, chubby cheeked smile that revealed a bright row of baby teeth.

"And you're here to stop them, along with Catherine and this other one?"

"No. We aren't powerful enough, but we can help."

The bell rang with more fervency, clanging out its desperate call across Independents. She stepped to the door. Samuel and her brother were talking to some of the other boys in town, now wielding their baseball bats once again. At least they were all fully dressed.

"If you can't stop them, who will?"

"He will."

Vanessa nodded and followed Margaret outside. Vanessa was a spiritual person. If anyone had faith that God would save them in their hour of need, Vanessa did. Margaret just wished she had some grasp of the overall plan. Her seventeen years of amnesia clouded her mind in a tumult of Molly decisions. The purpose was so unclear that Margaret had to believe it was a part of His plan. That didn't make her any more confident in her abilities to help save the world from total destruction.

They approached the boys in the street just as the ones with baseball bats took off. Samuel and Mark waited.

"Hunter got back into town not long ago," Samuel said.

Relief filled Margaret, and then settled into a happy, although guilty, contentment. Her discussion with Hunter was a lot closer than she'd wanted, but at least he was safe. "Is he okay?"

"He's fine. They just had a run in with the Britts. Apparently this dude, Famine, can turn kids into possessed killing machines."

"Are they all right?"

"Yeah, Catherine took care of them with the help of the new girl. I think your other saint just rode into town with Hunter. They also brought a bunch of kids from Cozad. That's where this Famine dude got his start."

"Everyone is gathering at Main Street," Mark said. "That's what the bell is about. We need to get a head count and set up defenses."

"Where is the baseball team going?" Vanessa asked.

"They're on patrol. Either they find this guy and take him down, or they help transport others safely to Main Street."

"They aren't safe," Margaret said. Everyone turned eyes on her. "No one is. We need to find out what Hunter knows. He's obviously been able to fight this new threat."

"Let's go then," Samuel said. "The sooner we deal with this dude, the sooner I can figure out some way to feed Independents and however many kids came here from Cozad."

The walk was fast and uneventful, except for the eerie ghost town feeling from the deserted streets. What made it even worse was the constant tolling of the bell. Whoever was ringing it was very enthusiastic. On and on it clanged, echoing over the houses. Little David grew annoyed by the noise and started squealing. Vanessa tried soothing the baby with distractions but he wasn't having it.

Margaret was worried about Hunter's arrival. What did it mean that he had found Barbara? What type of person would she be? Reincarnation was a tricky thing as Margaret's recent discovery had proved. Did Barbara suffer from the same memory loss? How old would she be? Considering Catherine was in the body of an eight-year-old and Margaret was seventeen, Barbara could be any age.

Why Hunter? He found Catherine and now Barbara. In a weird way, he'd even found Margaret. Maybe that wasn't the way to think about it. Margaret couldn't help feeling like she was missing something, and that she was in trouble for having a relationship with Hunter.

Oh, Molly, Margaret thought, *what did you do to me?*

As they drew nearer to the center of town, others merged with them on the path. The bell finally stopped as Margaret's group reached the brick cobbles where a crowd had gathered. The whole town, plus strangers from Cozad, milled about in two separate groups. The newly arrived kids looked like refugees away from their camp. Catherine and a couple others handed out bread and apples to the emaciated kids.

Then Margaret spotted Hunter with a pretty brunette girl draped over him, next to a couple of the Cozad kids. Something very Molly-like stirred inside of her and she quickened her pace across the street to where her boyfriend stood.

The girl caught sight of Margaret's approach and smiled in recognition. Margaret realized this was Saint Barbara wrapped comfortably around her boyfriend. Margaret slowed in an attempt to regain composure before charging in to challenge for the right to be Hunter's girlfriend, which she still was if anyone else had any doubts.

"Hello, Molly," Barbara said. "We were just talking about you."

Hunter stripped Barbara's hands off him and spun with a confused look in his eyes, like he didn't know what was going on. Margaret could share in that feeling.

"Molly," Hunter said, rushing over to her and enfolding her in a warm embrace that rivaled the August sunshine. Margaret laid her head on his shoulder and sighed, happy to have him back home. She breathed in his scent and contained her unsaintly thoughts.

Margaret opened her eyes and saw the pain and discomfort in the twists and turns of Barbara's face. Wanting confirmation, but afraid to ask such a delicate question, Margaret leaned back and stared at her boyfriend's face for answers. Her body went limp. Her knees left her and she slipped to the ground like a string of yarn cut from the ball. If Hunter hadn't helped her down she would have smacked her head on the cobbles.

"Molly, what's wrong?" Hunter cradled her.

Margaret looked at his face again. "You're Michael, the archangel."

Hunter nodded. "That's what they tell me."

"Hunter, we need a town council meeting, now," Billy said.

Margaret thought it sounded funny hearing Billy speak with such authority. She turned her head and remembered the strange thing about Billy when he came into Luis's last night and told her that Mark needed her help.

"Jimmy?" she said.

"Jimmy?" Ginger repeated, from where she helped hand out food to Cozad kids. The new mom dropped the basketful of green apples and they spilled across the cobbles, rolling to a stop at Billy's feet.

Jimmy pushed back his hat. Even if they couldn't see inside his soul, there was no mistaking Jimmy's mannerism in the small boy. His sad smile turned Billy's lips. "Hey, Ginger."

38.

SCOUT

Scout ran over when he heard the scream, ready to fight for Independents. What he found was Billy on top of Ginger, and that was pretty much all the justification he needed. Scout ripped the little troublemaker off and punched him in the face.

He didn't understand why someone clobbered him in the side of the head. Scout rolled to the ground and lay there panting from adrenaline rushing inside his body and madness burning through his mind. And he was even more surprised when that someone turned out to be a very pissed off Hunter.

"What the fuck is wrong with you, Scout?"

"Hunter!" Billy stood, wiping the blood from his busted lip with the hem of his already red-stained shirt. "Don't ever use that language around all these kids!"

"I've been telling him that for two days now," Barbie said, where she knelt tending to Ginger.

Ginger's eyes fluttered in unconsciousness. Apples littered the street, bright green on the brick cobbles. Billy walked back over to her side.

"Get away from her, Billy," Scout said.

Billy straightened his hat. There was something weird about the kid wearing a hat. Scout never saw him in one before.

"Scout, you don't know what's going on, so settle down until you do." Hunter reached down and offered Scout a hand up.

Scout slapped it away and regained his feet on his own. "No,

Hunter. You don't know what's been going on. Billy's been spreading lies all over town about how I got your brother killed. He was telling people that Raven was a spy, and now she's left me and gone who knows where." Scout balled his fist and stepped up in Hunter's face. "And now he's just attacked Ginger and you're standing up for him?"

Hunter's smile was so grim Scout couldn't tell if he was happy or was about to take a swing at him. Hunter leaned slowly into Scout and whispered in his ear, "Jimmy is Billy."

"Have you lost your fucking mind?"

Billy stomped over and got in the middle of both of them. His face twisted with rage. "The next person to use the F word in my street is going to spend a month cleaning outhouses."

Samuel walked over and bent down to Billy's eye level. "Jimmy?"

Billy patted Samuel's shoulder. "Hello, Samuel. Will you please get everyone on the council together?" He looked around. "We'll meet in Luis's for now. Have everyone else wait in Brittany's while we sort things out. Make sure everyone is accounted for. I want eyes on the street, but I don't want anyone wandering off on their own."

Samuel blinked. "Jimmy?"

Billy, Jimmy or whoever he was looked around again. Scout couldn't believe it. He shook his head as if that would be enough to clear away the confusion.

Hunter smirked at him. "Don't worry. It's going to get a lot more complicated in a minute. Jimmy coming back from the dead is the easy part to swallow."

"Hunter, please invite someone from Cozad to attend our council."

Hunter nodded and grabbed Scout's arm, dragging him over to where the Cozad kids waited for further instructions. Most of them stood around with apple cores in their hands. Hunter walked up to the scrawny boy and girl that had kept Chef Brittany at bay against the windshield.

"Hey, where can we put these?" the boy asked, dangling the well gnawed core by the stem.

"We'll find a compost bin in a minute. Henry, this is Scout. Scout, this is Henry and his sister Sophie. Henry here is kind of the unofficial leader of Cozad."

"I really didn't have a choice," Henry said.

Scout shook his free hand. "What happened to the other

leader?"

Henry dropped his head and lowered his voice when he answered. Scout didn't think he heard him right. Sophie covered her face and turned away.

"I'm sorry. Did you say she was eaten?"

"I told you it would get a lot more complicated," Hunter said. "Henry, will you come to the council meeting with me? Sophie can come too."

"All right," Henry said.

"Carissa," Hunter called to another scrawny girl. She walked over with another boy in tow. "Can you and Wesley get everyone from your town inside that building there? It's our cafeteria and we might be able to get you guys a little more to eat."

Hunter searched the crowd of Independents kids. "Brady. Emma."

The two parted from their respective huddles. Brady limped over and Emma sashayed.

"This is Carissa and her brother, Wesley," Hunter said.

"Brother?" Emma said, smiling like a lioness locking on her prey. Wesley looked like a deer in the headlights.

"Not now, Emma," Hunter said. "I want you guys to help the group from Cozad over at Brittany's. We need everyone not on the council to wait inside while we meet."

Hunter gave everyone their routes like a seasoned quarterback, leaving Scout wondering when his friend had become so responsible. Hunter never involved himself in council business or meetings of any sort. Scout tucked his hands in his pockets and reconsidered his friend's new attitude as something good. Now if Hunter could just lose his irritating, know it all smirk.

The crowds moved off in two directions towards Brittany's and Luis's, depending on their calling. Scout stopped Hunter on the way to council.

"Why was Billy, uh Jimmy, on top of Ginger?"

"She started fainting and he tripped on an apple trying to reach her. It was a miracle he was able to keep her from smashing her head on the ground."

"Why did she scream?"

There was that smirk again. "Wouldn't you if you just discovered your dead boyfriend had returned in the body of someone eight years younger?"

Scout nodded and followed Hunter up the street to Luis's.

*   *   *

"Is it okay to use the F word now, Jimmy?"

"No, Samuel, it's not. You of all people should know how I feel about that."

Scout's head spun from everything he had heard. Starting with Hunter and his fight with the demon sniper on top of the grain elevator in Cozad, through the explanation of how Jimmy had followed Samuel back from the dead, where he watched his son being born as a ghost, to there being not one but two other saints like Catherine. Saint Barbara, who preferred Barbie, was locked inside the previously mentioned grain elevator, and the other, Saint Margaret, locked inside the mind of Molly, who now preferred to be called Margaret. Then there was the fact that Billy had been possessed by a demon to serve the main bad dude, named Famine, who just so happened to be one of the Four Horsemen of the Apocalypse. Somehow Jimmy wound up possessing Billy and the demon was exorcised.

And the capper, the absolute unbelievable part, the last bit of information that probably had everyone in the room wanting to say the F word, besides the shorter version of Jimmy, was that inside Hunter rests the archangel, Michael—God's mightiest angel.

Yeah, the F word was the least of their concerns at the moment. Somebody should've brought out the straightjackets. Scout wanted his fitted with extra straps and buckles.

"So how do we take this dude down?" Samuel asked. "Does Hunter just grow wings and blow a horn or what?"

"I don't think it works that way." Hunter glanced over to Barbie, who shook her head. "It just sort of happened when the need came up."

Samuel sat forward. "What kind of need?"

"I have no idea. I'd say life or death, but I was pretty much fighting for my life all day yesterday and he only came out once."

"That's not really true," Barbie said. Everyone stared at her and she returned it like the confident new girl in school who's destined to break a lot of hearts. "Michael has regenerative capabilities now."

"What?" Samuel asked.

"It means his body heals from injuries, rather quickly."

"Cool," Samuel said. "You're like Wolverine, without the claws and metal skeleton."

"Who?" Hunter asked.

"Come over someday and I'll show you my comic book collection."

"All right, so now all we have to do is get rid of this new threat and then we can start preparing our winter food supply," Jimmy said. "Anybody have a plan to do this?"

"What's to plan?" Scout said. "We just wait for him to make his move and then Hunter can take care of everything. That sounds good to me."

Hunter leaned back in his chair and folded his arms across his chest. "I've already fought him once and the angel didn't come to my rescue then."

"What happened?" Scout asked.

"I had a broomstick shoved through my stomach." Hunter pointed at Henry. "They came out and chased him away."

Henry shrugged. "I guess we just needed to be inspired. We didn't have much hope until you arrived. We couldn't just let him kill you."

"Thanks."

"Maybe it's time to break out something better than baseball bats," Mark said.

"No," Jimmy said, before anyone else could jump in.

Samuel nodded along. Scout met Hunter's eyes and they both frowned.

"We stockpiled all those guns for when there was a need. I think this qualifies. We've seen what this guy can do." Mark placed his hand over his throat. "I've seen what this guy can do up close."

"I don't think we need to make this worse than it already is," Jimmy said. "It's just one bad guy. As long as they're not shooting at us, we'll do the same."

"They shot at me in Cozad," Hunter said. "You should see my jacket."

"That was Cozad. I'm sorry, but I still say no. We can vote, but I don't think the numbers have changed since the last time."

Scout scanned the faces of the council, and only one person looked like she had changed her mind about the gun control they enacted back when Greg was alive. Scout couldn't believe it was his sister.

"I've never liked guns," Vanessa said. "I saw my share of gang violence before the plague, and I still remember when all the adults died and all these stupid kids found guns and started shooting and robbing each other. It was a miracle Scout and I got out of St. Louis alive. But I'm not willing to let the father of my child face a horseman of the apocalypse with only a baseball bat for protection."

"I agree that we're up against some scary stuff," Samuel said. "But we got help now with the three saints. Dylan and I took it to that dude last night. When he comes back, we'll finish the job without shooting up the whole town."

Jimmy scooted out of his chair and paced, rubbing the back of his neck. Ginger stared at him with haunted eyes. Her silence was overwhelming since coming into Luis's to conduct this meeting. Molly, or Margaret, held little James, rocking the sleeping baby. Ginger wrung her hands like they were soaked with dishwater. Nothing about this was going to be easy, from the fight to the aftermath.

"Catherine," Jimmy said. "What can we expect after we beat this horseman?"

Catherine had remained quiet through the discussions. She was like that. Scout had even forgotten that she was sitting beside him. He regarded her now with her back to the chair, her hands folded in her lap, her legs straight out in the air, and the permanent grass stains on her toes. She scooted forward and her feet found the floor. "There's no point in thinking ahead right now, Jimmy. You have to take care of this and, like you said, create your winter food supply. What comes next is just another link in the chain. This is what's happening now."

"Okay, so how do we take care of the here and now?"

Catherine stood and walked through the middle of the circle to Jimmy. They were exactly the same height. She laid her hands on his shoulders and looked into his eyes. "We'll just have to wait and see, silly."

"You know more than that." He turned his head. "Doesn't she, Margaret?"

Molly stared at the baby and everyone in the circle guessed that Margaret knew just as much as Catherine about everything. The difference was that Margaret used to be Molly. She grew up with all the kids of Independents. Her friends should come before her secrets.

Scout broke the silence for everyone. "Molly, are we going to be able to beat this guy?"

Molly lifted her gaze. "My name is Margaret now."

Mark rocked forward in his chair. "You're still my sister, no matter what or who you were in a former life. If you know something, you have to tell us."

"No, Mark, I don't. All you need to know is that God is with us. He's seen to it that all the pieces are here at the right time to defeat this threat. I don't know how this will happen anymore than you do. I just know that you will defeat your enemies if you have faith."

Scout burst out of his chair. "This is total crap. Why are we the ones having to deal with all of this? Why not the kids in Denver?"

"Scout," Hunter said. "We're not the only ones who have to deal with this."

Scout followed Hunter's gaze to where Henry and his sister Sophie sat as the representatives of Cozad, their community decimated by this horseman called Famine.

"All right, you have a point, but what about all of us? I don't suppose we can call upon the power that the three saints are able to, nor do we have the power to heal ourselves and grow wings like angel boy, nor are we all going to be able to come back from the dead."

Jimmy squared up to Scout. "What's your point?"

Scout spread his hands. "My point is that most of us are just normal kids. How do we fight against this?"

"The same way you've fought since the start of the plague," Catherine said. "With everything you've got. We'll help you with the rest. You don't have to be a saint or an angel or—"

Dylan crashed through the door, his chest heaving and his eyes wide with fear. "They're here!"

"Who're they?" Jimmy asked.

"All the guys that were out looking for that dude are here with him. They're setting fire to the food storage building at the end of the block! Hurry!"

"I hope you grow some wings fast," Scout said to Hunter as they ran for the door.

39.

JIMMY

Jimmy ran behind Scout and Hunter. He skidded to a stop at the door and Mark slammed into him. Jimmy moved aside and looked back at Ginger still sitting in her seat. Margaret held their son. Jimmy went back to Ginger. "Let's get you and the baby someplace safe. Margaret, can you help?"

She shook her head. "I need to be out there with them."

Jimmy frowned, but understood. He searched the remaining crowd. Luis busied himself gathering some of his medical gear. "Luis, will you help me with Ginger and the baby?"

"Yes, of course." Luis rushed over with his bag packed.

"We'll all go together," Vanessa said, holding her baby. The older mother generated calm like a force of nature.

Henry and his sister stepped forward. "Can we follow you guys?"

Jimmy nodded. "Let's go, but stay close."

"Are you feeling better now?" Margaret asked Ginger. "Somebody else can carry James."

Ginger darted a glance at Jimmy and he felt a stab of regret for allowing his identity to be revealed so carelessly. Now he didn't know how to talk to her about it.

"I'm okay," Ginger said.

Margaret handed the baby to her and took off after the first wave already out in the street. Ginger's smile returned with little James back in her arms.

They left through the back door to the dirt alleyway where sunshine had been replaced by clouds rolling overhead, promising rain. The smell of smoke reminded Jimmy of the time when he thought Hunter had been caught in a house fire. The black column rose at the end of Main Street like a puffy chain. Jimmy hated the thought that the town he'd worked so hard to build might burn to the ground. He hoped the dark clouds above would unload and douse the fire.

Jimmy led the small party through a gate in a chain-link fence and into a backyard. They crossed quickly and skirted around the side of the house to the front. "We'll go to Ginger's house in case the fire gets out of control. Plus, you probably have stuff to take care of the babies, right?"

Ginger nodded. "Hunter and Scout have been bringing baby stuff over for months."

Jimmy made a mental note to thank Hunter and Scout when all of this was over. Would he still be trapped in Billy's body? He wished he was a foot taller so he could at least look Ginger eye to eye. She'd never take him seriously in this body. The cruel fate that brought him back must have been laughing at him.

Jimmy held up a hand when they reached the edge at the front of the house. He scanned up and down the block before waving the others to follow. Ginger's yellow house, her once colorful flowerbeds around the lone, leafless tree, had not survived the infestation this close to Main Street.

Bunched together, the little group crossed the street and started up the walkway when a groan, followed by a scratching sound, brought them to a quick halt. A shambling form paced in the dim shadows covering Ginger's front porch. The tall person's head drooped, touching its chest as if it were looking for something on the wooden planks. This looming figure rattled the doorknob, which failed to turn, and then it sniffed the air like it caught a familiar scent. The person turned slowly.

Caught in the open, the group stood with nowhere to hide.

"Who are you?" Jimmy called.

The person groaned and moved into the yard. Jimmy's heart stopped. His trembling knees threatened to buckle. Ginger screamed and little James began to cry.

Jimmy's corpse, buried these past five months, groaned again. His eyes were pale orbs and his gray mottled skin hung in loose folds. The shirt he wore was torn and dirty, as were his tattered jeans, but the boots looked to be in pretty decent shape.

Jimmy, the one occupying Billy, noticed that his dead body didn't wear a hat. That was something at least. "Ginger, Vanessa, I need you to run. I'll hold him off."

"I'll help you," Henry said.

Jimmy nodded. "Luis, you go with them."

"We can all out run this thing," Vanessa said.

"You get a head start. We'll be right behind you."

"Sophie, you have to let go of my hand," Henry said. "Don't worry, I'll be all right. Help them with their babies."

Jimmy didn't hear any complaints from the girl. He was too busy watching his dead body sniff the air and stare at them with those pale eyes. The thing opened its mouth, snapping it shut over and over like it wanted to talk, but the action only produced groans and small clouds of dust.

Ginger, Vanessa, and the rest backed slowly away to the street.

Dead Jimmy's eyes followed the flight of a butterfly as it flittered past his nose and down over the empty flowerbed. The corpse groaned once more and shambled in that direction like he wanted to chase the butterfly to pull its wings off. The group's slapping feet on pavement distracted him from the insect and his attention returned to them. When they began to leave, he groaned in great desperation.

Why had his corpse returned to Ginger's house? What would be controlling his body if his soul was inside Billy? Did his dead brain contain memories of his previous life? Whatever the deceased's intentions, Jimmy had news—Ginger and the baby were off limits.

The thing shifted his gangling walk towards the retreating mothers and their babies. Jimmy cut off his dead body's pursuit like a crossing guard halting traffic. The corpse towered two feet over him. Jimmy gagged and his eyes watered from the stench of his own rotten flesh. He breathed in through his mouth and balled his fists.

The creature stretched out an arm toward Ginger, and Jimmy felt an instant of sorrow for his body. Then the corpse looked down on Jimmy with those pale eyes. Like dirty motor oil in a pool of milk, the paleness turned black. The thing's mouth dropped open, releasing a hollow screech that split down the middle of Billy's little spine.

Jimmy covered his ears. The creature swung and clubbed him in the head. A stunned Jimmy dropped and shook the fuzziness away. Henry cried out, and then the creature fell beside Jimmy with Henry clinging to the corpse's knees. Jimmy rolled over and pushed up off the ground. His corpse groaned, twisted and swiped at Henry. After he kicked his body, Jimmy pulled Henry to his feet. The two boys backed away from the animated dead that wobbled like a turtle trapped in its shell.

They hustled to catch up with Ginger and the others at the end of the block. All around, screams echoed from Main Street. A crowd of kids ran towards them, chased by a couple of bat wielding boys that had been turned into pawns for Famine. Jimmy searched the sky for angels or lightning bolts—any sign that they weren't alone in the fight for their lives.

"Where should we go?" Vanessa asked.

Jimmy turned in a tight circle of panic and focused on the white steeple rising out of the neighborhood. "Let's go to the church."

They hurried and others joined their progress—Emma and some of the girls from town, along with some of the Cozad kids. Emma introduced Wesley and Carissa to those in the group who hadn't met them yet.

"What's happening back there?" Jimmy asked them.

Emma spoke first. "Hunter is fighting the big ugly kid with help from that new girl."

"Barbie," Wesley said.

Emma frowned at him. "Don't interrupt me." She turned back to Jimmy and rolled her eyes before continuing, "Catherine and Molly have been doing something to Scout, Samuel and Mark. They're glowing. They're trying to stop the other boys and put out the fire. Everyone else is running for their lives."

"All right," Jimmy yelled over the confusion of the growing group of frightened kids. "Everybody, get inside the church."

They followed Vanessa and Ginger through the doors. A lot of the kids gave Jimmy a funny look in passing. He wondered why before remembering whose body he inhabited.

Henry waited outside, helping Jimmy hold the doors open. "What now?"

Jimmy stared back at the billowing black smoke where orange flames licked the tops of the buildings at the other end of town. He saw the possessed boys fighting with Samuel, Scout, and Mark. Dylan was there too. The bats were gone and now they fought toe to toe with fists. The good side appeared to be winning.

"Go inside and lock the doors. Have someone guard every window and entryway. I'm going to see if I can help."

"You should stay here with us."

Henry probably thought Billy was too small to enter a fight. Jimmy reached up and patted him on the shoulder. "I'll be all right. This isn't my first rodeo. It won't be my last."

"What's a rodeo?"

"I'll tell you about it later."

Henry nodded and closed the door.

Jimmy left the churchyard and ran in a straight path for Main Street. He closed on Scout and Dylan as they finished knocking one of the kids unconscious. Catherine hustled over and began disrupting whatever controlled the enchanted boy.

Something heavy fell on him and drove him to the ground. Grass and dirt filled Jimmy's mouth and the taste of blood seeped out from his busted lip. Something grabbed his hair. His hat laid on the ground in front of him. He turned his head and looked over his shoulder, since the hand holding him by the hair allowed it. Jimmy's corpse held him tight, sitting on his back. The corpse groaned and then drove Jimmy's head into the ground, again and again, until the groaning ceased.

*　　*　　*

Jimmy floated out of Billy's tiny body. Billy's head didn't look right, but neither did the creature that lifted it one more time and smashed it into the ground.

Instead of floating away, Jimmy held himself together, familiar with the prospect of being a ghost.

"Hello, Jimmy," a voice said behind him.

Jimmy turned and found Billy's transparent spirit smiling at him.

"I couldn't believe it when I found you were inside my body. How cool is that?"

Jimmy shook his head, but smiled anyways. "Not very, but thanks for letting me borrow it for a while. Where've you been?"

"I've been hanging around. Catherine told me to wait because she was sure something would happen soon and I might get my body back."

Jimmy watched his own dead body move off of Billy's little dead one, lying face down in the bloody green grass. Jimmy's corpse stared down at the body and then looked around. For what, Jimmy had no idea.

"Sorry, Billy, I think I just killed you. This is really weird."

"Yeah, but hey, have you walked through a wall yet? That's pretty cool. The first couple of times I thought I was going to get stuck and that freaked me out a bit, but then you kind of get sucked out the other side and its okay."

Jimmy smiled. "I don't really enjoy it that much."

"Uh oh, looks like you're on the move."

Jimmy's corpse shambled over to where Scout and Dylan stood protectively over Catherine, unaware of the approaching danger. Jimmy grabbed Billy's arm, afraid to lose his little spirit friend.

"Catherine! Look out!"

The little girl lifted her head from her finished work and assessed the situation. "Scout, Dylan!" She pointed at Jimmy's corpse.

"What the hell?" Scout said.

"Jimmy?" Dylan said, with equal disbelief lighting on both of their faces.

"Famine must have raised Jimmy's corpse," Catherine stated the obvious. The two boys snapped out of their confusion, returning to fight mode.

"Why the hell would he do that?" Dylan asked.

Scout circled the walking dead body. Jimmy's corpse watched his progress as Scout came around behind him.

"Who knows," Catherine said. "He probably just wanted to scare us."

"I'm pretty freaking scared right now," Scout said.

"Me too," Dylan said.

Jimmy led Billy over to Catherine. "That thing just killed me. I mean it just killed Billy."

"I figured that out on my own. I'm glad you two found each other."

"Who are you talking to?" Scout asked in a shrill, un-Scout-like voice.

"Shush!" Catherine returned her attention to Jimmy, "Now, go get Margaret for me. She's over there finishing up with the last of the enchanted boys. I'm going to need her if we're going to put you two back where you belong."

"What do you mean?" Jimmy asked. "I don't want to be dead again."

She stood and wiped dirt off her knees. "You won't be dead, silly. This is all part of the plan."

"What plan?"

She tilted her head at him like he was simple. "You never pay attention, do you? Hurry and get Margaret."

The two spirits flew off. They heard Catherine order Scout and Dylan to take down Jimmy's corpse without killing it.

"Isn't he already dead?" Scout yelled.

Samuel and Mark were protectively sheltering Margaret when they found them. Like Catherine said, Margaret had just finished with the last of the enchanted boys.

"Margaret, Catherine needs your help."

Margaret looked up in shock and then understanding. "Oh, Jimmy, what happened?"

"Jimmy?" Samuel said, looking around.

Margaret waved him silent.

"Catherine says Famine raised my body from the dead. It just killed me. I mean Billy. I mean..."

Margaret stood and wiped dirt from her knees just like Catherine had done. "Show me." She waved Samuel and Mark to follow. "Boys, Catherine needs me. Come on."

"What about Hunter and Barbie?" Samuel said.

"What about the fire?" Mark asked.

Margaret smiled at them, grabbed each of their hands, and started pulling them along. "Everything is going according to plan."

Jimmy shook his head as he led the way back to his body. He glanced down Main Street before leaving and saw nothing but flames and dark smoke on either side. Hunter was nowhere in sight. Jimmy succumbed to the plan. Especially if it meant he might get to be alive in his own body again. Hopefully that meant without the mottled skin and pale eyes.

40.

HUNTER

Hunter burst through the door onto Main Street underneath overcast skies. He hoped his silent partner was about to swoop in for the rescue. Fifteen minutes later, he was still alone, fighting for his life.

Everybody paired off like a hoedown, leaving Hunter partnered up with the tall ugly guy at the dance. Scout and Dylan took one side of the street, glowing like light bulbs with help from Catherine. Samuel and Mark worked the other side, equally bright, with Molly backing them up with her new powers. The rest of the town scattered like ants after the log had been flipped over.

"We're having some fun now, huh?" Tommy swiped at Hunter with his deadly black talons. "You're going to watch your town burn as I spill your guts in the street."

Hunter jumped and dodged, wishing Tommy would shut up and fight. He'd tell him so if he could find the time to catch his breath. Barbie protected Hunter's back and helped guide kids away from the burning buildings. Tommy sliced open two kids who ran close by in the confusion. Hunter stepped inside Tommy's reach and head butted him in the nose, sending the perv reeling backwards. Barbie healed the injured kids quickly and moved them along. It appeared the three saints had an abundant supply of their miracle stuff working overtime, because none of them had passed out. Sure would have been nice if someone would get off his angelic butt and mop this place up.

Tommy returned, holding his nose with one hand, springing forward and clawing Hunter across the chest with the other.

Hunter gasped from the jagged rip and rolled away from Tommy's second attempt. He scrambled on hands and knees until he was able to regain his feet. His shirt hung in bloody shreds, but his wounds closed mere seconds later.

Tommy stalked him with slow determination. "You're not getting away. You're all alone. Nobody will help you."

Hunter searched his surroundings, verifying his solo role against the horseman. Smoke rolled through the streets, separating him from the others. Barbie had disappeared in the chaos of the fight. Survival mode kicked in and Hunter decided the only option was to flee. The wall of smoke would provide the needed cover for escape. But then what? Who else was trapped here on the street with this monster? Where would Tommy turn next if he wasn't focused on Hunter? Who else would Tommy pervert into his little band of monsters?

The buildings of Independents burned. The noise of the flames tearing through the heart of the town rose as roofs caved in and windows popped under the intense heat. Support beams gave way and whole buildings crumbled. Hunter coughed from the black smoke filling his lungs, created by the plumes that darkened the day.

What he wouldn't give for some rain.

Thunder rolled and the answer to his silent prayer arrived. Fat drops pelted him from above, lifting Hunter's spirits in the circle of smoke that kept him hidden from Tommy. Hunter pulled his shirt collar over his nose and ducked down as he sped in an arc around the monster stalking him. He needed a weapon. He had his lock blade in one pocket and his Zippo in the other. He pulled out the knife and flicked it open. He'd creep in close and hope Tommy didn't spot him coming.

The rain drove down in a torrent. The smoke surrendered under the assault, replaced by a rank smelling fog. All around, the air steamed and hissed as the rainfall doused the flames. Hunter shuffled sideways, focused on where he thought Tommy stood in the swirling turmoil.

The smoke cleared, revealing Barbie with her arms stretched to the heavens. Her dark hair was plastered to her face and lightning crackled from her fingertips. She had called down the rain to save what remained of Main Street. Hunter couldn't spot Tommy anywhere around.

The rain caused a different kind of hazy blindness. Shadows moved within the wall of water brought down from the clouds. Tommy slipped into view with a terrible lustful smile and raked his claws across Barbie's back and the other over her stomach, ripping her open like an orange as bright blood shot out everywhere. Barbie dropped onto the wet brick pavement.

Hunter screamed, rushing forward. He stepped on a discarded aluminum baseball bat and skated across it until he landed on his face. His knife was knocked loose, clattering off, lost in the fog. He sucked in quick breaths. The bruises and painful scrapes on his face quickly started healing. He pushed up as a foot connected with his forehead, flipping him onto his back. His thoughts spun out of control and threatened to shut down production all together. He stared into the sky, wondering why the angel hadn't come.

Tommy leaned over, with his deadly claws drumming a steady rhythm on his knee caps. He blocked the cool rain from Hunter like an unwanted umbrella. His horrible mouth of pointed teeth smiled down.

"She's gone, but don't you worry. You'll be following her shortly. I promise."

Hunter rolled to one side and tried to stand.

Tommy grabbed his arm and forced him down. "You're finished. What did you think was going to happen? You're on the wrong side. This world is going to hell, but you won't be around to see it."

Why was this happening? Was there a plan or was all the crap about angels and saints for nothing? Why didn't the angel come? Why didn't Hunter get the chance to make all this right?

"Are you ready?" Tommy asked.

"You must be Tommy."

A flash of silver swung through the storm and slammed into Tommy's chest, knocking the horseman backwards. He fell to the ground, sitting there stunned with a goofy look on his hideous face.

A tall shadow wielding a baseball bat stepped over Hunter and hit Tommy again in the shoulder with a sickening thump.

Tommy howled in pain and fell all the way to the ground.

Hunter sat up, shaking his head in disbelief. It looked just like him, but the whole thing was impossible. The tall guy whacked Tommy two more times before Hunter put together the voice, the posture, the conviction. *That's my brother!* Jimmy was alive and in his own body. The same body Hunter had buried months ago. Unbelievable joy swept over him, healing his spirits as whatever inside of him healed his body. By the time Hunter reached his feet and took a couple of breaths, he was fully revitalized and ready to finish the fight.

Screaming at the top of his lungs, Jimmy laid the aluminum bat into Tommy's body over and over.

The kid that was Tommy the Perv twisted from the continuous rain of blows, crying out in torment. Jimmy was relentless. Finally, even Hunter had enough. He rushed over and grabbed Jimmy's arms. His brother snarled and broke out of his grip.

Hunter backed away with his hands out, trying to calm his brother. "Jimmy, you got him. That's enough. He's not hurting anyone anymore."

Jimmy panted as if possessed. "You're right about that." He turned his back on his brother and brought the bat high. "You will never hurt my family again."

Pain burst through Hunter's back and something else took over.

The angel had arrived.

*   *   *

Instead of blacking out this time, Hunter's consciousness was shoved to a corner in the back of his skull. The angel swept forward with grace and grabbed the downward swinging head of the baseball bat right before it struck its intended target. Tommy had no opportunity or will of his own to stop his impending death, but the angel did. With a jerk, the angel ripped the bat free from Jimmy's hands.

"This is not your way, James."

"Hunter, what are you doing?" Jimmy stopped. The fury in his eyes cleared and he stepped back. "We can't allow him to leave. We can't let this monster live."

Hunter felt his head nod and the strange sensation of his wings folding in on themselves as they settled upon his back. The voice in control answered, "That is not your decision. You are not meant to kill. You are meant to lead. This creature is beaten. I will decide his fate according to our Father's will."

Jimmy narrowed his eyes. "What about my brother? What have you done with Hunter?"

The angel smiled.

"I'm right here," Hunter said, and was surprised when he spoke aloud.

"He's right here," the angel copied his words. "My presence is only temporary. Your brother will not be harmed while I am with him."

"What are you talking about?" Hunter spoke. "I was getting my ass handed to me before you decided to show up."

"You were doing just fine on your own."

Hunter found himself unable to voice another comment. He figured the angel knew what he had in mind and most of the words were made up of four letters.

"So what happens now?" Jimmy asked.

"Now you must rebuild. This battle is won. You understand the hardships this winter will bring. There is no time to rest."

Jimmy surveyed the smoking ruins. Half the buildings of Main Street were destroyed. The rainwater pooled in the cobbled street. Jimmy raised his face when the sun broke through the fleeting gray clouds. He smiled. "I guess the first thing I need to do is find me a new hat."

The angel laughed. "Yes, James. You do have your priorities."

Hunter felt trapped with the sensation of joy and happiness he was unable to express. He wished the angel would depart now that the trouble had been averted. Hunter desperately wanted to hug his brother.

The angel turned quickly. Barbie lay silent in her own pool of blood some twenty feet away. The angel went to her and knelt beside the wounded saint. He brushed a lock of her dark hair from her eyes.

Barbie blinked and tilted her head. "I'm bleeding."

"I see that."

She frowned at him. "And?"

The angel placed Hunter's hands on Barbie's wounds and bowed his head. "Dear Father, please bless Your servant and heal her so she may continue to serve Your will."

Blinding light poured from Hunter's hands. The angel filtered the power, channeling it through Barbie's body and mending the torn flesh. The healing took seconds, and soon as the light winked out, Barbie stood and hugged the angel.

Hunter felt awkward from the affection he'd been forced to partake in. He tried keeping his thoughts as pure as possible with Barbie pressing her body against his, given the fact that the angel probably wouldn't appreciate Hunter taking pleasure from their embrace.

"Michael, about the conversation we had last night," Barbie said.

"Yes, I accept your desire for a normal life. I won't be in the way any longer."

Barbie crossed her arms, looking cold, tired, and also very sad. "You sort of are in the way though."

Hunter really wanted off the tracks to wherever this conversation was headed. He had his own relationships to deal with without being embroiled in the tangle between Barbie and her angel boyfriend. That thought alone left him queasy in the corner of his head. How did they even hook up in the first place? Weren't angels supposed to be in Heaven instead of dating human chicks? Of course, Barbie was more heavenly than earthly because of her sainthood.

Hunter fell back into the conversation as the angel nodded their collective head. "I see. When I have finished with this horseman, I will step out of the way. Our Father only allows me access to Hunter when needed. You may pursue whatever course you desire. I too understand how hard our relationship has been."

Barbie reached out and touched Hunter's arm. "And you're okay with this?"

The angel smiled. "I will live."

"Thank you."

The angel and the saint embraced one more time.

"Now I will take this creature someplace safe and return Michael to you when we have finished."

Hunter wondered what the angel meant by that last bit. The angel walked over to where Jimmy had been standing wary guard over the fallen horseman.

"James, remember to keep hold of your goodness when everything around you seems lost. Your leadership will save the children in the end. Use this rare gift of a second life wisely."

"I will. Thank you."

"Don't thank me."

Jimmy nodded.

"Are we going on a trip?" Hunter asked, finally able to rejoin the conversation.

"We are indeed, Michael. I hope you're not afraid to fly."

"Dude, I was born to fly."

41.

SCOUT

The rain slowed with big fat drops thumping Scout in the head. Sunlight parted the dark clouds, ending the storm. Humidity rose from the ground, thick in the air. Puddles made finding a dry path tricky. At his feet, Catherine and Molly lay sleeping after performing another miracle. Billy slept in a tight ball beside Molly with his tiny fist curled under his chin. He looked innocent, like a little boy should.

The freakiest thing Scout tried wrapping his head around was seeing Jimmy shoot off the ground after Catherine finished. Jimmy, healed and alive, didn't say a word, but tore off running towards Main Street.

"Did Jimmy just get up and run off?" Dylan asked.

"That's what I saw," Mark said. "This has been one hell of a day."

Samuel's laughter rolled like a train off its track. "That's the greatest understatement in the history of mankind."

"Let's carry everyone to the church." Mark gave Samuel a funny look when they both bent down to pick up Molly. "I can get my sister, Samuel."

Samuel stepped back, scratched his head, and slipped a goofy grin on his face. "Okay, sure. I'll carry Catherine. She's lighter anyways. I mean, not that your sister is heavy or anything. Please don't tell her I said that. I mean, I don't want her to get her feelings hurt or anything because I said something stupid."

"Are you okay?" Scout asked. "You're being kind of jumpy."

"It must be stress." Samuel scooped up Catherine and walked away without another word.

Mark shook his head. He stood with his sister and grunted from the effort. "She is heavy." He smiled nervously before following after Samuel.

"I'll carry Billy." Dylan lifted the little kid and caught up to Mark and Samuel.

Left alone, Scout turned the other way for Main Street, keeping his feet out of the water. His shoes squished over the damp earth. He avoided the muddy road and was happy once he finally stepped on the brick cobbles.

Scout's mouth dropped open in shock and disbelief. Hunter stood in the middle of town with a pair of large brown wings protruding from his back. At first Scout thought his imagination was running wild, until they flapped. Then Scout realized he'd stopped moving altogether and felt really stupid when Jimmy waved him over. Every step Scout took toward the amazing creature Hunter had become seemed like an eternity.

There was no smirk when Hunter looked his way and nodded. "David, it is a pleasure to meet you at last."

Scout fell to his knees and bowed his head.

A strong pair of hands gripped him under his arms and lifted him up. Scout slowly raised his head. The smirk was there. "That's the first time you ever showed me any respect."

"Hunter?" Scout said, searching the familiar face of his friend.

"I'm going to get to fly," Hunter said.

"Please allow me to speak without interruptions. I have something important to say."

"Who are you talking too?" Scout said.

"He's talking to me."

"Who's talking to you?"

"I am," Hunter said.

"I'm confused."

"Join the crowd. We're all inside my head."

"Please, both of you," Hunter said.

Scout was afraid to speak. Hunter released him and stepped back. The wings rose above Hunter's shoulders and tapered down his back. This time, he gave him a normal smile.

"David, we are proud of the work you have done here. We know your faith was tested as it always will be. We are happy that you have chosen to believe."

"Who are we?" Scout asked.

Hunter's smile widened. Scout thought his friend glowed and realized who "We" must be, and his legs trembled.

"David, keep strong in your faith. Your flock will need that in the coming days and beyond."

"I will. I promise."

"Good," the angel said. "Now, I understand that you're the one to ask for rope."

"Rope?"

"Yes, rope. I need this creature bound for transport."

"Transport?"

"He wants you to tie this dude up so we can fly him somewhere for safe keeping," Hunter said, regaining his voice behind his smirk. "Go get some rope."

Scout ran to his room, thankful that it survived the fire. He gathered enough rope to tie up all four horsemen and ran right back down, his heart hammering in his chest the entire round trip.

Wings stretching behind him, Hunter held the tall creepy dude while Scout lashed his arms and legs together. Scout finished and stepped back. Hunter walked over to the girl, Barbie. Scout finally noticed Jimmy standing beside him.

"Pretty amazing," Jimmy said.

"If I woke up in my bed right now, I wouldn't be surprised," Scout said, staring at the wings on his best friend's back.

Jimmy nodded. "I don't ever want to sleep again."

Hunter hugged Barbie. Scout didn't understand the sadness involved, but why should that be any different. With a nod towards Jimmy and Scout, Hunter lifted the tied-up creepy dude and leaped into the air, beating his wings and creating a rush of wind. Scout heard Hunter cry, "Wahoo!"

Jimmy walked over and placed his arm around Barbie. Her eyes were a blurry mess and she buried her head in his chest. Scout waited for them to come over to him, figuring space was needed, if not required.

"What now?" he asked Jimmy.

"Now we rebuild and replant and prepare for winter. But first I'd like to go spend some time with my family."

Scout watched Jimmy leave with Barbie, helping her along the path back to the church. When they were gone, he looked up and down the empty stretch of Main Street. The thick smell of smoke mixed with the scent of the recent rain. Scout spun in a tight circle trying to figure out where he was needed and where he wanted to be. Everyone else was at God's house, creating the perfect opportunity for spiritual connection with his congregation. It was selfish, but Scout needed to be alone.

Back in his apartment, he found his sermon on the table and after a cursory glance he ripped out the notebook pages, crumpled up the message, and made a perfect three-point shot into the wastebasket.

Scout stared at the wall, waiting for something that wasn't coming as memories of Raven chased him around the room before he fell to his knees and buried his head in the couch cushions. He prayed, for a long time.

When night arrived like an ominous shade, Scout lit a candle, searched for hope, and then he wrote a different sermon.

42.

JIMMY

Jimmy's hand shook as he reached for the handle on the church door. The sun hung high overhead, drying the water from the land. He figured that's why he was sweating so much. It was either from the humidity or the thought of Ginger totally freaking out over his resurrection.

He tamped down his fear and opened the door. A ripple of excitement followed as he entered. Some who hadn't heard about his return gasped, and others calmed them as they dealt with the surprise.

Vanessa walked up and embraced him. "I don't believe it, but I'm glad it's true."

"Me too," Jimmy said, keeping his thoughts as still as an untroubled pond so he wouldn't be overwhelmed by his emotions.

Mark hugged him, and then a progression of Independents kids surrounded him, gripping his arm, reaching out to touch him and welcome him back.

Samuel stood from where he sat next to a sleeping Molly. He walked over and punched Jimmy a staggering blow to the shoulder. The crowd took a huge step back.

"That's for not taking me to Denver with you," Samuel said. Then he wrapped his arms around Jimmy and squeezed. "I'm never leaving your side again, unless you're going to the outhouse. Then you're on your own until you come out."

Jimmy patted Samuel on the back. "I missed you too."

They broke apart and Samuel returned to his seat next to Molly. Jimmy followed.

"Are Catherine and Molly okay?"

"She's called Margaret now," Samuel said. His face turned red as he regarded the sleeping Margaret. "I think so. They've been asleep since bringing you and Billy back from beyond."

"Bringing people back from the dead isn't easy," Barbie said from behind Jimmy. She knelt next to Catherine and felt the little girl's forehead. "They'll be okay after a while. I'll watch over them." She leaned against the wall and closed her eyes.

Jimmy nudged Samuel's foot. "The food storage building is gone. The fire wiped it out."

Samuel's eyes bugged out and his mouth dropped open. "That Famine dude really F'd us up for good."

Jimmy nodded, okay with Samuel using "F" as a word instead of saying the "F word." "Do you have seeds we can use to start crops?"

"Yeah, but I don't think there's enough time for anything to grow. We'll have to greenhouse everything and we'll need to build a bigger one. I might have another option that I've been looking into since you died. Only problem is the process requires a lot of electricity. It's called hydroponics and we could grow our vegetables indoors away from bug threats."

Jimmy frowned at Samuel. "Please tell me you're not growing weed in our basement."

Samuel squirmed and looked around, probably for eavesdroppers. He lowered his voice. "Man, I've been dealing with a lot of stuff, starting with the death of my best friend."

"You told me the same thing when you started making your homemade wine right after Greg died."

"Yeah, well. I'm a big boy now. I can make my own decisions."

Jimmy stared at Samuel and Samuel stared right back.

"Setting up a hydroponics system would be a good option if we can figure out the electricity. Maybe we can find some solar panels, wind turbines or something like that. We'll start with the greenhouse first."

"I guess we should get to work."

Jimmy scanned the crowded church of soon to be hungry kids, but Ginger and his son were missing. Vanessa caught his attention and pointed to a closed door. Jimmy nodded before turning back to Samuel. "I think we can take the rest of the day off. We'll start early tomorrow."

Samuel smiled. "Good luck."

Panic rose in Jimmy's chest. "Do I need it?"

The smile dropped. "You were dead, dude. That took some getting over. But she loves you. Go talk to her."

Samuel's pep talk didn't help. Tension and stress strung Jimmy's nerves tighter than a banjo string. One pluck and all the emotions he'd lost in death would play like a forgotten tune.

Barbie suddenly snored so loud that the blue and green stained glass window above her rattled. She opened her bleary eyes and wiped the drool off the corner of her mouth. "What?"

"Nothing," Jimmy and Samuel said in unison.

Barbie closed her eyes again.

Jimmy departed. Vanessa met him at the door and held him up. "Let me go inside and tell her you're here. She's still a little shook up."

Jimmy waited by the door while Vanessa went in to check if it would be okay for Ginger's resurrected boyfriend to visit. He leaned against the wall, trying to settle his shaky limbs.

The crowd in the church headed toward the exit. With the bad guy defeated, everyone appeared ready to get on with surviving. Jimmy's plans hinged on the reception he may or may not receive.

Vanessa returned and left the entrance open. "You can go on in. She's ready."

Jimmy hesitated.

Vanessa patted his arm. "It's going to be okay."

Jimmy stepped inside the bright room and found Ginger seated on a couch, holding their son. She was staring into the baby's round, sleeping face. He looked so peaceful that Jimmy believed Independents now had two angels. Jimmy moved silently toward the center of the room. He stood there waiting, unable to come up with anything intelligent to say.

"I've missed you," Ginger said, still not looking at him.

"I'm sorry I ran out on you. I couldn't let my brother die. I never wanted to leave you."

Ginger faced him, stopping Jimmy's heart with her beauty. "Don't do it again."

He spread his hands. "I won't if I can absolutely help it."

"Come hold your son."

Jimmy sat next to Ginger and took the sleeping baby in his arms. Little James was wrapped in a fuzzy blue blanket. He smelled like warm summer sunshine, and Jimmy kissed him on the forehead.

Ginger placed her hand on his cheek and kissed the other. It was hard to keep his tears from spilling over her hand and lips, so Jimmy didn't even try.

43.

MARGARET

Long evening shadows filled the church when Margaret finally awoke. Samuel sat next to her on the floor. They were the only two there. She wiped sleep from her eyes and smiled at him.

"Is everything okay?"

Samuel stretched in the grip of a giant yawn. "You missed a whole day of excitement."

Margaret sat up and joined him in a stretch. Her thoughts were still hazy from exhaustion after healing Billy and retuning his spirit. Catherine was nowhere around. She probably recovered a lot quicker. From her past lives, Margaret knew her body would adjust to the healing process with repetition.

"The fire burned down the food storage building and everything inside that the Britts had managed to can for the winter. If you're hungry, we should probably get over to Brittany's before all the food is gone. Those Cozad kids are starving."

"Were any of the other buildings damaged from the fire?"

"No, we got lucky there. I'm told that Barbie brought down a monsoon. The fire didn't have a chance."

"I remember that. I was in the middle of things with Billy. Is he okay?"

Samuel sat next to her. "He's shook up about Preston, but other than that he's alive and back in control of himself."

Margaret folded her hands in her lap. She hadn't even thought about Preston and how that might affect Billy. Even though she knew who she was now, she also remembered who Molly had been to this community and how much she was helping kids deal with life. Margaret would have to continue that mission, starting with Billy.

"How are you doing?" Samuel asked.

Margaret tilted her head and gave the question some proper reflection before answering.

Samuel must have gotten nervous. "Margaret?"

"I'm okay."

"Just okay?"

"Just okay. I have a lot to figure out and haven't really had the chance to do that. Now that everything is over, for a while..."

They sat silently. Margaret knew she and Samuel had been forming some type of closeness. She hadn't realized how close their relationship had become until now. She felt comfortable in his presence. It was very unlike the tumultuous feelings she had in Hunter's presence earlier.

"Where is Hunter?"

The atmosphere around them changed as Samuel shifted side to side. "He, or rather the angel, took that Famine dude somewhere safe. That's what Jimmy told me. I guess they flew off west. They didn't say when they'd be back."

Margaret nodded, unsure of what to do next, until her stomach rumbled. "Well, maybe we should go eat something. You haven't been here with me the whole time, have you? You must be hungry."

"I'm okay. Mark didn't want you to be alone when you woke up."

"Mark likes to worry."

"He and Jimmy have that in common."

"What about you?"

Samuel turned his head and she looked into his eyes. They were a soft brown with that mischievous sparkle he now tried to hide without success.

"Were you worried about me?"

Samuel played it off with a laugh. "No, I knew you'd be okay."

Margaret stood and took his hand, pulling him off the floor. "Let's go eat. On the way you can try to convince me that I'm okay."

* * *

Dinner ended and Margaret escaped the crowd to be alone in the still night air. The steady beat of wings sounded in the distance and grew louder until she watched Hunter settle smoothly on the ground. He fell to his knees, moaning in pain as the wings on his back disappeared. When the process finished, he was left lying there, panting.

Margaret stepped quickly to him. "Are you all right?"

Pain registered in his eyes. "I think I'm going to live." He accepted her hand and stood on wobbly legs. "That was a lot of flying."

"Where did you go?"

"We flew all the way to the mountains and dumped Tommy in a cave. Then Michael brought the entrance down. He said it was best that way because if Tommy died, then that horseman would just find somebody else. At least Tommy wanted what happened to him."

"How do you know that?"

Hunter shrugged. "I don't. It's just easier to think that, I guess."

Margaret made no move to hug Hunter like she would have done by now if she was her old self. For some reason it just didn't feel right anymore. She loved Hunter, she just wasn't in love with Hunter. She couldn't shake the feeling that their relationship was about something else. These were the lies she'd been telling herself through dinner in preparation for this moment.

Hunter smiled at her, his white teeth reflecting the moonlight. He had all his teeth again.

"What?" she asked him.

"If you thought a little louder I would probably be able to hear you."

"Hunter, I'm a different person."

He nodded. "It's okay. I am too. This has been the craziest two days of my life. I flew to the mountains on a pair of wings that grew out of my back."

"That is pretty crazy," Margaret said. "Yesterday I found out that I've been alive for seventeen years without knowing who I was before."

"So when you say you're a different person, you really mean it?"

Margaret sighed. "I'm still Molly, but I'm also a reincarnated saint who's lived several different lifetimes and has just woken up to discover that I haven't been in control."

"And that's bad?"

"No, it's just different."

This was not going exactly like she had planned or thought she wanted. Everything confused her now, yet everything had cleared like morning fog when the sunshine broke. Only the sun had faded an hour ago and nighttime was going to be here for a while. Margaret wanted to make the changes in the dark. That way it might be less painful, she hoped.

"I saw the way you looked at her," Margaret said.

"Barbie? I don't think that's my fault. She and the angel had a thing."

"Yes, I knew about that. What do you mean had?"

"She broke up with him before we left. I have no idea why. He didn't feel like talking about it on the trip. I promise, Molly, I didn't do anything with her."

"My name's Margaret now."

He didn't respond.

"I love you, Hunter."

"But it's different."

"Yes."

"Okay, I understand."

"Do you?"

"I think I do," he said. "Did you want the apartment? It was yours."

"No, you can keep it. I owe you since I burned your house down. That way you and Scout can still be neighbors."

"Fantastic."

Margaret wanted to leave. The Molly side of her was already crying and Margaret didn't know if she could keep herself together much longer. She'd committed herself to go this far. She couldn't go back and do this to either of them again.

"I'm going to go talk to Jimmy."

Margaret was glad for the change of topic, if only to delay the upcoming heartache. She felt it before as Molly. She recognized the warning signs: the shortness of breath, the building of tears, and the terrible feeling of a definite ending.

"You should. He seemed really happy at dinner. They left early and went back to Ginger's house."

"What will you do?"

"I'll go pack a few things from the apartment. Then I'll stay at Mark's tonight until I get settled somewhere."

That did it. She had to go. She gripped his arm as she passed and continued walking as the tears flowed down her face. She became a full blown, sobbing mess by the time she reached their apartment. Margaret closed the door behind her, thankful that Hunter hadn't followed.

After a while she reigned in her crying enough to pack a small bag. She rinsed away the sadness from her face and was preparing to leave when she spotted one other item and grabbed it.

The walk to the edge of town was familiar. He sat on the porch, staring into the darkness when she arrived. His smile was hesitant but brightened as she approached. Margaret sat next to Samuel on the steps and returned his shirt.

44.

HUNTER

Nighttime felt strangely disturbed. Exhaustion from the past two days caught up to Hunter like the gust of wind that whipped through town and brushed its hot breath in his face. He was alone again, the way he liked it.

He walked through the empty streets, past the houses where candlelight flickered. Hunter knew the candles would burn late tonight. It had been one of those days where some extra light provided safety to those who were afraid of the dark. However the dark wasn't the only time that badness happened. The kids of Independents found out that terrible things could walk right down the middle of Main Street on a sunny day.

Hunter rolled his shoulder and worked his arm in a circle. The ache returned, but now he knew why it was there thanks to his angelic hitchhiker. Nothing like having an angel on your shoulder. The pain served as a reminder to always try and be good, and to balance out the bad. That's what the angel had told him on their long flight to the mountains and back. Funny, Hunter never would have guessed that an angel would have a sense of humor.

He stopped on the street when he reached Ginger's house. Jimmy was inside with his family—probably happy.

Hunter thought about Molly and experienced another type of ache. She had become his family, or at least the hope for the future. Now that was gone, again.

Hunter let her go. He had too. He knew things had changed

between them. They'd changed, and it was better this way. End it quick and move on.

He stepped halfway up the walkway and stopped. He couldn't see his brother just yet. Too much stuff roiled inside of him. Let Jimmy enjoy his homecoming.

The front door opened and light from a lantern inside flooded into the yard, washing over Hunter. Jimmy filled the frame. He closed the door, which swallowed the light and left them in the dark together.

Jimmy's tall, lean body looked unscathed for having been underground in a wooden box. He worked fresh creases into the bill of his baseball cap before slapping it on.

"Hey, Jimmy."

Jimmy almost jumped out of his boots. "Hunter! Are you trying to kill me?"

Hunter didn't know how to answer that. A streak of guilt wormed inside his guts. "I never meant to kill you."

Jimmy left the porch. He stopped a couple of feet short and stuck his hands inside his jean pockets. "I didn't mean it like that. And you didn't kill me. Everything that happened back in Denver happened for a reason."

"I don't believe that."

"Why not? Look at all the things that came from that day. Look at yourself and the amazing thing that happened to you."

"What? I've been invaded by someone that doesn't help out when I'm getting my ass handed to me. I just heal up and keep taking it." Hunter shifted his feet and shoved his own hands into his pockets.

Jimmy stared at him with unwelcomed scrutiny. "What happened?"

Hunter's body convulsed and he stumbled away, not wanting to talk about anything with anyone. This was his mess—his life. Hunter was always alone. He accepted that long ago when his parents died, regardless of how much Jimmy had been there to help him through it. The greatest thing that ever happened was when Hunter rode his motorbike out of Independents for the first time. He was free in that moment to do whatever. He didn't have to return. Not really. Not if he didn't want to.

Jimmy grabbed his arm before he stepped into the street. "What happened?"

"You left me!" Hunter said. "Just like Mom and Dad." He couldn't stop the pain from ripping out of him. "I was the one who was supposed to leave, but instead you took that from me. I'm afraid."

Jimmy dropped hold of Hunter's arm, but he remained close. "Afraid of what?"

It was a simple question. What was it? Hunter had been trying to figure this question out for so long. He was not scared of anything. Scared meant you ran. Hunter never ran. He would never back down.

But he was afraid, and that was something totally different. Being afraid meant you didn't want to face something intangible.

"I'm afraid of being home."

Jimmy's silence was loud.

Another brush of hot air ran over them, prompting Hunter to continue. "I can't be the only one left when this is over. I can't come back here and find everyone gone. But I can't stay and do nothing. I have to take this fight away from here."

"Where is all this coming from?" Jimmy asked.

"Damn it, Jimmy, don't you see? I'm the reason all this is happening here in Independents. It's like you said, these things happen for a reason, but I'm the one that it's all circling around. I find Catherine, Molly, and now Barbie. I die and when I come back I have this archangel inside of me. Maybe if I leave, then the rest of you will be saved."

"But this is your home," Jimmy said.

"And that's why I have to leave."

"Leave?"

"I can't allow this to follow me home anymore."

"Look, you're putting too much on yourself. We need you, Hunter. Regardless of what you think, this is happening to all of us, not just you and not because of you. This is happening for bigger reasons that don't have anything to do with us. We just have to survive. We're all in this mess together. You going away would not change that."

Hunter nodded, but inside he knew he was right. He saw it with a clarity that shocked him. If he left, Independents would be saved. He'd never convince Jimmy. He didn't have to.

"Hunter?"

"You're right." He sighed, trying to release some of the tension, but he already felt most of it slip away. If he was wrong about this, wouldn't the angel inside tell him? "I'm just a little upset right now. Molly and I broke up."

"When did this happen?"

"About fifteen minutes ago."

"Why?"

Hunter shrugged and told the truth. "Because of all the changes."

Jimmy rested his hand on his brother's shoulder. It made Hunter feel like the younger brother again. "Why don't you come inside? We have room."

"No, I'm ready for a good night sleep in my own bed. Molly said I could have the apartment. I've actually been thinking about my bed for the past couple days."

Jimmy smiled at him. "See, it's not so bad being home."

Hunter rubbed the back of his neck. Being in his bed and being home were two very different things to him. His bed would be a relief for his many aches and pains. The loss of a true home would never heal properly.

Jimmy pulled Hunter close and hugged him fiercely.

Hunter returned the love with just as much strength. "I'm glad you're back alive."

"I'm glad you're here with me."

*   *   *

Hunter slowly climbed the top step to his apartment. His whole body felt trashed. Someone stepped out of the shadows and Hunter thought Molly had a change of heart. Maybe she wanted to forget about all that breaking up mess.

Barbie moved into the moonlight. "I was starting to worry."

Hunter smiled. "Oh yeah? What about?"

"I didn't think you were coming back."

Hunter tilted his head, trying to read her face in the dark to see if she had guessed. But then he thought she meant something else. "Are you talking about me or him?"

She closed the small distance between the front door and the top step. Barbie looped her arms around his neck and leaned close to his ear. "I wanted to see you, Hunter."

Hunter circled his arms around her and held her close. It felt right this time. He opened the door and followed her inside.

A candle was lit on the coffee table, sending a soft glow throughout the room. Catherine sat on the couch in her pink pajamas holding a teddy bear.

"Where have you two been?"

"I had to drop Tommy somewhere safe," Hunter said. "What

are you doing in here?"

"I wanted to let Jimmy be with his family tonight. I think tomorrow Barbie, Margaret and I should find a house to live in. What do you think, Barbie?"

"I..." Barbie began to say and looked at Hunter and then at Catherine, who was busy fussing with her teddy bear's fur. "You're right. That would probably be best."

"Great," Catherine said and stretched into a giant yawn. "We're going to steal your bed tonight if that's okay, Hunter? You don't mind sleeping on the couch, do you?"

He stared at the couch as the girls left him there for the comfort of his bed. He turned in time to see Barbie closing the door, staring at him with a blank expression. Then she was gone and Hunter was alone in the night, wiped out from his trip to Cozad and his flight to the mountains. He sat down on the couch and waited for morning. When sleep finally came, he passed into it thankfully, and once again found his parents living in his dreams.

45.

SCOUT

The next day Scout sat with his knees bouncing, reading over his sermon again, making sure it sounded right. The congregation shuffled into the pews while Vanessa powered through old hymns on the church piano that desperately needed tuning. There were more kids filing in than Scout had ever seen on a Sunday morning, plus with the addition of Cozad, every row was packed full. The stained glass windows were open and a breeze drifted from one side of the building to the other, flapping pages in the open hymnals. Sweat moistened the collar of Scout's white button-up shirt, which he absently swiped a finger around. After scriptures and singing, Scout stood at the pulpit.

"I believe in God. I can't tell you why exactly. Maybe it's because my parents taught me to. Maybe that's good enough. It's comforting to know that one of the things my parents taught me before they died was to believe in God.

"You may not believe like I do, and that's okay. You woke up this morning and came to church looking for answers. It starts with questions. I'm still searching for answers just like you.

"I put my faith in God. Everything we are going through will be so much easier if we all put our faith in Him.

"Why?

"Because I believe it will. I believe in God.

"Belief isn't easy. It's so much easier to not believe, to give up and let the Big Bad roll right over you. But I believe in God, and that means I put my faith in front of my fear. My faith shields me from all the fears that would swallow me whole without my belief in Him.

"Every chance we've ever taken is because we believe that the outcome will be something good. When our parents died from the plague, why did we leave our homes and follow the road that eventually led us here? It was belief that something better waited for us if we had the courage to go out and find it.

"That's what faith is. Faith is courage.

"God is waiting for us to ask for His help. He has seen to our needs every time, even when we didn't know what those needs were. So now we have a big need. A long winter lies before us without our normal food supply. We will ask for God's help and, with His blessing, we will survive like we have since the plague took our parents.

"Will bad things continue to happen?

"Yes.

"Why?

"Because that is the nature of the world, the nature of being human. That is the price we must pay to earn our place by God's side in Heaven.

"You might say that's not fair. Why us? Why can't He just give us what we need? Why does it all have to be so hard?

"Life has to be, because he gave us something special when he gave us life. We were given the freedom to choose between what's right and what's wrong. Everyone has that choice and it makes us stronger. It will make us worthy when the time comes to stand in God's presence and say I did the best I could.

"That's what I believe. I don't pretend to know all the answers. I believe in God and I'm asking you to have faith with me. Have faith in God.

"I believe that God also has a plan for each of us. I know he has one for me. I don't know what it is, but I know He's working in me so I can become something better than I am. He does that with all of us. It's our choice to follow the path He's laying out for us. I know the path is hard, but with God's help, with His blessing and His guidance, we can survive anything. He will help us through the dark times when we feel all alone.

"God's first action was to bring light into the world. God is the light. He is the shining candle in the pitch black that holds every one of our futures.

"There was a time I doubted God's plan. It wasn't that long ago either. I doubted His existence because we were living in a dark place. Our parents were dead and everyone else was dying. I asked myself how God could allow this to happen, and when no one responded, the doubt crept in and the world became darker. I couldn't see His light for a very long time.

"And then I met a little girl. She brought light back into the darkness, shining bright with God's light, bringing his healing power to my friend, Hunter. Not once, but twice she healed him. And in those moments I realized that God's light had been shining the whole time. I was just too blind to see. I was too busy following my own plan, wanting things back the way they were before, instead of realizing that God had been there protecting me, giving me strength through my sister, guiding us through dark times across the Big Bad, to deliver us safely into Independents.

"So what does God have planned for you? I don't know. I think life is about finding the path that God has laid out for you from the moment you were born to the moment you die. Sometimes we go off course, and sometimes things happen or don't go the way we plan. That's when we need to stop, look and listen for God's plan to come to us.

"That's what I believe.

"I don't know what you believe. I'm just glad you're here. I hope my words will shine a light for you to find God's path. I hope you're looking. God has a plan for you."

*   *   *

Everyone filed past Scout into the sunshine. Some shook his hand, and some even met his eyes as they did. Not everyone had heard his message, and that was okay. They had come for one reason or another, but at least they had come.

Too bad Raven had left before hearing the sermon. Scout thought she would have liked it, but she was off following her own plan. Whether that was God's intention, Scout didn't know. He missed her and he wasn't going to question her leaving, at least not with God. Time, a lot of it, was needed to shed the hurt of her absence.

The Brittanys served lunch outside, setting up the tables on the brick cobbles in the middle of Main Street after passing them through the empty window frames. They covered the tables with an array of colorful tablecloths. Vibrant bolts of fabric were rolled out and hung from the buildings. These crossed the street and provided cool shade under the August sun.

They served the food hot, buffet style, and Scout was amazed at the fare. Dylan had brought Chef Brittany hams from the smokehouse that Famine had not destroyed. Jimmy and Samuel had spent the morning before church digging in the fields for potatoes and carrots and beets that lay beneath the ground, protected from the grasshopper onslaught. Everyone loaded up a full plate and found a chair.

They asked Scout to give thanks and bless the food. Scout knew the kids of Independents had already been blessed, making the thankful part important.

Scout ate with Hunter, planning a trip into the Big Bad to start bringing back items desperately needed by the town. They talked about where they had seen the things they needed. They would search for livestock, mainly chickens and hogs, to replace the ones that were lost. They would look everywhere for things to eat, and then they would look everywhere again.

Jimmy walked up with little James asleep in his arms. Fatherhood suited Jimmy, but the whole town saw their leader as Dad anyways. Hunter smiled and pulled the tiny blanket back for a better peek at his sleeping nephew.

"You guys are heading out tomorrow." It wasn't a question. Jimmy knew the best thing for the town was to get Hunter and Scout out into the Big Bad as soon as possible, looking for stuff to bring home. "If you're done eating, I want you guys to go meet Mark at that farmhouse where you found the baby furniture and sewing supplies last year."

"Why?" Scout asked.

"He's going to give you guns and you're going to learn how to shoot and how to care for them. I don't want you in the Big Bad unprotected anymore. When you get back from your trip, I want you to help Mark teach the rest of us what you've learned. We have to prepare."

Hunter and Scout nodded.

Jimmy looked down at his sleeping baby boy. "War is coming."

EPILOGUE

MARGARET

Margaret was awoken in the predawn light by a rough shake to her shoulder. She rolled over, focusing on the golden haired intruder. "What?"

"We have to go. It's time."

Margaret threw off the covers and grabbed her pants from the chair as the little girl stood by the bedroom door, tapping her foot. She drew her belt tight, finding the need to poke another notch, or find a smaller belt later. Using the mirror, she brushed her hair quickly and saw Catherine throw up her hands before leaving the bedroom.

Margaret's stomach rumbled complaints about the meager dinner from the night before at Brittany's. It happened frequently, and her stomach was not the only one complaining around Independents these days. She slipped on her snow boots, coat, gloves and stocking hat without any real eagerness to travel out into the cold. She found Catherine already by the front door, turning the knob as soon as Margaret entered the living room.

"Good. Let's roll out."

They left the house, hurrying over the compacted snow that had refused to thaw over the past month. Margaret followed along, noticing Catherine's snow boots and wondering if the grass stains on her feet would survive the winter. A cold wind tore its way through her as they rounded onto Main Street, forcing her to pull the coat tightly around her body.

Candles were already lit inside Brittany's and she saw Jimmy sitting in his usual spot. She scanned the interior for signs of Samuel, and then chastised herself after the letdown of not seeing him. It was bad enough that Molly filled her every thought with desires for Hunter. Samuel complicated matters, and Margaret wasn't prepared to handle the emotions that arose with issues of the heart.

"Quit stalling. We're on a tight schedule," Catherine called from the stairs that led up to the apartment where Molly used to live with Hunter.

Margaret stopped dead in the middle of Main Street. Going into that place held the same appeal as walking through the fires of hell. "Wait, what are we doing?"

Catherine's eyebrows pinched together in annoyance. "We're going to make contact with Raven. We need Michael's help, just like the last time in France." She placed her hands on her hips. "I thought we discussed all this before we went to bed. She's getting close to my tree."

Catherine turned and vanished up the stairs. Apparently the discussion was over.

Margaret followed, but she wasn't very enthusiastic about the climb. Each step brought her closer to the one person she'd been avoiding for the past three months since he returned from Cozad and she had been changed from the girl who loved him into Margaret. She walked through the door and froze.

Hunter stood in the middle of their apartment, his brown wings folded against his back, his white t-shirt stretched tight across his chest. He wore blue jeans and bare feet, but this person was not her ex-boyfriend. Michael gave her his heavenly smile and Margaret felt the ache deep inside where Molly stirred.

"Hello, Sister Margaret," he said. "He thinks of you all the time."

Margaret frowned at him. "You mean Molly."

"Is there a difference?"

Margaret's frown deepened. "Is there a difference between you and Hunter?" Even his name on her lips brought raw emotions laced with memories. She took a deep breath. "We're not here to talk about this."

"No we're not," said Catherine, holding their hands. "She's almost there. It's time, Michael."

"Yes, Catherine." Michael offered Margaret his other hand to complete the circle.

She stared at the familiar palm like it was a live hand grenade. After closing her eyes, she held hands with the angel, telling herself over and over, *it's not Hunter.*

She opened her eyes to golden flames signifying God's presence. Michael led them from the holy fire engulfing Catherine's tree that burned without causing physical harm. The red motorbike rolled to a stop at the same moment, with the fiery sunrise breaking the horizon behind the familiar rider.

Raven's eyes widened with surprise. Margaret considered the angel and his wings, unable to fathom what Raven must be thinking. It wasn't everyday three of your friends popped out of a burning tree to say hello.

"Hi, Joan," Catherine said, skipping over and giving the stunned girl a crushing hug.

Raven slipped an arm through the embrace and gasped for air. "Did you just call me...?"

Catherine took her hand. "Joan, we need you to join us now."

Golden light filled their grip as Catherine called upon God's grace, spreading slowly outwards until both were encompassed in the Lord's holiness. Raven's knees shook and then Michael was there, lending support so she wouldn't fall.

Margaret really didn't know why she had been invited. They needed Michael to bring them here, and Catherine called forth Raven's reincarnation, or rather Joan's, like she had for Molly.

Margaret shook her head in agitation. She meant Margaret. *There is no more Molly*, she tried convincing herself. She looked at Michael holding Raven, sorting through memories of times spent in those arms.

The process of bringing forth Raven's reincarnated persona finished with nothing more spectacular than a slow dousing of the light. Raven lost complete consciousness and Michael lifted her slack body gently into his arms.

Catherine caressed the sleeping girl's cheek. "She's ready now, Michael. Do you have a place picked out?"

"I do, Sister Catherine. Hunter knows of a sound location that will suit our purpose. I shall return swiftly to give you passage back to Independents."

"What about her stuff?" Margaret asked.

"She will not need those items. God shall provide for her."

"Yes, but what if Scout comes out here and finds her stuff lying around all over the place and no Raven? It might not help the transition."

"Who's transition," Catherine asked. "Raven's?"

"No, Scout's. I take it Joan will be returning to Independents to help fight War?"

"That's right. We talked about all this right before bed last night."

"Yes, I know, Catherine, but as usual you left a lot of blanks in the processing of your plan. When Michael returns, he can take Raven's motorbike and gear to her. We can wait."

Catherine folded her arms, giving Margaret all the grumpy she could squeeze together.

Margaret held her ground. Now she understood why she was needed. If they were going to tear these kids apart for the sake of this War, then Margaret would make sure that all those affected received the proper attention. Molly would have wanted that.

Michael sat on the red motorbike with Raven cradled in his lap, her gear strapped to the back of her seat. He gripped the handlebars. "I shall hurry." And the angel climbed into the air with a beat of his mighty wings, Raven and her bike safely in his charge.

Margaret watched him fly away in the western sky until he was a dot in a field of blue.

The holy fire in the tree died with his absence. Catherine stepped over to her friend, resting her cheek on the bark. She sighed like the whole world was crushing down on her. "Hello, tree. I missed you."

ABOUT THE AUTHOR

Ted Hill grew up in the front pew of the Methodist church in Denton, Texas where he honed his scribbling skills on the church bulletin. He peaked as a senior in high school when he became Class President, Homecoming King, All-District Offensive Tackle, and Class Clown. He also failed Spanish II and Geometry, but graduated because of football credits.

Ted then took his talents to Bethany College in the middle of Kansas where he fell in love with the heartland.

14
BY PETER CLINES

Padlocked doors. Strange light fixtures. Mutant cockroaches. There are some odd things about Nate's new apartment. Every room in this old brownstone has a mystery. Mysteries that stretch back over a hundred years. Some of them are in plain sight. Some are behind locked doors. And all together these mysteries could mean the end of Nate and his friends. Or the end of everything...

"A riveting apocalyptic mystery in the style of LOST."
—Craig DiLouie, author of The Infection

PETER CLINES

PERMUTEDPRESS.COM

DAY BY DAY ARMAGEDDON
GREY FOX
BY J.L. BOURNE

Time is a very fluid thing, no one really has a grasp on it other than maybe how to measure it. As the maestro of the Day by Day Armageddon Universe, I have the latitude of being in control of that time. You have again stumbled upon a ticket with service through the apocalyptic wastes, but this time the train is a little bit older, a little more beat up, and maybe a little wiser.

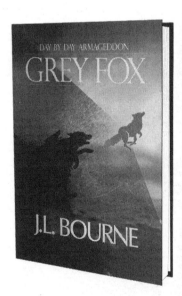

DAY BY DAY ARMAGEDDON
GREY FOX
J.L. BOURNE

DEAD TIDE
BY STEPHEN A. NORTH

THE WORLD IS ENDING. BUT THERE ARE SURVIVORS. Nick Talaski is a hard-bitten, angry cop. Graham is a newly divorced cab driver. Bronte is a Gulf War veteran hunting his brother's killer. Janicea is a woman consumed by unflinching hate. Trish is a gentleman's club dancer. Morgan is a morgue janitor. The dead have risen and the citizens of St. Petersburg and Pinellas Park are trapped. The survivors are scattered, and options are few. And not all monsters are created by a bite. Some still have a mind of their own...

DEAD TIDE RISING
BY STEPHEN A. NORTH

The sequel to Dead Tide continues the carnage in Pinellas Park near St. Pete, Florida. Follow all of the characters from the first book, Dead Tide, as they fight for survival in a world destroyed by the zombie apocalypse.

BREW
BY BILL BRADDOCK

Ever been to a big college town on a football Saturday night? Loud drunks glut the streets, swaggering about in roaring, leering, laughing packs, like sailors on shore leave. These nights crackle with a dark energy born of incongruity; for beneath all that smiling and singing sprawls a bedrock of malice.

PERMUTEDPRESS.COM

TANKBREAD
BY PAUL MANNERING

Ten years ago humanity lost the war for survival. Now intelligent zombies rule the world. Feeding the undead of a steady diet of cloned people called Tankbread, the survivors live in a dangerous world on the brink of final extinction.

THE ROAD TO NOWHERE
BY BILL BRADDOCK

Welcome to the city of Las Vegas. Gone are the days of tourist filled streets. After waking up alone in a hospital bed, everyone seems to have fled, leaving me behind. Survival becomes my only driving force. Nothing was as it should have been. Things seemed to lurk in the buildings and darkest shadows. I didn't know what they were, but I could always feel their eyes on me.

PERMUTEDPRESS.COM

ZOMBIE ATTACK: RISE OF THE HORDE
BY DEVAN SAGLIANI

Voted best Zombie/ Horror E-books of 2012 on Goodreads. When 16 year old Xander's older brother Moto left him at Vandenberg Airforce Base he only had one request - don't leave no matter what. But there was no way he could have known that one day zombies would gather into groups big enough to knock down walls and take out entire buildings full of people. That was before the rise of the horde!

THE INFECTION
BY CRAIG DiLOUIE

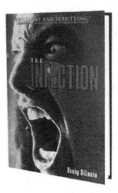

The world is rocked as one in five people collapse screaming before falling into a coma. Three days later, the Infected awake with a single purpose: spread the Infection. A small group—a cop, teacher, student, reverend—team up with a military crew to survive. But at a refugee camp what's left of the government will ask them to accept a dangerous mission back into the very heart of Infection.

PERMUTEDPRESS.COM

THE KILLING FLOOR
BY CRAIG DiLOUIE

The mystery virus struck down millions. Three days later, its victims awoke with a single violent purpose: spread the Infection. Ray Young, survivor of a fight to save a refugee camp from hordes of Infected, awakes from a coma to learn he has also survived Infection. Ray is not immune. Instead, he has been transformed into a superweapon that could end the world … or save it.

PERMUTEDPRESS.COM

THE INFECTION BOX SET
BY CRAIG DiLOUIE

Two full #1 bestselling apocalyptic thrillers for one low price! Includes the full novels THE INFECTION and THE KILLING FLOOR. A mysterious virus suddenly strikes down millions. Three days later, its victims awake with a single purpose: spread the Infection. As the world lurches toward the apocalypse, some of the Infected continue to change, transforming into horrific monsters.

THE BECOMING
BY JESSICA MEIGS

The Michaluk Virus has escaped the CDC, and its effects are widespread and devastating. Most of the population of the southeastern United States have become homicidal cannibals. As society rapidly crumbles under the hordes of infected, three people--Ethan, a Memphis police officer; Cade, his best friend; and Brandt, a lieutenant in the US Marines--band together against the oncoming crush of death.

―――――― PERMUTEDPRESS.COM ――――――

THE BECOMING:
GROUND ZERO (BOOK 2)
BY JESSICA MEIGS

After the Michaluk Virus decimated the southeast, Ethan and his companions became like family. But the arrival of a mysterious woman forces them to flee from the infected, and the cohesion the group cultivated is shattered. As members of the group succumb to the escalating dangers on their path, new alliances form, new loves develop, and old friendships crumble.

―――――― PERMUTEDPRESS.COM ――――――

THE BECOMING:
REVELATIONS (BOOK 3)
BY JESSICA MEIGS

In a world ruled by the dead, Brandt Evans is floundering. Leadership of their dysfunctional group wasn't something he asked for or wanted. Their problems are numerous: Remy Angellette is grief-stricken and suicidal, Gray Carter is distant and reclusive, and Cade Alton is near death. And things only get worse.

DOMAIN OF THE DEAD
BY IAIN MCKINNON

The world is dead, devoured by a plague of reanimated corpses. Barricaded inside a warehouse with dwindling food, a group of survivors faces two possible deaths: creeping starvation, or the undead outside. In their darkest hour hope appears in the form of a helicopter approaching the city... but is it the salvation the survivors have been waiting for?

PERMUTEDPRESS.COM

REMAINS OF THE DEAD
BY IAIN MCKINNON

The world is dead. Cahz and his squad of veteran soldiers are tasked with flying into abandoned cities and retrieving zombies for scientific study. Then the unbelievable happens. After years of encountering nothing but the undead, the team discovers a handful of survivors in a fortified warehouse with dwindling supplies.

PERMUTEDPRESS.COM

DEMISE OF THE LIVING
BY IAIN MCKINNON

The world is infected. The dead are reanimating and attacking the living. In a city being overrun with zombies a disparate group of strangers seek sanctuary in an office block. But for how long can the barricades hold back the undead? How long will the food last? How long before those who were bitten succumb turn? And how long before they realise the dead outside are the least of their fears?

ROADS LESS TRAVELED: THE PLAN
BY C. DULANEY

Ask yourself this: If the dead rise tomorrow, are you ready? Do you have a plan? Kasey, a strong-willed loner, has something she calls The Zombie Plan. But every plan has its weaknesses, and a freight train of tragedy is bearing down on Kasey and her friends. In the darkness that follows, Kasey's Plan slowly unravels: friends lost, family taken, their stronghold reduced to ashes.

————— PERMUTEDPRESS.COM —————

MURPHY'S LAW
(ROADS LESS TRAVELED BOOK 2)
BY C. DULANEY

Kasey and the gang were held together by a set of rules, their Zombie Plan. It kept them alive through the beginning of the End. But when the chaos faded, they became careless, and Murphy's Law decided to pay a long-overdue visit. Now the group is broken and scattered with no refuge in sight. Those remaining must make their way across West Virginia in search of those who were stolen from them.

————— PERMUTEDPRESS.COM —————

SHADES OF GRAY
(ROADS LESS TRAVELED BOOK 3)
BY C. DULANEY

Kasey and the gang have come full circle through the crumbling world. Working for the National Guard, they realize old friends and fellow survivors are disappearing. When the missing start to reappear as walking corpses, the group sets out on another journey to discover the truth. Their answers wait in the West Virginia Command Center.

PAVLOV'S DOGS
BY D.L. SNELL & THOM BRANNAN

WEREWOLVES Dr. Crispin has engineered the saviors of mankind: soldiers capable of transforming into beasts. ZOMBIES Ken and Jorge get caught in a traffic jam on their way home from work. It's the first sign of a major outbreak. ARMAGEDDON Should Dr. Crisping send the Dogs out into the zombie apocalypse to rescue survivors? Or should they hoard their resources and post the Dogs as island guards?

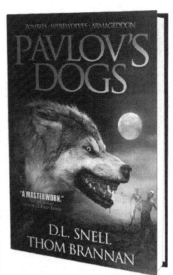

THE OMEGA DOG
BY D.L. SNELL & THOM BRANNAN

Twisting and turning through hordes of zombies, cartel territory, Mayan ruins, and the things that now inhabit them, a group of survivors must travel to save one man's family from a nightmarish third world gone to hell. But this time, even best friends have deadly secrets, and even allies can't be trusted - as a father's only hope of getting his kids out alive is the very thing that's hunting him down.

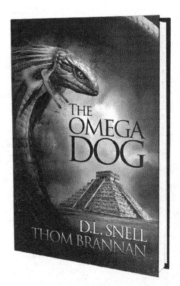

DEAD LIVING
BY GLENN BULLION

It didn't take long for the world to die. And it didn't take long, either, for the dead to rise. Aaron was born on the day the world ended. Kept in seclusion, his family teaches him the basics. How to read and write. How to survive. Then Aaron makes a shocking discovery. The undead, who desire nothing but flesh, ignore him. It's as if he's invisible to them.

PERMUTEDPRESS.COM

AUTOBIOGRAPHY of a WEREWOLF HUNTER
BY BRIAN P. EASTON

After his mother is butchered by a werewolf, Sylvester James is taken in by a Cheyenne mystic. The boy trains to be a werewolf hunter, learning to block out pain, stalk, fight, and kill. As Sylvester sacrifices himself to the hunt, his hatred has become a monster all its own. As he follows his vendetta into the outlands of the occult, he learns it takes more than silver bullets to kill a werewolf.

PALE GODS
BY KIM PAFFENROTH

In a world where the undead rule the continents and the few remaining survivors inhabit only island outposts, six men make the dangerous journey to the mainland to hunt for supplies amid the ruins. But on this trip, the dead act stranger and smarter than ever before and the living must adjust or die.

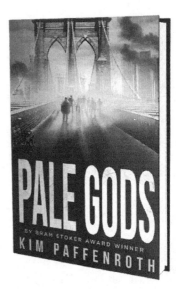

PERMUTEDPRESS.COM

THE JUNKIE QUATRAIN
BY PETER CLINES

Six months ago, the world ended. The Baugh Contagion swept across the planet. Its victims were left twitching, adrenalized cannibals that quickly became know as Junkies. THE JUNKIE QUATRAIN is four tales of survival, and four types of post-apocalypse story. Because the end of the world means different things for different people. Loss. Opportunity. Hope. Or maybe just another day on the job.

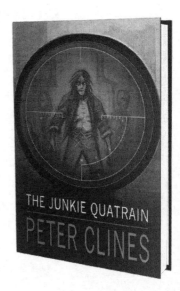

BLOOD SOAKED & CONTAGIOUS
BY JAMES CRAWFORD

I am not going to complain to you about my life.

We've got zombies. They are not the brainless, rotting creatures we'd been led to expect. Unfortunately for us, they're just as smart as they were before they died, very fast, much stronger than you or me, and possess no internal editor at all.

Claws. Did I mention claws?

PERMUTEDPRESS.COM

BLOOD SOAKED & INVADED
BY JAMES CRAWFORD

Zombies were bad enough, but now we're being invaded from all sides. Up to our necks in blood, body parts, and unanswerable questions...

...As soon as the realization hit me, I lost my cool. I curled into the fetal position in a pile of blood, offal, and body parts, and froze there. What in the Hell was I becoming that killing was entertaining and satisfying?

THE KING OF CLAYFIELD
BY SHANE GREGORY

On a cold February day in the small town of Clayfield, Kentucky, an unsuspecting and unprepared museum director he finds himself in the middle of hell on Earth. A pandemic is spreading around the globe, and it's turning most of the residents of Clayfield into murderous zombies. Having no safe haven to which he can flee, the director decides to stick it out near his hometown and wait for the government to send help.

— PERMUTEDPRESS.COM —

THE KING OF CLAYFIELD 2
ALL THAT I SEE
BY SHANE GREGORY

It has been more than a month since the Canton B virus turned the people of the world into hungry zombies. The survivors of Clayfield, Kentucky attempt to carve out new lives for themselves in this harsh new world. Those who remain have been hardened by their environment and their choices over the previous weeks, but their optimism has not been extinguished. There is hope that eventually Clayfield can be secured, but first, the undead must be eliminated and law and order must be restored. Unfortunately, the group might not ever get to implement their plan.

— PERMUTEDPRESS.COM —

THE KING OF CLAYFIELD 3
FIRE BIRDS
BY SHANE GREGORY

For weeks, he has fought the undead and believed that he was Clayfield's sole survivor. But when odd things begin to happen in the town, it becomes clear that other healthy people are around. A friend returns full of trouble and secrets, and they are not alone.

Something bad is coming to Clayfield, and there could be nowhere to hide.

INFECTION:
ALASKAN UNDEAD APOCALYPSE
BY SEAN SCHUBERT

Anchorage, Alaska: gateway to serene wilderness of The Last Frontier. No stranger to struggle, the city on the edge of the world is about to become even more isolated. When a plague strikes, Anchorage becomes a deadly trap for its citizens. The only two land routes out of the city are cut, forcing people to fight or die as the infection spreads.

PERMUTEDPRESS.COM

CONTAINMENT
(ALASKAN UNDEAD APOCALYPSE BOOK 2)
BY SEAN SCHUBERT

Running. Hiding. Surviving. Anchorage, once Alaska's largest city, has fallen. Now a threatening maze of death, the city is firmly in the cold grip of a growing zombie horde. Neil Jordan and Dr. Caldwell lead a small band of desperate survivors through the maelstrom. The group has one last hope: that this nightmare has been contained, and there still exists a sane world free of infection.

THE UNDEAD SITUATION
BY ELOISE J. KNAPP

The dead are rising. People are dying. Civilization is collapsing. But Cyrus V. Sinclair couldn't care less; he's a sociopath. Amidst the chaos, Cyrus sits with little more emotion than one of the walking corpses… until he meets up with other inconvenient survivors who cramp his style and force him to re-evaluate his outlook on life. It's Armageddon, and things will definitely get messy.

THE UNDEAD HAZE
(THE UNDEAD SITUATION BOOK 2)
BY ELOISE J. KNAPP

When remorse drives Cyrus to abandon his hidden compound he doesn't realize what new dangers lurk in the undead world. He knows he must wade through the vilest remains of humanity and hordes of zombies to settle scores and find the one person who might understand him. But this time, it won't be so easy. Zombies and unpleasant survivors aren't the only thing Cyrus has to worry about.

MAD SWINE: THE BEGINNING
BY STEVEN PAJAK

People refer to the infected as "zombies," but that's not what they really are. Zombie implies the infected have died and reanimated. The thing is, they didn't die. They're just not human anymore. As the infection spreads and crazed hordes--dubbed "Mad Swine"--take over the cities, the residents of Randall Oaks find themselves locked in a desperate struggle to survive in the new world.

"EXTREMELY WELL-WRITTEN"
—Zombie-Review.com

PERMUTEDPRESS.COM

MAD SWINE: DEAD WINTER
BY STEVEN PAJAK

Three months after the beginning of the Mad Swine outbreak, the residents of Randall Oaks have reached their breaking point. After surviving the initial outbreak and a war waged with their neighboring community, Providence, their supplies are severely close to depletion. With hostile neighbors at their flanks and hordes of infected outside their walls, they have become prisoners within their own community.

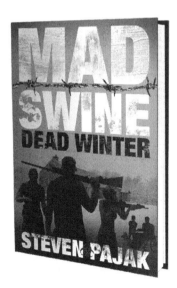

RISE
BY GARETH WOOD

Within hours of succumbing to a plague, millions of dead rise to attack the living. Brian Williams flees the city with his sister Sarah. Banded with other survivors, the group remains desperately outnumbered and under-armed. With no food and little fuel, they must fight their way to safety. RISE is the story of the extreme measures a family will take to survive a trek across a country gone mad.

PERMUTEDPRESS.COM

AGE OF THE DEAD
BY GARETH WOOD

A year has passed since the dead rose, and the citizens of Cold Lake are out of hope. Food and weapons are nearly impossible to find, and the dead are everywhere. In desperation Brian Williams leads a salvage team into the mountains. But outside the small safe zones the world is a foreign place. Williams and his team must use all of their skills to survive in the wilderness ruled by the dead.

DEAD MEAT
BY PATRICK & CHRIS WILLIAMS

The city of River's Edge has been quarantined due to a rodent borne rabies outbreak. But it quickly becomes clear to the citizens that the infection is something much, much worse than rabies... The townsfolk are attacked and fed upon by packs of the living dead. Gavin and Benny attempt to survive the chaos in River's Edge while making their way north in search of sanctuary.

PERMUTEDPRESS.COM

ROTTER WORLD
BY SCOTT M. BAKER

Eight months ago vampires released the Revenant Virus on humanity. Both species were nearly wiped out. The creator of the virus claims there is a vaccine that will make humans and vampires immune to the virus, but it's located in a secure underground facility five hundred miles away. To retrieve the vaccine, a raiding party of humans and vampires must travel down the devastated East Coast.

AMONG THE LIVING
BY TIMOTHY W. LONG

The dead walk. Now the real battle for Seattle has begun. Lester has a new clientele, the kind that requires him to deal lead instead of drugs. Mike suspects a conspiracy lies behind the chaos. Kate has a dark secret: she's a budding young serial killer. These survivors, along with others, are drawn together in their quest to find the truth behind the spreading apocalypse.

AMONG THE DEAD
BY TIMOTHY W. LONG

Seattle is under siege by masses of living dead, and the military struggles to prevent the virus from spreading outside the city. Kate is tired of sitting around. When she learns that a rescue mission is heading back into the chaos, she jumps at the chance to tag along and put her unique skill set and, more importantly, swords to use.

LONG VOYAGE BACK
BY LUKE RHINEHART

When the bombs came, only the lucky escaped. In the horror that followed, only the strong would survive. The voyage of the trimaran Vagabond began as a pleasure cruise on the Chesapeake Bay. Then came the War Alert ... the unholy glow on the horizon ... the terrifying reports of nuclear destruction. In the days that followed, it became clear just how much chaos was still to come.

— PERMUTEDPRESS.COM —

QUARANTINED
BY JOE MCKINNEY

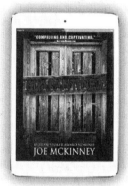

The citizens of San Antonio, Texas are threatened with extermination by a terrifying outbreak of the flu. Quarantined by the military to contain the virus, the city is in a desperate struggle to survive. Inside the quarantine walls, Detective Lily Harris finds herself caught up in a conspiracy intent on hiding the news from the world and fighting a population threatening to boil over into revolt.

— PERMUTEDPRESS.COM —

THE DESERT
BY BRYON MORRIGAN

Give up trying to leave. There's no way out. Those are the final words in a journal left by the last apparent survivor of a platoon that disappear in Iraq. Years later, two soldiers realize that what happened to the "Lost Platoon" is now happening to them. Now they must confront the horrifying creatures responsible for their misfortune, or risk the same fate as that of the soldiers before them.

Made in the USA
Charleston, SC
12 March 2016